SOMEWHERE A CHILD IS BORN

Conversations Beyond Belief

WOLF STANLEY

CARACATUS LLC

Contact Me

wolfstanley.com

wolf@wolfstanley.com

Subscribe to my newsletter and/or
receive your free copy of the classic book:

As a Man Thinketh by James Allen

https://dl.bookfunnel.com/fs7wqwjqrz

Contents

Introduction

"A bird does not sing because he has the answer.
He sings because he has a song." ~ Unknown

I have had a lifelong fascination with the astounding accomplishments of rare human beings. Every time I would read about ordinary people performing superhuman feats, I would always think that every other ordinary person is capable of the same. But I look around me and I see it isn't so.

Then, I began to wonder … What is the difference? Could *my* mom lift a car off of one of my little brothers? Could I? Under what circumstances would I be able to perform such a miracle?

World-class athletes break old records continuously. Human beings constantly push themselves beyond previously held beliefs about physical limitations.

How much further can we go from here?

With physics that were contrary to what we believed, I knew these phenomena had everything to do with the mind and beliefs.

I also began to wonder what kind of person could develop without the limiting beliefs of the collective consciousness. How much of collective consciousness is real and how much is an illusion?

"Do not be conformed to this world but be ye transformed by the renewing of your minds." ~ Romans 12:2

We are programmed to believe certain concepts about our world. The programming comes to us from the people who raise us as well as outside influences. Most of us were raised with heavy influence from TV programming.

We each have a unique worldview. I was raised to believe that illness is an illusion; that the key to health is a healthy mind that does not accept the suggestion of dis-ease.

Mind creates the body. Physical health begins with mental health. Dis-ease begins with emotion. There is an emotional root to physical disturbances in the body.

I have mostly read non-fiction books on these topics, and I love reading them. But they are not for everyone. Stories are more fun to read and are easier to remember. It's human nature.

Fictional presentations of the material always seemed to either skim the surface or were too cryptic. I wanted to write a book that presented the material in an entertaining way that would deliver on multiple levels. Each time you read this book, you will discover something new.

The odd chapters of this book demonstrate the extraordinary mind of an ordinary child, Elias, raised with empowering beliefs.

The even chapters are a series of conversations in a classroom setting and one-on-one therapy sessions.

If you consider the possibility that what we believe to be reality is an illusion based on the programming of others false beliefs, you may begin to question your beliefs.

Have you ever been to a stage hypnosis show? As you are walking in, the induction has already begun. In fact, the hypnotic induction began as soon as you became aware of the show. There may be a part of you that is curious to see a hypnosis show, and you were attracted to it.

Everything about the show is designed to bring you into an altered state of mind. People are hypnosis machines. We go into the alpha state many times a day.

Some people are more suggestible than others, and some people are more suggestible about certain things than others. A distinction can be made between the degree of suggestibility and the topic on which a hypnotized person will accept suggestion.

ALL people are hypnotizable and will accept suggestion.

ALL hypnosis is self-hypnosis. You can accept or reject any suggestion. The difference is in who your subconscious is following. Is it your own mind or someone else's illusion?

The most effective presentations use the elements of hypnosis. Church services, political rallies, sporting events, rock concerts, educational lectures, movies, and even good books, communicate directly with the subconscious mind to guide people into the Spirit of the Thing.

In the hypnosis show, the music is chosen to entrain your mind to an alpha state. Small suggestibility tests are given to the audience to see who is responding.

You might think you do not want to go up on stage and make a fool of yourself. The good news is, if you really do not want to go up, you probably won't. They are looking for the most compliant, most suggestible people to come up on stage to make the hypnotist successful.

They are also looking for people who do want to go up on stage and make fools of themselves. It makes for good theater. It is a show, after all. The people who go up on stage at a hypnosis show want to be a part of the show.

Whatever their reasons, they will allow themselves to go along with what is suggested. They could resist, but they don't want to. What would be the fun of that?

Modern humans are conditioned to respond to the formula of fear and repetition. Advertisers and politicians know how to use this formula to direct your thinking and feeling.

Evoke an emotional state to get the attention of the subconscious.

Repeat the suggestions incessantly.

If you don't direct your own subconscious mind, someone else will.

You can use your subconscious mind to create Heaven or Hell.

You already do. Live from choice, not by default, but by design.

You may not agree with what I say. I may not be any more correct than billions who have gone before me, but what if ...?

Would you argue with Dali over the shape of clocks?

Can you imagine how powerful a human being can become with only empowering beliefs?

WHO IS ELIAS?

Matthew 17:1 – 13

ELIAS!

I

"ELIAS! LEAVE GRAMMIE'S GECKOS alone. Come in here for a minute; these people want to meet you."

The little boy, with blond surfer curls hanging past his shoulders, was pouring a pail of water across the lava rock that had naturally solidified into channels. The water formed a pool at the bottom for the geckos.

He had given up trying to get the uncooperative geckos to sleep in the huts he had made for them out of ti leaves.

After a long pause, he looked back toward the house and, smiling, said, "Coming Gramma Chrissy." He was always excited to meet new people.

He ran barefooted through the garden, across the gravel drive, and up the stairs to the house.

As he started through the kitchen door, Gramma Chrissy stopped him with, "Ah, ah, ah. Feet."

Elias looked down at the crust of lava dust on his feet. "Not that bad," he thought, then protested aloud, "But the bottoms are clean from the wet grass. I won't get any dirt on the floor."

"Since when have you been afraid of a little water?"

"Oka-ay. I'll wash my feet." He ran back down the stairs to the outdoor shower with the foot wash he had just rushed past.

As he again tried to enter the kitchen, Gramma Chrissy put her hand on his chest to stop him. "Hang on a sec, sweetie. Let's see if we can do something with that hair of yours."

Raking her fingers through his hair proved to be impossible, so she did the next best thing: She open-palm gathered and somehow managed to pull all of Medusa's snakes into the same compass point and deftly banded them together.

With a licked thumb, she wiped a smudge off his cheek, looked him over, and said, "Here, put this shirt on. They're in the front room waiting for you."

"Who are they?" he asked curiously.

"People from the state who are here to see Papa. He told them how smart you are. They want to ask you some questions."

"Like a game?"

"Of course. Life is a game. Now go have some fun."

Kamakani Angel

II

Puget Sound, eight years earlier.

Driving across the bridge, Dr. Anders Starkstrom felt the cleansing winds of change blowing hard. "The harder the wind, the bigger the change." He knew something big was about to happen.

The spray of seawater dried quickly in the wind, leaving a layer of salt on his windshield. Long drives along the familiar highway usually led him to think about his life and where he has been.

The drive to the Bowman Bay Training Center had been uneventful. Not even the seasonal tourist traffic could upset the mood he was in today.

It was a beautiful Spring morning. The sun glistened off the water like a field of diamonds on the crests of the wind-swept waves.

"Whatever this wind brings, it is going to be *amazing*!" he said to himself excitedly.

He had never been to Bowman Bay before, though he had driven past it hundreds of times. As he drove down from the highway, through the trees and into the basin, he began to notice what a delightful area this was indeed.

On some level, he felt as though he was being watched, that there was someone, or some *thing*, just waiting, watching. He somehow felt that whatever it was, the spirit was friendly.

He drove into the training facility. Blessed contractors were parked all over the place. Now, where was he supposed to go? Ah, there, building C. According to his contact at the base, it wasn't a classroom, but it was dry and mostly clean.

Curiously, this was the first building finished. He didn't know why they didn't start with building A. That would have made more sense to him. "Who can rationalize military intelligence?" he wondered.

As he walked from his truck to the building, he could see one of the cadets sitting at a makeshift registration table by the door. She was not unattractive. She seemed eager to start the day, her face lit up in joy as he got closer.

When he got close enough, he smiled and said, “Good morning.”

“Good morning.” As she smiled back at him, she stood and extended her hand for a handshake.

As they shook hands, they each instinctively felt an undistinguishable familiarity; both glanced down at the union of hands they had just formed. They brought their attention back up and looked each other directly in the eye.

“Truly,” she said. “I mean, Cadet Murphy, sir.”

“Good to meet you, Truly Murphy. That’s an unusual name. I like it. My name is Anders—I mean Dr. Starkstrom, ma’am.”

To the casual observer, there was nothing remarkable about this first encounter between these two. To each of them, however, there was ... something ... neither could quite put their finger on.

“Oh, yes. How can I help you today, sir?”

“I'm looking for my classroom, in Building C.”

“Well, you’re in the right place. This is your classroom, here. I read your name on the course description, but when you came up, I thought you were a contractor. You are not what I expected.”

“I used to be a construction contractor. Now, I’m an instruction contractor.”

“Clever. I’m in this class, but I’ll be the last one in. I unlocked the door. I’m checking in the cadets as they arrive. Everyone gets a packet. Do you have any specific instructions?”

“Yes. Remind them to smile.”

“Yessir.” she smiled a smile that seemed to originate from her very core.

As Starkstrom entered the classroom, he could hear what sounded like the whine of a high-end motorcycle engine at top speed, off in the distance but getting closer quickly. “Sounds like a BMW in a big hurry,” he thought to himself.

Murphy was to be in the first group of cadets who would begin to learn something about themselves they had never even considered before. They were about to explore the inner workings of their own minds. They were about to discover not who they thought they were, but who they really are.

Because Starkstrom had condensed his syllabus to fit the narrow, three-day training window, they had little time to waste. It was nearly time to begin, and most of the seats were filled.

From his backpack, he pulled out a Bluetooth speaker and with his phone began playing *The Grand Illusion* by Styx, as the cadets continued to take their seats.

He would play the same song every time class was about to begin. This would be the auditory anchor the cadets would recognize as the beginning of learning time.

The cadets couldn't help but smile a little as Starkstrom danced at the front of the class. Not what anyone would call a good dancer, but it didn't matter to him. He would do this little dance every time he played the song. This would be a visual anchor that would also let the cadets know it was time to learn.

Back outside, the roar of the Beamer got louder, amplified by the shape of the valley, until the black and silver two-wheeler pulled into view and its rider, without hesitation, parked next to the table at which Murphy sat.

"You're going to kill yourself on that thing, Benjamin."

"No worries, love. I am invincible," he said as he tossed his key to her.

"Don't call me love. What is this for?"

"You'll see. I have to go. Time for class," he said as he slipped through the door.

No sooner had the door closed when a security cart pulled up to the table. The driver had followed the disruptive vehicle into the lot and said, "You can't park that scooter there."

"It's not mine."

"Still can't be here."

Murphy looked at the classroom door, then down at the key in her hand, gave a little grin as she nodded her head, and said, "I got this."

As the rest of the cadets had already gone inside, Murphy thought, "I think Benjamin needs a lesson in humility."

"I'm going to be late. Can you follow me and give me a ride back?"

"Sure," replied the driver.

She climbed on the bike and started it with her thumb, revved the engine a couple of times, and started to drive the motorcycle up toward the farthest reaches of the parking lot.

"This should teach him." When she reached the top of the lot, she parked under a tree. The roar of the man-made beast had scared off a few seagulls formerly roosting in it.

Murphy got off the bike and jumped into the passenger seat of the little golf cart with the blue stripe on the side, which identified it as base security.

The driver, who seemed concerned with the fate of the glistening two-wheeler, asked Murphy, "You know those birds will be back?"

"I know," she said slyly.

"Well, whoever owns that bike is going to have a mess. Seagulls are nasty."

"I know. He made his decision. I made one too."

When they got back down to Building C, Murphy got off the cart and thanked the driver.

Now in a hurry, she did a quick hair and makeup check of her reflection in the side window. "Fabulous!" she asserted as she smiled and walked to the slightly opened door.

Class had already started. Good, maybe she can get in without anybody noticing. She heard the instructor saying, "… a training program, specifically for military use, to protect trainees from PTSD and other demons that attack unprepared minds."

She eased the door open and saw that everyone was distracted. Looking to take advantage of that, she quickly stepped into the room. She tripped. *CLANG*! The ringing of the steel wastebasket as it collided with the concrete floor turned all eyes in her direction.

"Good morning!" the instructor greeted her cheerfully.

"Good morning," she mumbled, getting up from the floor.

"Pardon me?"

"Sir, good morning! Cadet Truly Murphy reporting for duty, sir!" as she snapped to attention.

"You may address me as sir, but I am a civilian, cadet." With his hand, he directed her attention to the upper left-hand corner of the whiteboard where his name was printed and, as though they had not already met, said, "My name is Dr. Anders Starkstrom. Why are you here, cadet?"

She stammered a little and then gathered herself, "My orders are to report here at oh-eight-hundred."

He paused a beat, still sensing there was something extraordinary about this cadet, glanced at the clock on the wall (08:03), and said, “Well, you’re here. You got it half right.”

“Yes, sir. I was … I just had to …”

“Please stop,” he calmly interrupted her, holding up his hand and smiling, “Save it for the coffee shop. What I meant was, why are *you* here? What do you want? What are you here to learn?”

“Sir, I understand that this module will help me deal with the expected as well as unexpected challenges of space travel. I want to explore outer space, *and* inner space! I am a space traveler.”

“You’re a space *cadet*, Murphy,” quipped the young rider in the front row, causing the rest of the class to chuckle.

“Okay,” Starkstrom said to the class, and then, “Take a seat. Anywhere you want, Murphy.”

The only open seat was up front next to the smart ass. Her eyes narrowed at Benjamin. The key bounced off his chest and dropped into his lap as she sat down next to him.

Starkstrom turned his attention to the outspoken young man in the front row. “Thank you for volunteering to go next. What is your name, and why are you here?”

“Sir, my name is Cadet Benjamin Coyote. I have been studying the mysteries of the mind since I was in middle school. Your expertise is well-known in the field of Mental Science. *Sheer Genius* is pure genius. I plan on reading your other books as well, and it's an honor to be here.”

“Suck up much?” asked Murphy.

Starkstrom, ignoring Murphy’s payback, looked Coyote directly in the eyes and asked, “For what purpose?”

The young cadet’s eyes started moving around the room, zigzagging back and forth, first up high, then a little lower, then down low, apparently scanning the room for an answer. Unable to find a response to the question, he said, “I guess I don’t know.”

Starkstrom: “Excellent! Let’s begin with that. Everybody needs a sense of purpose. Not a vague, general direction that you are kind of going in, that you *hope* will work out for you someday, but a *purpose*, a reason for getting up in the morning, excited to take on the challenges of the day, in love with your life. A sense of purpose is the key to happiness. By the time we're done here, you will know the answer to that question.

"As I was saying, before I was so rudely interrupted," smiling at Murphy, "when I heard about the formation of Space Force, I put together a five-day pilot program of various proven NLP techniques to prepare your minds for deep space travel. The government gave us three days."

Cadet: "What is NLP?"

Starkstrom: "NLP stands for Neuro-Linguistic Programming. It is the science of the programming language used by the human mind and neurology. It is the study of your operating system.

"You are not aware of it, but you have been exposed to some bad programming.

"Contrary to popular belief, cancer, phobias, suicide, eating disorders, PTSD, and just about any other malady (which means a bad song) you can think of all begin with a similar root cause.

"That is, unresolved emotional issues attach themselves to other unresolved emotional issues, until a person gets overwhelmed.

"People get so involved *subjectively* that they cannot view themselves, or their circumstances, *objectively*.

"As time goes by, more unresolved issues attach themselves to the earlier ones, creating a complexed web of false beliefs. By the time a person reaches that stage, it's difficult, though still possible, to help them get back on track.

"We are going to take the ounce-of-prevention approach. We are going to optimize your mental hard drives by clearing out some unproductive apps that are running in the background of your minds.

"With these NLP exercises, we will clear out some of the past trauma and bad programming, and then we will focus your energy into obtaining a goal of your choosing.

"Now, I don't just want to take you through the exercises. I want to teach you the science behind these processes so you can repeat them. So, let's begin with Eye Accessing."

He drew the outline of a face on the whiteboard. Then he drew a dotted line horizontally across the brow, just above the eyes. Then another dotted horizontal line just below the chin.

In the space above the brow, he wrote VISUAL, in the middle space, AUDITORY, and below the chin, KINESTHETIC.

Starkstrom: "Our senses are tuned to receive vibrations within certain frequencies. Light operates on higher frequencies, sound on middle frequencies, and matter on lower frequencies."

Above the drawing, on the left, he wrote CREATIVE and, on the right, REMEMBERED.

Starkstrom: "Generally speaking, people organize their images according to their relative brain functions."

Cadet: "Is that like what the FBI uses to tell if someone is lying?"

Starkstrom: "Yes, but for that to be effective, you have to calibrate the person to see how they process information. For some people, this is reversed." He pointed to the words CREATIVE and REMEMBERED.

Cadet: "How do you do that?"

Starkstrom: "By asking questions. I can ask you to describe your car, and you will likely look to your VISUAL/REMEMBERED location.

"Then I can ask you to tell me what it would look like if it had a lift kit and flames painted on the front fenders. Then you will likely look to your VISUAL/CREATIVE location to create that image in your mind."

Cadet: "What if my car does have a lift kit and flames?"

Starkstrom: "You probably would have told me that when I asked you to describe your car. If that were the case, I would have you imagine some other modifications.

"By observing the eye-accessing cues when you ask questions that you already know the likely answers to, you can see which way they process information.

"Notice where they look when they are trying to remember, and where they look when they are creating.

"Now, in all directions from our center," he brought his hands together at his heart, "we have our sphere of awareness." He swept his arms outward with palms flattened as though pushing against the insides of a man-sized ball, fingers outstretched. Twisting at the waist, he rotated his arms like a street mime trapped in a bubble.

Starkstrom: "We have different locations for storing thoughtforms in our awareness." He started randomly indicating various locations with his hands.

"When I asked Coyote, 'What is your purpose?' he looked up here," pointing to the upper right of the drawing, "to *see* if he had an image of that.

"Then, he glanced over here," pointing to the upper left, "to see if he could make something up. Quickly abandoned that idea, and his eyes went over here to *listen* for some inspiration, then back over to the creative side. Found nothing.

"Finally, he looked down over here to check on his feelings and slowly worked his way across through his kinesthetic awareness to make sure he didn't miss anything." Each time, Starkstrom pointed to a different location relative to the face on the board.

"We're going to use this information in a unique way.

"We all have different experiences and as many ways of relating to those experiences. We have places that we use to organize and store those experiences. We also have a direction for organizing our past and a direction for our future.

"We can move images around like Tony Stark does with J.A.R.V.I.S. We can make them larger and brighter and more important. Or we can make them smaller and push them further away, making them a smaller part of our paradigm and less influential.

"Do you know that your creative imagination is what forms your physical reality? THOUGHTS ARE THINGS.

"We all create our worlds, moment by moment. Yesterday, you created today. Today you create tomorrow. You can drift around on the sea, subject to the tides and the wakes of other ships. Or you can choose a destination, input the coordinates, and move in that direction.

"My purpose is to teach you how to operate your mind, to integrate your conscious with your subconscious to remove limiting beliefs and clear negative emotions.

"Do you know what emotions are? One way of looking at it is like Bob Proctor says, 'Our emotions are our awareness of the frequency at which the body is vibrating.'

"I don't expect you to understand that the first time you hear it, but there has to be a first time you hear it.

"Some of our emotions are what we call positive: happy, excited, hopeful, valuable, grateful, love.

"Those emotions set us vibrating at a certain frequency, which attracts more of the things that are vibrating on that frequency. The things we are in resonance with flow to us, and we to them.

"The emotions we call negative—anger, greed, fear, guilt, hate, resentment, envy—these emotions set us vibrating at lower frequencies, which makes us feel bad, and attract more of the things vibrating on those frequencies.

"Feeling is a kinesthetic awareness. We *feel* our body vibrating at a specific frequency. Much like we sense firmness or heat with our body, we also sense the frequency of our emotions.

"The government wants *me* to teach *you* how to control your emotions by changing your thoughts, because it is in its best interest for you to attract good things and *not* bad.

"Yes, you in the back."

A cadet with brilliant red hair stood up and said, "Sir, my name is Cadet Hector Alonzo. Your bio says you are a hypnotist. Are you going to hypnotize us? I've never been hypnotized before."

Starkstrom: "You've *never* been hypnotized before? With a show of hands… How many of you think you have never been hypnotized before?"

Everybody raised their hand.

Starkstrom: "What if I were to tell you that in the first seven years of your life you were in a constant state of hypnosis?

"Every night when you go to sleep, and every morning when you wake up, you are in a state of hypnosis. Several times a day, you naturally drift in and out of the hypnotic state.

"Hypnosis is simply a brainwave frequency of natural relaxation. I believe your question is more about suggestibility, an important one, and we will talk about that later.

"I'm going to show you how to enter and travel through *multiple* levels of mind at will. The hypnotic state itself is a super learning state that gives us the ability to acquire knowledge quickly.

"So, we believe everything we become aware of during the first seven years of our life. Then the guardian-at-the-gate comes on duty to sort and sift information from then on."

Alonzo: "You mean babies believe *everything*? Well, that explains a lot about my little brother."

Starkstrom: "Yes, up to age seven, we don't have a developed critical faculty, and we believe that everything we experience is real. Believe me, you guys are full of shit. We are going to dig down deep and flush out the sediment. Shall we get down to business?"

"Let's dig up some shit!" shouted another cadet.

Kūpuna

III

"Elias is an ordinary boy. He gets extraordinary results because he doesn't accept self-imposed limits like the rest of us," Elias heard his father saying as he walked into the front room.

Two ladies were sitting together on the loveseat, and one gentleman was sitting on a chair. They were wearing business clothes and seemed to have their game faces on a little early. So serious.

Elias: "Aloha uncle and aunties." He nodded respect to each.

Anders: "Elias, these folks are from Honolulu. They're here to evaluate for our new school. It seems I've raised their curiosity about your skills, so they want to ask you a few questions. Have a seat, son."

Elias whispered to Anders, "Papa. He looks like Pele."

Anders: "In what way, Elias?"

With his hands forming the base of a mountain, rising up and narrowing at the peak, he said, still whispering, "He is brown honua on the bottom, red lava in the middle, and gray vog on top." He continued moving his hands straight up and then out, imitating a volcano steaming.

Anders: "Yes, I see what you mean. Be especially kind to people who radiate those colors, Elias. They are usually hurt and afraid. Bless him with love. See him bathed in the golden light."

Elias: "Okay, Papa."

As Elias jumped up into his chair, Anders introduced Mr. Halemalia, Mrs. Bellamy, and Mrs. Kurosawa. His feet dangled freely, so he began swinging them, just because. "Gramma Chrissy says we're going to play a game, a question game."

Mr. H: "Yes Elias, that's right. We are going to ask you a few questions, and you are going to do your best to answer them. Is that all right with you?"

Elias: "Sure. What's the object of this game? And what are the rules?"

Mr. H: "We would just like for you to answer the questions the best you can. We are going to ask you some questions about your math, reading comprehension, and writing skills."

Elias: "The three Rs? Around here, we call that a test. I love to test!"

Mr. H: "Yes, I guess you could call it a test. We just didn't want you to get nervous."

Elias: "What's to be nervous about? A test just lets me know my level of awareness."

His words were met with blank stares.

Through the Portal

IV

Starkstrom: "All right, cadets. Now, if you can trust me enough and trust yourselves enough to know everything that happens in this room is for your highest good, yeah?

"We are going to expand your limits and stretch your minds to the point where they can never go back to the way they were. You will see things in a different way and the world will be a different place.

"*Be aware* and accept that, here and now, you are going to clean out the back of your closet and get that clutter out of the attic. Do I have your permission to proceed?

"Before we begin to go into the state of hypnosis, I wonder if we can all take a deep, cleansing breath, you know, the kind where you fill up your lungs completely, and hold it for a couple of seconds, and then just let it all out.

"That's right. Again, take another deep, deep breath, hold it to the mental count of three, and just push it all out. Good.

"Now that you are feeling more relaxed, I want you to imagine a sphere in which you are the center. Imagine what it would be like if you had an omnidirectional heads-up display, waiting for your commands, on the bridge of your ship. That's right.

"You have complete control over everything in your life. There are buttons and knobs, levers and switches, dials and readouts; there are images and soundbites, thoughtforms and beliefs, and everything else you need to adjust, delete, or enhance any or all of it. That's right. Just continue relaxing.

"Allow your imagination to unfold. You control your perception of everything that has ever come into your awareness.

"You don't have to know how it all works right now. Just enjoy your new awareness of this control center. We can move images around, change their size, adjust their color and brightness.

"You may also notice that we have a direction for storing our past memories, and a direction for storing our future memories.

"However you do that is perfect. There is no right or wrong way. Your past may be before or behind you. Some people have their past right in front of them, large and in charge.

"If you can, I want you to get a sense for which direction you store your past, trust yourself, and extend your palm in that direction. Then extend your other palm toward your future, which may be in the opposite direction, or not.

"You may be comfortable with where your timelines are now. Or you can move them with your hands to different locations. Whatever works for you is perfect.

"It is your system for organizing time.

"Just go ahead now, relax your hands, and allow yourself to float up. Float up, out of your body, above your timeline and look out over your past.

"From this position, you can see your life from an *objective* point of view, without emotional attachment. Notice the dark spots and the bright spots, and when you are ready, you can turn and look out over your future. Some of you may be afraid to see into the future, but you will soon learn to use this skill in a very powerful way.

"Now, let yourself float back down into your body and begin to bring your awareness back to this room.

"Take a deep breath, and as you let it out, open your eyes, feeling energized and alert. How was that?"

Cadet: "That was so *awesome*!"

Starkstrom: "Isn't it? Is anybody here ready to get rid of a negative emotion, right here, right *now*? Phobias? Anger issues? Anybody want to get rid of programmed-in guilt? Murphy, how about you?"

Her eyes opened wide. "Me?"

Starkstrom: "Yes, come with me … up here. We all encounter situations in our lives that we react to based on our beliefs. Oftentimes, we have reactions that may not get the results we want, right? Reacting may not be the most effective way of responding.

"When something happens and comes into our awareness, it causes us to feel a certain way, which causes us to react to that stimulus. That reaction is based on *learned* responses to that stimulus.

"When a person gets angry and acts out, it's often because that behavior has worked for them in the past. Usually, they learned that behavior by observing someone else getting what they wanted and subconsciously adopted it as a strategy in their own lives.

"They will continue to employ that strategy, even if it does not get them *all* of the results they want. They have made it a part of their subjective mind, a part of their paradigm."

Cadet: "What *is* a paradigm?"

Starkstrom: "A paradigm is a collection of thoughts and beliefs that literally control the decisions we make and the actions we take. Your paradigm controls your perspective, how you see the world. Most of what you think you know … is *garbage*.

"How many of you would hook up a brand-new computer—not just some cheapo, but a top-of-the-line model, some of you know the kind, with the fastest speeds and largest capacities—to the internet with no security software? Just a rapid learning app that lets it learn *everything*… for seven years.

"Compare and contrast that with a human baby. Believe it or not, a human baby has speeds and capacities at infinitely higher levels than the most advanced computer ever developed by man. Yes, that little blob of flesh, giggling at the dog eating their oatmeal, is a genius. All of them are.

"Imagine placing several computers at various public locations around the world and hooking them up to the internet with no security software. We want them to learn quickly, so we won't put any limitations on them yet.

"The input at each location will be from the people in those locations who speak a certain language, think a certain way, and act out certain behaviors.

"Aware only of its immediate environment, it learns, without filtering, specific human behavior. It also assumes the language, way of thinking, and taking action.

"That is its *reality*. This computer is connected to the internet, but it is limited by the interests of the people it communicates with.

"Some of those interests may not be the kind you want your computer exposed to, but there they are. Many of them are beneficial, but some of them are viruses, and some of them are malware. Each one of those computers will have unique programming.

"Just for the fun of it, let's say it is *your* personal computer. Which means you will be doing some of the programming yourself by choosing apps and customizing settings, the language, location, and so on. But it will always be open to input from other sources. You can't stop the learning process.

"You can input what you know, but what do you know? Do you have life all figured out? Chances are, you don't.

"You learned everything you know from people who also didn't have everything figured out. You are aware of systems and strategies that have helped people get from birth certificate to death certificate. Some of the information that you input is outdated. Some of it doesn't apply, and some of it is just incorrect.

"During the times when we are not tending to our baby computer, it is subject to input from other sources. Sources that may be helpful or hurtful will continue to write to the hard drive. All of them are skillfully conditioning the mind and embedding certain ways of thinking.

"If you plop it in front of a TV, you input the programs advertisers and others want you to believe.

"All of these lines of code are etched into our brains through repetition.

"It is like randomly loading the world's most advanced supercomputer with poorly developed or half–thought out software. Some of the apps are the best they can be, based on the developer's knowledge.

"Some of the apps will perform adequately, and some will even excel, but some are so poorly conceived that they actually hold you back. It's much easier to travel forward if you untie the mooring lines. We want to optimize performance.

"Having said all that, let's get back to the task at hand, which is to clear past negative emotions."

Murphy: "Are you saying we can go back and change the past and change our history?"

Starkstrom: "I'm saying you can go back into your past and change how you *relate* to your history. You can change the way you think and feel about those past experiences, and that will change the way you think and feel about future experiences.

"Murphy, is there one of these negative emotions on the board that has an impact on your life, that you want to change?"

Looking thoughtfully at the board, she said, "Anger sometimes gets ahold of me."

Starkstrom: "Okay, good. Anger sometimes gets ahold of you. Tell me something that causes anger to get ahold of you."

Murphy: "Well, sometimes I get really angry when people don't listen to me."

Starkstrom: "All right, so what are you saying that people don't listen to?"

Murphy: "Like when I tell people, 'There is a storm coming in. Don't go out around the point.' What do they do? They take their boat out around the point, and the storm comes in! Then I either have to go out to help them or pick up their bodies from the beach the next day."

Starkstrom: "On a scale of one to ten, where would you say your anger is?"

Murphy: "If nobody gets hurt, I'd say about seven or eight. If somebody gets hurt, it's going to be about *ten,* or sometimes 11."

Starkstrom: "Okay, seven or eight, ten, or sometimes 11. Now, just go ahead and close your eyes when you are ready, take a deep breath, and as you let it out, allow yourself to relax… Now I want you to remember where you keep your past. Just get a sense of where your past is, relative to where you are, right now. Got it?"

She nodded her head.

Starkstrom: "In your mind's eye, I want you to feel yourself floating up, out of your body, and float back into your past, moving along your timeline. Go all the way back to your first experience of anger. If you were to know, was it before, during, or after your birth?"

Murphy: "Before."

Starkstrom: "Was it in the womb, or before?"

Murphy: "In the womb."

Starkstrom: "Okay. Now I want you to go back to just *before* this first event, float down into your body, and notice… Is there any anger?"

Murphy: "No."

Starkstrom: "Okay, so you are before your first experience of anger. Float back up above the event. Since we are in front of the class, please don't reveal any details.

"There is a lesson here for you. You didn't understand it at the time, but now, you can see the event from a new perspective. What you couldn't process before, you have the wisdom to process now.

"Now, go down into that event with the understandings that you have now, as an adult, and share that wisdom with your younger self.

Learn what you needed to learn in this situation, take that understanding through each of the subsequent events associated with anger, and release those feelings, moving through your timeline, all the way back to … *now.*

"Take a deep breath. Let me know when you are back." After a few seconds, she nodded her head.

"How would the world be different if animals could talk?"

She opened her eyes and blinked twice, "What?!"

Starkstrom: "That was a 'break-state' question. It doesn't matter. How do you feel?"

Murphy: "I'm not sure. I feel different."

Starkstrom: "Okay. Think about something that makes you angry, or would have made you angry, in the past."

Her eyes moved back and forth as though scanning the floor for an answer.

Murphy: "Can it be a different event? Something else popped up."

Starkstrom: "This is your stuff. Process is more important than details. Go with the flow."

Murphy: "Yeah. I don't feel angry about it. It's more like, I'm disappointed, but I understand that what he did, he did out of ignorance, and now I just feel pity for him."

Starkstrom: "On a scale of one to ten, where are you now?"

Murphy: "Maybe a two. I'm not going to let someone else's ignorance ruin *my* day."

Starkstrom: "Nice. Thank you, Murphy," as he motioned for her to return to her seat.

"Let's have some more fun! Pair up and alternate between practitioner and client."

Cadet: "Client? Am I getting paid for this service I am providing?"

Starkstrom: "Oh, you most certainly will be repaid in kind. When it is your turn to be the client, riches will flow by barter.

"Use your workbook diagrams to guide your client through the process. Let's go over the ten steps quickly.

1. RELAX and orient yourself to your timeline. It might be easier to face the future with the past behind you.
2. ASK 'What is my first experience with anger?' Go with the answers that come up. Trust your subconscious.
3. FLOAT up above your timeline, back to the first, first time you experienced anger.
4. LOOK at the event, floating above it; see yourself before, during, and after the event.

5. USING the information and understanding that you have now, that you didn't have then, what did you need to learn from that situation?
6. TAKE that understanding down into that earlier you and see how that feels now.
7. BRING that understanding forward, through all the subsequent events when you experienced anger, and allow that understanding to change the way you now feel about that situation.
8. YOUR subconscious mind wants to do this and can do so quickly.
9. BRING yourself back to the present.
10. SEE yourself in a future situation where, in the past, it would have caused you to feel anger, and see if you can feel it now. Is it gone?

"Go through each of the five negative emotions listed, in whichever order you choose. Any questions?"

Cadet: "It says here, 'Was it in a past life, or genealogical?' How do we know if they are really going back into a past life?"

Starkstrom: "We don't, but it doesn't matter."

Cadet: "Why doesn't it matter? If they are going into a past life, for *real*? Whooa. That's…"

Starkstrom: "It doesn't matter to *us*. *We* are not the ones who are processing the event. The client is the one who is digging down into the deepest, darkest penetrations of their mind, to pull the black bags into the light.

"However it is that their subconscious mind wants to structure that to keep them feeling safe makes no difference to *us*. So, it doesn't matter if we share their beliefs. We guide them through whatever works for them.

"Their *problem* lies in their imagination, and their *solution* lies in their imagination."

Cadet: "So, follow them into whatever rabbit hole they go down, and that will help them find their answers?"

Starkstrom: "You've got it. Enter their world and speak their language."

Cadet: "If I get rid of my anger, does that mean I won't ever get angry again?"

Starkstrom: "Good question. You will be able to experience any of these emotions again. *All* emotions are useful in helping us relate to the physical world.

"Even if we tried, we could not *remove* any emotion. We are not removing your ability to feel anger, guilt, or fear. We are uncovering the black bags, or repressed memories."

Cadet: "What do you mean, black bags?"

Starkstrom: "The ancient Hawaiians had an interesting way of thinking about the subconscious mind.

"The subconscious, or unihipili, is our inner child, or animal self, and takes care of all the autonomic functions of the body.

"It is in charge of our emotions and keeps track of our memories. It stores events, and the emotions attached to them, in a filing system that resembles bunches of grapes, with associated thoughtforms grouped together.

"Would you agree that, as we are growing up, we have experiences that just don't make sense?

"The conscious mind is supposed to sift and sort information for the subconscious to make associations, so it knows where to file everything.

"If the conscious mind does not understand and cannot explain something to the subconscious, the subconscious is embarrassed that it cannot do its job. It shoves that event into a black bag and buries it in the backyard. That is known in psychology as repressed memory.

"Every once in a while, an event will occur in our life that has a similar vibration to one of the events in the black bags, and the subconscious will haul it out of the depths of hell and present it to you again to see if you can make sense out of it.

"And you say, 'Not now! I'm trying to deal with *this* situation.' The reason that stuff comes up at that time is that the events are related by frequency and are magnetized to each other.

"So, what we are going to do today is excavate some black bags, tear them open, and file the memories where they belong."

Cadet: "Is this going to hurt? Old memories can be painful."

Starkstrom: "What is it that's painful about an old memory?"

Cadet: "Having to live through those feelings again."

Starkstrom: "Living through a bad experience again can be painful when you *feel* it subjectively, but you are going to process these events objectively.

"NLP is about structure and process. As an outside observer would, you will teach your inner child what you needed to learn back then to be able to deal with similar situations.

"You will still be able to experience all of your emotions. What you will change is the way you *relate* to those emotions.

"It may take you a little time, the first time through the process, but you will quickly get the hang of this exercise, and your subconscious is going to love it. Then it can go extremely fast. Let's get started."

A COUPLE OF HOURS LATER (during which time, you were entertained by a montage of cadets guiding each other through the exercises):

Starkstrom: "It looks like everybody has finished. Let's take our seats. Our time is up for today.

"Now, you may find when you go back to the world outside that some things are different. That is because you will see the world from a new point of view, a new perspective.

"You have been controlled by your past. Your past thoughts, feelings, and actions have formed into you and your surroundings. You have created your world to this point.

"Your body, your environment, and your beliefs about health, religion, money, are all created by you. Your world reflects your mind. It is literally how you see the world. It is your paradigm.

"One of the principles of Huna is ikea, which means the world is what you *think* it is.

"Questions? None right now? As they come up, which they will, write them down."

Griffin: "Cadet Beth Griffin, sir. I have a question. What kind of doctor are you?"

Starkstrom: "I have a PhD in Religious Studies.

"Whatever images just flashed across your minds when you heard that title are likely of the people who are afraid of me. They consider me a heretic.

"Religion isn't part of this module, but my way of thinking will appear throughout. Regardless of your beliefs about God, most of you will probably find it difficult to understand my concept of God."

Griffin: "Why would I have a hard time understanding your concept of God?"

Starkstrom: "Do you believe God watches over you; that he has a plan for you; that if you are a good person, you will go to heaven?"

Griffin: "Yes, of course."

Starkstrom: "Then you have many misconceptions about God."

Griffin: "That's harsh. My family are all good Christians."

Starkstrom: "Ah, Jesus, my favorite heretic."

Griffin: "How could Jesus be a heretic?"

Starkstrom: "A heretic is someone who speaks out against the Church. That was why they killed him, wasn't it? He spoke out against the Church and called out the hypocrites. They killed him for it."

Griffin: "Still, how can so many people be wrong?"

Starkstrom: "The world is what you think it is. People get attached to their beliefs. The worst kind of ignorant is the one who refuses to unlearn and relearn.

"I don't claim to know everything. I don't have a congregation, but I have earned the doctorate and title, therefore I am.

"That's enough for today. Go home and read *As a Man Thinketh*, by James Allen. It's a short but powerful book. You'll find it in your syllabus. Reprinted from the public domain. Meet back here at, what time, Murphy?"

Murphy: "Oh-eight-hundred." She smiled to herself.

Starkstrom: "Oh-eight-hundred. See you in the morning. Class dismissed."

Murphy: "I have to secure the classroom. I'm waiting for everyone to clear out.

Starkstrom: "If you'll excuse me, I need to make a pit stop before I leave."

Murphy: "Do you have everything?"

Starkstrom: "I think so. If not, I'll be back tomorrow."

Murphy: "See you then."

Born in a Pu'u

V

Mr. H: "Well, all right then. Shall we begin? Elias, if you don't mind, I would like to record this. So, for the record, will you please state your full name and your age?"

Elias: "I am Elias Murphy Starkstrom. At your service and as you please, sir. I was born in Kealakekua Bay seven years ago."

Mr. H: "You mean you were born in Kealakekua Village, yeah? Elias, would you say you are better at reading or math? We can start with whichever you prefer."

Elias: "No, uncle, I was born in a pu'u in the bay. I don't know which I'm better at. They're both fun. We can start wherever you want."

Mrs. B: "Elias, do you know your multiplication tables?"

Elias: "Yes, auntie."

They asked him grade-level questions, which he answered easily.

Anders: "I think you may get a better understanding if you ask him more challenging questions like this, Elias, what is the cube root of 649,461,896?"

Mrs. Bellamy pulled up the calculator on her phone and began entering the numbers as Elias said, "866." She paused, pushed a few more buttons, and stared at Elias.

Anders: "Elias, how far off-line is a 200-yard golf shot that misses by three degrees?"

Elias looked toward the ceiling. "Ten and a half yards."

Mrs. B: "That's trigonometry. How did you know that?"

Elias: "I'm just good at it. Papa, what was the time of my birth?"

Anders: "You were born on Christmas Day, at 8:37 AM."

Elias looked at the clock on the wall. After looking up at the ceiling a couple of seconds, he looked back at Mrs. Bellamy, and said, "That means I was born 3,756,188 minutes ago."

She pushed some buttons on her calculator, "Elias, you are off by 2,880 minutes. The answer is 3,753,308."

Elias whispered, "You forgot the two leap years, auntie."

That's Not What Happened

VI

Coyote stood looking around the parking lot, and asked, "Where is my bike, Murphy?"

Murphy: "How should I know?"

Coyote: "I heard you move it."

Murphy: "Oh, yeah. The last time I saw it, it was up there," She waved toward the upper parking lot.

Coyote: "All the way up?"

Murphy: "To the top."

He shook his head, angry and amused at the same time. "Thanks! I could use a good hike," he said sarcastically as he cinched his backpack and started his journey up the levels to the remote reaches of the parking lot.

While opening the door to her truck, Murphy saw Starkstrom walking past, and said, "See you in the morning, sir."

He stopped and asked her, "Where's a good place to eat around here?"

Murphy: "What do you want?"

Starkstrom: "I'm open to suggestions."

Murphy: "If you just want a good place to eat, you could go over to Maggie's. It's right off the highway. If you're feeling adventurous, there's Fisherman's Alibi on the other side of the river."

Starkstrom: "I'm feeling adventurous. How do I get there from here?"

Murphy: "Go back up to the highway, take a left. When you see the sign that says Mutiny Bay, take another left. After you cross the river, take another left and follow Smugglers' Cove Road to the end."

Starkstrom: "Two wrongs may not make a right, but three lefts do."

Murphy: "If you go by boat, you can just take a right."

Starkstrom: "Thanks. Do you want to come with me?"

Murphy: "I'd like to, but I should probably go home and start reading," She pointed over her right shoulder with both thumbs. "Thanks, anyway."

Starkstrom: "OK. See you in the morning." And then added, "Oh-eight-hundred."

Murphy: "Oh-eight-hundred. Bye."

They each got into their own vehicle.

As Anders began driving up the narrow road out of the Bowman Bay basin, he heard the familiar wail of Coyote's motorcycle in the distance and getting closer. He slowed down for the first of many switchbacks needed to ascend the steep hillside. He could see that Murphy had caught up and was directly behind him.

The motorcycle sounded close now. The rider cut into the inside, oncoming lane, which was nearly vacant this time of day, to pass them both. He barely avoided becoming a hood ornament on a maintenance truck heading for the shed.

Anders tapped the brakes to provide cushion between them, and said, "Careful cadet. Whatever it is, it isn't worth it." The truck's horn announced its driver's displeasure.

He could hear the banshee scream reverberate off the mountainside as the motorcycle accelerated its way up. And then, suddenly, the noise ceased. "What in the world?" he wondered out loud.

When he got to the next hairpin turn, he could see a small group of people standing around Coyote, who was lying at the base of the granite wall, next to his brand-new bent motorcycle. There was a scenic lookout at this turn with enough room for a couple of cars, so he pulled over, and Murphy followed.

Starkstrom: "Call base security. They'll get someone here before the 9-1-1 dispatcher can."

Murphy: "Yessir."

Starkstrom: "Hey, Coyote, what happened? Did you forget you painted that fake tunnel on there?"

Coyote: "Almost made it. How did that dog not hear me coming?"

Starkstrom: "I can help you, if you do exactly as I say. Okay?"

Coyote nodded his head, "Yeah, yeah."

Starkstrom: "You cut your leg pretty bad on those rocks, but you're going to be all right."

As he applied pressure with a folded hankie, he said, "Take as deep a breath as you can.

"As you let it out … you may begin to notice that … just as you can slow down your breathing … you can also begin to allow your heart rate to slow down … that's right … just allow your heartbeat to slow … down.

"Take another deep, deep breath … and as you let it out … allow your heart to slow down even more … and as your heart begins to slow down … that's right … just like that … you can begin to notice … that your blood vessels … the ones that have been damaged … are beginning to constrict … to close down … to keep your blood in your body, where it's needed.

"Now … continue breathing deeply … as you also thank the nerves for sounding the alarm … for letting your brain know that something has happened. And as you are aware that something has happened, you can allow the nerves to stop sending the signal of pain. That's right, you can turn off the signal of pain … and … just relax.

"Allow your body to release the flow of endorphins. Conserve your energy to send it where it is needed. Notice how the pain is no longer needed.

"Take in another deep … deep breath … and this time … as you let it out … feel yourself … sinking … deeper … and … deeper into relaxation … and as you do … allow your body to slow the blood flow to the damaged blood vessels. Your body knows how to do this. Conserve your blood for now.

"Now … I want you to do something … that might seem a little silly … but … I want you to imagine yourself in a movie theater … that's right … yes … that's a nice theater ... remember that?

"Can you smell the popcorn? … hear the gurgling, swishing sound of the soda machine? As you take your seat … you feel the firmness of the seat cushion … and begin to notice the lights are dimming … the show is about to start.

"As the projector turns on … I want you to see yourself up on the screen … see yourself in the moment after the accident … like a still photograph of you … just after the accident. Good.

"Now … allow all of the color to drain out of that image … just let the color drain right out … until the image is entirely black and white … that's right … Now you can see the image up on the screen … in black & white.

"Now, I want you to float up, out of your chair, into the image on the screen. Be the person in that image.

"From this freeze-frame, play the movie in reverse. That's right, feel yourself going through the entire event in reverse, with some silly circus music playing, going backward through the entire event, all the way back to before you got to this curve.

"Pause here for a moment.

"Now, you can let the movie begin to move forward … at normal speed. Bring the colors back into this image. As you watch and feel yourself moving forward, you may begin to notice that there is something about this scene that has a lesson for you.

"What is it that you need to learn from this experience? What could you have done differently … that would have prevented you from hitting the wall? Do you now know what you needed to learn then?

"Now … in your mind's eye … see yourself successfully going around that turn the way that you want, having made that correction … and learning what you needed to learn *before* you made that turn.

"Then bring yourself back to just before the turn, and repeat going around the turn successfully.

"Then do it again, and again, faster each time. Each time you do this, your body is automatically beginning to repair itself and your mind is becoming more aware."

Murphy: "Security and medics are on their way." She felt a little queasy from seeing the puddle of blood on the ground.

Starkstrom: "Thank you, Murphy. Coyote, I want you to stay in this pain-free state while your body continues to repair itself."

Coyote: "I'm not going anywhere."

Murphy shot a puzzled look at Starkstrom, "Wait, I thought he was hypnotized. How can he talk?"

Starkstrom smiled knowingly, "You can talk when you're hypnotized."

Murphy: "How could he be hypnotized so fast anyway?"

Starkstrom: "He was already in a state of shock from the accident. I just converted his confused altered state into a productive altered state. Also, we have an established rapport, not to mention that he has been going in and out of deep trance all day."

Murphy: "It seemed pretty simple. Why don't they teach it to first responders?"

Starkstrom: "I have taught it to EMS. A couple of them listened. Most of them resist because it bumps up hard against their own beliefs. I keep trying anyway."

The security detail, blue lights flashing, stopped their vehicle in the middle of the road. The driver got out and said, "Folks, we need to clear the area for the medics. Did any of you see what happened?"

A young couple with a dog raised their hands. The young man said, "She was chasing a bird and ran right out in front of him. I'm so sorry."

Security: "This isn't an off-leash area. Will you two and your dog please step over there to answer a few questions? Anybody who didn't see what happened, please get back in your vehicle and clear the area.

"Ma'am, I'm going to have to ask you to move your vehicle as well."

Murphy: "I'm with him," she motioned to Starkstrom, who was still applying pressure, and talking to Coyote.

Security: "Well, can you help me get some of these people out of here?"

Murphy: "Sure."

When the medics arrived, Coyote lay motionless on the ground, seeming too comfortable for someone who had just crashed a motorcycle into a wall of granite. One of the medics said to the other, "He must have passed out from the pain."

Coyote: "No, I'm just resting. I don't feel any pain right now."

Medic: "Let's bandage you up and get you to the hospital."

After the ambulance leaves …

Anders turned to Murphy, "I hope I didn't come across as too forward when I asked you to join me for dinner."

Murphy: "That's a pretty fancy ring. Is it an antique?"

He glanced down at the ring. "My wife gave this to me after her father died. He was one of my mentors. We were married for over 40 years, my entire adult life. She died five years ago of cancer. I still wear it in remembrance of them both."

Murphy: "You're widowed? I'm sorry to hear that. I just don't want *anything* to do with a married man."

Starkstrom: "Yes. I was just asking if you would join me for dinner."

Murphy: "I know, but I feel like it's something more than dinner. I don't know what it is, but it's like you have some kind of vibe going on. But this new information shines a different light on things."

Starkstrom: "It always does. There is something special about you, too. I don't think I've ever felt quite like this before. We only met this morning. I don't mind breaking rules, but I don't want to violate your trust."

Murphy: "Well, you aren't in Space Force, so it's not fraternizing. Do you mean the teacher/student taboo, or the age gap? I'm okay with both of those. I don't feel like I'm breaking any of my rules. It's my choice, and age is just a number."

Starkstrom: "When I'm around you, I feel 20 years younger."

Murphy: "That would still make you about 15 years older than me."

Starkstrom: "You're a real math whiz, aren't you?"

Murphy: "I'm just good at it."

Starkstrom: "Age is just a number. Dinner is just a meal."

Murphy: "I am going to eat anyway, and I could really use a drink right now."

Starkstrom: "Fisherman's Alibi? Let's do it. Lead the way."

Mathemagician

VII

Anders: "Elias, what is 7 trillion, 686 billion, 369 million, 774 thousand, 870 *times* 2 trillion, 465 billion, 99 million, 745 thousand, 779?

"While he's working that out, Mr. Halemalia, is there anything else you need from me?"

Mr. H: "I think we have what we need from you. I am curious to hear more from Elias. Do you mind if we stay for a while? We have a few more questions."

Anders: "You are welcome to stay as long as you like. I believe Elias can answer all your questions. I have some editing to take care of. If you need anything, I'll be in my study, and Chris is in the kitchen."

Mr. H: "Thank you, Dr. Starkstrom."

Elias: "18 septillion, 947 sextillion, 668 quintillion, 177 quadrillion, 995 trillion, 426 billion, 462 million, 773 thousand, 730."

Mrs. B: "My calculator doesn't even go that high. I'll take your word for it, Elias."

Elias: "This is fun!"

Mrs. B: "Elias, how do you know the answers so quickly?"

Elias: "I see the numbers as they are called out, until the answer reveals itself."

Mrs. K: "Where do you see the numbers?"

Elias: "On my screen. Where else?"

Mrs. K: "And all of those numbers just appear? Do you know where they come from?"

Elias: "All things come from one source."

Fisherman's Alibi

VIII

Starkstrom: "This is fantastic! Can we sit down there?"

He pointed to the table beside the terrarium with the rock fireplace, a stream trickling into a koi pond, and floor-to-ceiling windows that kept the cold winter wind from chilling a body to the bone.

A hand-painted sign above the windows boasted, "The Most Vibrant Sunsets in Heaven."

The server greeted them. "Hi, my name is Katie. We have just that one table left, sir. You are very lucky."

Starkstrom: "I know I'm lucky, but why do you say that?"

Katie: "This table has a standing reservation for the owners. She just called to say they won't be in tonight, so you are very lucky."

Starkstrom: "See how lucky we are?"

Murphy: "Do the owners ever feel guilty about taking the best table every night?"

Katie: "No reason for them to feel guilty. None of us would be able to enjoy any of this, if it weren't for them."

Starkstrom: "I would have no qualms about taking the best table either, and I don't." He pulled out her chair.

She was a little surprised and taken aback by the gesture. "Most people don't do that anymore."

Starkstrom: "I'm not most people."

Murphy: "No, you are not."

Katie: "What can I bring you to get started?"

Starkstrom: "What do you think about a Jameson's Irish Coffee?"

Murphy: "No coffee. I'd rather have a beer. I'll take a shot of Jameson's, though."

Starkstrom: "Two beers and two shots of Jameson's, if you please."

Katie: "Coming right up."

Murphy: "This has been a peculiar day."

Starkstrom: "Big winds bring big changes."

Murphy: "I wasn't talking about the wind. I was talking about my mind."

Starkstrom: "Same thing. The air element rules the mental plane. Wind can literally blow your mind."

Murphy: "Yeah, well, it feels like a hurricane came into my head and uprooted everything."

Starkstrom: "You'll get used to the new landscape. You seem like the adventurous type, so I'm not surprised, but why did you choose the Space Force?"

Murphy: "My grandpa was a ship's captain. I want to pilot a starship."

Starkstrom: "You know we don't have those yet, right?"

Murphy: "I know, but I want to be ready. When we *do* have them, I want to be the first starship captain."

Starkstrom: "Admiral-able."

Murphy: "I'm in the S.T.A.R. program for flight officers. I'll be shuttling astronauts to and from the space station and sometimes staying up there for months at a time.

"By the time they get the station complete, I should be a captain, ready for my starship. After that, I plan on going until I get to the top."

Starkstrom: "What do you consider to be the top?"

Murphy: "Is there anything higher than Commander-in-Chief?"

Starkstrom: "Ladies and gentlemen, President Truly Murphy."

Murphy: "Are you making fun of me?"

Starkstrom: "Not at all. In fact, I can show you how to get there."

Murphy: "How about you? Do you have children?"

Starkstrom: "Yes, I have two amazing sons. If we're going to eat, drink, and talk about family, do you mind if we go by first names? Most people know me as Anders. My friends call me Andy."

Murphy: "I think I'd like that, Andy."

Sam: "Here you go folks. Two Irish boilermakers. I'm Sam, your bartender. Katie will be back to take your order when you're ready."

Anders: "Thank you, Sam."

Truly: "Any grandchildren?"

Anders looked down as if he was imagining what it would feel like to have a grandson, "No," he said solemnly. "They both have told me they will never have children. I don't understand that decision. To me, it's a disturbing anti-life philosophy.

"I'm not sure of the source of that fear-based thinking. They got programmed by TV and school like everybody else. I always believed in the school system, but now I've lost faith.

"Now I feel like I have done more harm than good by sending them to government schools."

Truly: "What do you mean by that? Going to school is a good thing."

Anders: "Generally speaking, it is. There is no better way to improve yourself than through education. Some information can only be learned from people who have spent decades studying their field.

"The question isn't *that* they are learning in school, it is more of a question of *what* they are learning in school. Knowing what I know now, I would home school my children.

"I think public schools are teaching counterproductive philosophies, elitism, and victim mindsets. I don't agree with any of that. They're also preparing our children to be cogs in the machine. I gave them authority status over my children by endorsing the schools. That's on me.

"Of course, there are many good teachers, but the system itself is corrupt. And teachers who hold mistaken beliefs persist. It's difficult to unlearn when you think you are right.

"Schools should teach children how to think, not what to think."

Truly: "Parents should take care of that."

Anders: "Through no fault of their own, most parents don't know how to think themselves."

Truly: "True dat."

Anders: "Institutions with good intentions have devolved into the machines that grind people down."

Truly: "To devolution!" she says raising her cup.

Anders: "Yes, to devolution. We have people raising people under false beliefs. Sometimes it seems like we're moving in the wrong direction."

Truly: "That sounds pessimistic. Where's the optimistic attitude? You're supposed to be an example to your students."

Anders: "An example? You mean a role model, like Jesus?"

Truly: "Maybe not that extreme."

Anders: "Do you believe in God?"

Truly: "I don't know. Too many things don't add up. It's hard to believe that there is this one Great Puppet Master out there controlling everyone and everything. Maybe if the Chelseas would stop bugging Him about getting on cheerleading squads, He would have time to take care of the starving babies."

Anders: "God has all the time there is. So, you can't accept the concept of God as presented to you by the world. Me neither."

Truly: "It seems like most people believe in God, in some form or another."

Anders: "Arguing over the form of God is one of the biggest problems with the God debates, because God has no form, yet is all forms."

Truly: "What does that even mean? No form, yet *all* forms?"

Anders: "People think God is an outside force with an individual personality. The universal cannot be an individual. 'For a unity to acknowledge anything outside of itself is to cease to be unity.'"

Truly: "There is no 'I' in team."

Anders: "Right. From the team perspective, the team and the players do not see each other as outside of themselves. The team sees all the players as part of itself. It would not be *that* team, if it did not have *those* players.

"Each one of those players is an individual expression of that team, bringing something unique every time. Just as we are all individual expressions of God forming a unity."

Truly: "If God is a unity, why doesn't everyone agree on one concept of God? I mean, He controls everything and everyone. He could just make everybody happy and nice."

Anders: "We have free will. We each have the divine ability to think positively or negatively, to create Heaven or Hell."

Truly: "It would be nice if we could agree on the guidelines to follow. Maybe if we had a role model?"

Anders: "We already have that. In fact, we've had many great teachers step up, tell us all about it, and show us how. After 2,000 years of energetic evolution since Jesus did, we humans *still* argue about His teachings.

"Some people argue that His teachings are fictions, made up to control the masses. Others argue that He is God, or God as man, and that's the reason He could do all those things. All the time unconsciously stating that they are *not* God, and therefore can*not* do all these things.

"That's not what He said. He said all these things and more shall you do."

Truly: "Are you saying I can walk right out across that cove to the other side?"

Anders: "Does that feel like a natural thing for you to do?"

Truly: "No, I don't think so."

Anders: "Then you don't really believe you can do it. Jesus *believed* he had no limits. 'All things are possible to him that believes.'"

Truly: "I believe I'll have another beer."

Anders: "It is already done." He motioned to Katie.

Katie: "Are you guys ready to order now?"

Anders: "Truly, what do you recommend?"

Truly: "Of course, the fish 'n chips is excellent here. I'll have that."

Anders: "Two fish 'n chips and two more beers. Do you want another shot?"

Truly: "No. I'm good."

Katie: "Two fish 'n chips and two beers coming right up."

Anders: "I'll be right back, too. I'm holding too much water element."

¡No Entres en Pánico!

IX

Mrs. B: "Elias, do you know how to read?"

Elias: "Ha ha, yes, that's a silly question. I read every day."

Mrs. B: "What do you like to read?"

Elias: "It depends on my intention. Sometimes I want to learn about something, and sometimes I just want to read some jokes. Mostly, I like to read stories."

Mrs. B: "Are you reading chapter books already?"

Elias: "What are chapter books? Don't all books have chapters."

Mrs. B: "What was the last book you read, and what is your favorite?"

Elias: "Let's see. *The Prince and The Pauper* is esoteric *and* funny. I just finished *The Picture of Dorian Gray*. Interesting concept, to have a painting take the stripes for you.

"I have a lot of favorites, but I really like *The Hitchhiker's Guide to the Galaxy* series. For some reason, it's funnier in Spanish. ¡No entres en pánico!" Giggling, he held his hand out, palm facing away like a traffic cop.

Mrs. B: "You can read Spanish?"

Elias: "I understand all languages. I read nine, but I only speak seven. Nobody speaks Latin or Aramaic anymore. Give me a break."

Tatsu

X

On his way back to the table, Anders stopped to chat with Sam, the bartender. "This is a unique little hideaway. Gorgeous view. The spirit of this place is calming."

Sam: "We are protected here."

Anders: "Do you mean by the cliff walls?"

Sam: "The cliffs protect us from the northerly winds. The rocks protect us from the wrath of the ocean. The trees protect us from the hot afternoon sun. Tatsu protects us from evil spirits."

Anders: "Tatsu? I'm intrigued. Tell me more about this Tatsu."

Sam: "Every place has a genius loci, or the spirit of the location. When you enter a new area, you should always introduce yourself to the spirit of the place."

Anders: "Right, every place has a guardian spirit, just as every person has a guardian spirit assigned to each of us at birth. Our genius. But what is Tatsu? Is that its name?"

Sam: "Tatsu is a water dragon. Water dragons are protectors. My family has lived here since my great-great grandfather, Sam, discovered this grotto when he was young. I was named after him.

"We would all sit right down there, next to that stream when our grandfather would tell us stories. I don't know how much of it was real or made up, but he told us that his grandfather has fished this river since he found this spot.

"This stream feeds that river, which flows into the bay where it blends with the ocean as the tides flood and ebb. It symbolizes the flow of money to and through us."

Anders: "That is an amazing visual. I'm going to keep that one in my 'Frequently Used' folder. Please continue."

Sam: "Great-Great-Grandfather would fish all day. Friends would stop by to help him prepare the fish, and they would all sit down to eat together.

"They all brought what they could bring. One friend, Iron Mike, brought his steam shovel down here and moved these boulders around. Mother Nature didn't stack them up like that.

"Two brothers, who were carpenters, built this trestle table. None of the chairs survived. Then, they built this longhouse, and they all lived here. Eventually, the others began moving out on their own, until only my grandfather and his family were left.

"As people moved to the other side, upriver, he began converting this front part of the longhouse into a restaurant; then he added the bar, all built around this little stream of life. We still live in the back. My father had all this glass put in. It used to be an outdoor bar."

Anders: "Fascinating. This used to be a village? How many people live here now?"

Sam: "We have the rest of the house divided into two sections. My family lives in one side, and Auntie Myrtle lives in the other. Auntie Sarah and Uncle John don't live here, but they run the restaurant. You're sitting at their table. Cousin Jimmy makes plank salmon for Harvest Potlatch that you wouldn't believe."

Anders: "Isn't a potlatch like a Thanksgiving feast?"

Sam: "We have potlatches to give thanks to the creator for the First Salmon and the Fall Harvest. We follow the old ways. Potlatch means to give. In my family, we give thanks for our daily bread."

Anders: "Are you a Christian?"

Sam: "That's a simple question with a complicated answer, my friend. I don't believe all those things they do about their church, but I believe Christ is a model of what we can be. I haven't figured it all out, but he did say 'All these things and more shall ye do.' Didn't he?"

Anders: "He did indeed."

Sam: "We never thought of our way of life as a religion. It's just how we live. Most of it is similar to what Jesus was teaching his people. Missionaries came in and wanted our people to wear their clothes, cut our hair, and pray to their God; made us go to their Sunday school. Elders said, 'We don't need their God.'"

Anders: "Isn't it amazing how some people think they know what is best for everyone else? I've found that when you strip religions down to their core, you find many of the same principles expressed in different ways. You said you follow the old ways. Any miracles yet?"

Sam: "We have excellent health, and we are supplied with everything we need. What some call miracles are ordinary to us. Your friend may figure it out, but I'm not going to try to walk across that bay."

Anders: "You heard that, eh? You said the Tatsu is a water dragon. I like the sound of it. Is that a tribal belief from your ancestors?"

Sam: "All bodies of water have a spirit protecting them. My grandfather named this one Tatsu. It's a Japanese word for dragon. My people have great respect for the spirits. Just because we cannot see them, does not mean they are not there. Their existence does not depend on people believing. They protect us anyway."

Anders: "Is there any artwork of the dragon?"

Sam: "You mean like that drawing up there?"

Looking up, Anders saw a long, narrow charcoal of a dragon hanging above his head. "Oh, right there above the snake bite kit."

Sam: "My great-grandmother drew that when she was just 13 years old."

Anders: "Did she see it in a vision?"

Sam: "You could call it a vision. She was known for her ability to see the spirits. As a chief's daughter, she had tremendous mana. When she came into puberty, she was isolated for three months for everyone's safety."

Anders: "To protect against what, exactly? Really bad PMS?"

Sam: "To protect her while she is especially vulnerable and to protect the village from her, while she is accruing her new power.

"When a girl goes through these changes in her physical body, her emotional, mental, and spirit bodies change as well. The other girls in the village may only get isolated until the cycle stops, but the chief and his family have more mana, so the chief's daughters, especially the first-born daughter, are secluded for three cycles. It was during this time that she drew Tatsu."

Anders: "I find it interesting that you use the word mana. What kind of powers are we talking about that the village needs to be protected against?"

Sam: "The people were afraid of the spirits. During this period of change, the girl is not capable of rational thought because she is in metamorphosis on many levels.

"While her consciousness is preoccupied with that, she is wide open to outside influences. Free-roaming spirits, and those that cling to other people, could influence her while her guard is down."

Anders: "They were afraid she would become possessed?"

Sam: "Not only that, but she has not learned how to control her emotions."

Anders: "She won't grow out of that soon."

Sam: "She has *no* control at this point. She has a blossoming emotional body that amplifies the force of the thoughts emanating from the blossoming mental body.

"If someone makes her angry, she could have thoughts of doing harm, which, amplified by newfound emotional power, makes her extremely dangerous."

Anders: "Keeping them away from everyone else can only work for so long. Then what?"

Sam: "At the end of the isolation period, they would do a purification ritual to cleanse the physical and etheric bodies."

The sound of boots, dim at first but getting louder and coming up behind him, was an early warning signal that he had been talking too long.

"Hey! Where's my damned beer?" hollered Truly.

Sam: "Coming right up."

Truly: "What's with the fur coat in the glass case?"

Sam: "It's been in my family for generations. My great-great grandfather, was the so-called 'chief' of this longhouse. This was his robe. Otter pelts were the most valuable furs of his time, and only the leaders would wear them."

Truly: "Fur is murder."

Anders: "Murder means to kill a human being unlawfully with premeditated malice."

Truly: "It also means to kill wantonly."

Sam: "Is that how you think furs are harvested? Men with no conscience, killing for the pleasure of the kill? Some may enjoy the rush of the kill, or are motivated by money, but it was a different way of life back then.

"Hunting, trapping, and fishing were acts of survival. Nobody could go to the mall or shop online for jackets made from plastic pop bottles."

Truly: "It's still cruel. Hi, I want to wear your skin because you look so warm and beautiful. Turn your head this way please."

Sam: "I guess it's a matter of where you want to draw the line. At what point in the intelligence scale do we say, 'From this level, down, we can do what we want.?'"

Truly: "I'm okay with fish, but cute and furry seems like a good place to draw that line."

Anders: "In Genesis it says, 'And God blessed them, and said to them, 'Have *dominion* over the fish of the sea, the birds of the heavens, and over every living thing that moves on the earth.'"

Truly: "Somewhere, it says, 'He has given you every plant on the face of the earth, and every tree with its fruit. You shall have *them* for food.'"

Anders: "Doesn't it also say, after that, 'Every moving thing that liveth shall be meat for you?'"

Truly: "I don't know about that. I just know my friend, Janice, used to say that in the cafeteria."

Anders: "We were given dominion over the animal kingdom."

Truly: "Dominion doesn't mean do whatever you want, like kill and eat them. It means to take care of."

Sam: "I will still hunt, but I promise you I will not kill any animals just for their fur. Okay?"

Truly: "Deal. Let's head back to our table."

Sam: "Katie will have your fish out in a minute."

Anders: "Thanks, Sam."

Body As an Instrument

XI

Mrs. K: "Elias, what can you tell us about the screen where you see the numbers. I find that fascinating. Are you saying you have a screen in your mind that shows you the answer?"

Elias: "Yes, we all have a screen that surrounds us. It is our screen of perception. That is how we perceive the 3D world."

Mrs. K: "Aren't we living in a physical world? Knock on wood. It's real. I'm just wondering how you get those answers to come up so quickly."

Elias: "We are not just a physical body. We are consciousness using a body and brain to express different levels of mind.

"Mind is God. Body is an instrument through which God expresses Himself. A part of my mind is connected to infinite knowledge."

Mrs. K: "Why do you think you were chosen to receive this special gift?"

Elias: "You have the same gift, auntie. Inside, we are all the same. We all have the same gifts. The difference is in perceived limits.

"We are spirit before. We are spirit after. I came here with a purpose. No fire and brimstone, just water and wine. I chose these two as parents for obvious reasons."

Mr. H: "Are you saying you selected this life before you were born?"

Elias: "You have to admit, I made some good choices. This is pretty sweet. We need a physical vessel to interact with the physical world. We need material receptors to experience Heaven on Earth."

Mr. H: "Not everyone can be born into this kind of life, Elias."

Elias: "Nobody else can be me, that's true. Everybody does have the ability to reshape their world with the power of their imagination.

"You chose to have this earthly experience. Your parents, this body, this life, you have chosen. What are you going to do with it all now? What choices will you make?"

After-Hours Alibi

XII

Truly: "Did you hear that guy back there?"

Anders: "The guy at the bar with that chick?"

Truly: "Yeah. Did you hear that? He said, 'Can you imagine me going down on you, exactly the way you like it?' Who does he think he is?"

Anders: "It sounds like part of a rapid seduction pattern to me. It also appeared she was responding favorably. If things keep going that way, they're going to have a great evening."

Truly: "With a line like that? Shouldn't he say that more privately? If a guy said something like that to me in a bar, he would probably end up with my knee going down on him."

Anders: "You didn't hear the context. We just heard him say one sentence, and I saw a twinkle in her eye. They've been talking for a while. They were sitting there when we came in."

Their conversation was momentarily disrupted by Katie placing two plates on the table.

Katie: "Two fish 'n chips. Sam said you got your beer already. Can I get you anything else?"

Anders: "We're good, thank you."

Truly: "Wait. Can I get some extra tartar sauce for my fries?"

Katie: "I'll bring you some. Enjoy your meal."

Truly: "Do you think they knew each other already?"

Anders: "Maybe. If you do the techniques properly, it doesn't matter."

Truly: "Techniques? You mean he's scamming her? I still might go over and introduce my knee to his sack."

Anders: "Easy there, tiger. Like I said, if he knows what he's doing, they both will have an amazing night."

Truly: "Tonight, maybe, but what about after that? If he's just trying to trick her into sleeping with him, so he can dump her in the morning, that's not cool."

Anders: "Done properly, he can connect with a part of her that most men wouldn't care about, even if they knew it existed. A master of seduction can weave beautiful imagery for the subconscious mind.

"You never know, this could possibly end up being the most powerful sexual experience of her life. Even if it is just a one-night stand, she may never forget how she feels tonight. Also, you don't know what she wants. Maybe she wants someone just for tonight."

Truly: "Yeah, I get that. Been there. How did you learn about seduction? I thought you were married all your life."

Anders: "The two are not mutually exclusive. Shortly before my wife got diagnosed with cancer, she stopped enjoying sex. It was painful for her, but I didn't know that.

"I thought maybe it was me. I thought maybe she had gotten bored with me as a partner after all these years. So, in an effort to improve our sex life, I began studying seduction, tantric sex, and various other lovemaking techniques."

Truly: "Oh, do tell. Like what? Did you learn how give her multiple, mind-blowing orgasms?"

Anders: "It's not as difficult as you might think. But how many ever take the time to find out? People should learn how to seduce each other. It takes sexual relations to multiple exquisite levels of enjoyment. Sexual energy heals the body and the mind."

Truly: "It's good for the spirit too."

Anders: "I learned how we could both have multiple simultaneous orgasms. An experience I'll never forget, I can tell you. And, yes, it was very good for the soul."

Truly: "Wait, how can a man have multiple orgasms? Don't you have to wait a long time in between?"

Anders: "To understand the concept of multiple male orgasms, you first have to make the distinction between orgasm and ejaculating."

Truly: “Aren’t they the same?”

Anders: “You've probably realized I don’t mistake common knowledge for truth. Most people think a man has an orgasm by ejaculating, then he’s done.”

Truly: “Yeah. And?”

Anders: “They are linked, but an orgasm is not dependent on the spasms of the muscles. When you learn how to circulate the energy, and specifically train the muscles to respond differently, you can postpone ejaculation and experience multiple orgasms.”

Truly: “But isn’t that the best part, shooting your gun? That’s the part they seem to be in such a hurry to get to, and then it’s ‘Thanks, see ya. I gotta go.’ Not exactly fair, when you don’t even get one, let alone multiples.”

Anders: “There are levels of orgasm that are far superior to physical muscle spasms.

“Seduction expands the sexual experience. It can begin with a glance, or a touch as simple as a handshake. When two people connect on an unconscious level, it’s usually because they’re operating on similar frequencies, so they resonate with each other on a deeper level.

“Do you know how it feels to be magnetically attracted to someone the first time you meet them?”

Truly: “Yes, I felt that recently.”

Anders: “Right, you can’t quite put your finger on why, but you instantly feel comfortable with them. You know you haven’t met this person before, but something seems remarkably familiar.

“You just want to be near this person. It happens spontaneously when people have aligned themselves to attract certain people into their lives, consciously or unconsciously. They are magnetically attracted to each other.”

Truly: “Magnetically attracted? You know how magnets are attracted to each other, don’t you? Opposites attract. That’s why relationships fail. Opposites get together, feed each other for a while, then they start feeding on each other, until there is nothing left.”

Anders: “We attract what *appears* to be opposite, because the other person has qualities that we want to develop in ourselves. Couples who are unhappy have stopped living and giving. You have to give love to receive love.”

Truly: “I’ve seen it too many times. My parents haven’t been happy for a long time. They’re getting a divorce now. That’s why I’m never getting married or having kids.”

Anders: "People aren't necessarily unhappy in marriage. The institution of marriage is not the problem. A lot of people are happy in their marriages for decades. It's entirely up to the individuals themselves to *be happy*. You can't make anyone happy but yourself."

Truly: "Speaking of happy, those two are getting ready to leave. Look at her. I see what you mean about the twinkle in her eye. She's *all* lit up. He did that just by talking to her?"

Anders: "Yeah. More accurately, she did that to herself with his guidance. She could reject his suggestions, but it feels better to follow along. Seduction patterns are a powerful way of communicating with the subconscious."

Truly: "That sounds interesting. What are seduction patterns?"

Anders: "The term *patterns* refers to language patterns. One of the many aspects of NLP is the study of how words, and combinations of words, affect physical responses in our bodies."

Truly: "Words cause physical responses?"

Anders: "Stop for a second … and remember what it's like to bake chocolate chip cookies. You're mixing the dough while the oven heats up. Once you get all the ingredients blended, and you are putting dollops of dough on the sheet, you just can't resist popping a little ball of cookie dough in your mouth. Yum-m-m.

"You put your sheet into the oven and let it bake. As the cookies bake, that sweet smell fills the entire house. And you start to feel the excitement, which builds and builds, as you anticipate the pleasure of that warm, sweet, melted chocolate on your tongue. Your whole body begins to fill with *ecstatic* energy and anticipation.

"Then you hear the timer go off. As you open the oven door, a wave of warm, sweet goodness embraces you. With your oven mitts, you remove the cookies from the oven, and set them down to cool."

Truly: "I'm not going to lie. I really, really, want a chocolate chip cookie right now."

Anders: "That was a simple language pattern that got you to stop what you were thinking about, and start thinking about and feeling, the experience I wanted you to have.

"With my word choices, and the sequence in which they were delivered, by telling a story, I guided you from the state you were in, to the state you are in now, which is desire."

Truly: "And you can do that with sex too? I want to be seduced."

Anders: "Sure, we all do. I'm just not so sure this is the right thing for *us* to do."

Truly: "What are you hung up on? You claim to have special skills. I'm calling you out. Can you deliver, or not?"

Anders: "I can definitely deliver. I don't think you realize how powerful this technology is. Love chemicals are highly addictive. You will feel things you have never felt before."

Truly: "I want to feel things I've never felt before."

Anders: "Have you ever been in love?"

Truly: "I think so. I'm not sure if it was actually love. It was fun … for a while."

Anders: "I've heard that men fall in love when they are with someone, and women fall in love when they are away from them."

Truly: "That sounds like a generalization."

Anders: "It is. Falling in love is partially a thought process. Women tend to be more guarded in their conversations with men. A person can only hold about seven thoughts at a time.

"If a woman is thinking about how she presents herself and the safety of her surroundings and evaluating the person she is with, she is not likely to process thoughts of love consciously."

Truly: "Isn't it more like a feeling?"

Anders: "Sure it is. 'In love' is a state of being. Every state has qualities that define it. The qualities of a state are the steps to achieving that state.

"The qualities of the state we call being in love are certain thoughts and certain chemicals that produce specific vibrations that we recognize as a specific emotion. Like, I'm sure you can remember the best parts of being in love. All of your senses sing in harmony. You feel too good to feel bad."

Truly: "How are those the steps to getting there?"

Anders: "You can separate the state into its component states. Each time you achieve a component state, you are another step closer to being completely in that state, to becoming it. The easiest way to begin is to match the breathing of it."

Truly: "You mean like, I'm breathlessly in love. I can't stop thinking about you. My heart goes pitter pat. I'm not even hungry anymore."

Anders: "So, you do know the qualities of being in love."

Truly: "Yeah, but how do you just call them up whenever you want?"

Anders: "The words you use to describe a quality vibrate in harmony with that quality, and pluck the string that causes that vibration in the brain. Each one of those qualities has qualities that define it.

"What I really love about being in love is the cocktail of chemicals your brain and body release. Endorphins block signals of pain. Serotonin, dopamine, and oxytocin flowing through your system push out any negative feelings. You feel motivated to take on challenges.

"Those chemicals are the creative force that motivates us to mate, which perpetuates the species. We are designed to enjoy sex. You know how, when you're in love, everything looks brighter and more beautiful?"

Truly: "Yeah. I want those feelings."

Anders: "When you reach that level of ecstasy, you become addicted to it. You want to feel the excitement of pure energy flowing through you more and more. You will become a different person."

Truly: "I'm going to become a different person anyway. I might as well go out with a big bang."

Anders: "Okay. I have one condition, though. After tonight, except for in the classroom, we won't get together again for thirty days."

Truly: "Who says we are going to get together again? I thought we were only talking about tonight?"

Anders: "We are. Just make a commitment in your mind and promise yourself you will wait thirty days."

Truly: "That's not a problem. I've gone longer than thirty days before. So, yeah, I promise."

Anders: "You don't have to go without for thirty days, just without me. It can be a powerful addiction. It's better if you and I wait. Just a precaution."

Truly: "It seems so arbitrary. Like I said, I'm good with that. Enough of baking cookies. Seduce me. Now, what was that you were saying about how words affect our bodies?"

Anders: "The guy who pioneered these techniques ingeniously applied NLP techniques to making women feel good, so they would sleep with him."

Truly: "I don't know whether that makes him an angel or a devil."

Anders: "It's interesting. Women call him angel and men call him devil.

"Whether a technology is used morally or abused immorally depends on the intention of the operator. It's easier to sway the subconscious with language than you might think.

"His argument is women use makeup, clothing, and accessories to glamour men into lowering their guard. And believe it or not, women also tell stories."

Truly: "But women get dolled up for men. They do their hair, put on all that makeup, and their best perfume for men."

Anders: "Do they? Or is all that presentation to get men to give them something they want even more?"

Truly: "Like what?"

Anders: "Attention, if it's the right kind, builds self-esteem. Everyone wants to be loved. All I'm saying is that women have traditional ways of seducing men. Men can step up their game by evoking images that create an environment and stir emotions using language patterns. Words.

"I never practiced enough to get good at it, but I learned some of the basics. He had this one, called the Discovery Channel Pattern. It was fascinating. It went something like this: Have you ever watched the Discovery Channel, Truly?"

Truly: "I used to watch it, when I was little."

Anders: "I don't know if you saw it, or would even remember it, but there was this one episode where they were talking about roller coasters. Do you like roller coasters, Truly?"

Truly: "Oh, yeah. I love roller coasters."

Anders: "They had a roller coaster design expert on the show. He was saying there are three main factors that make up an amazing roller coaster ride.

"He said, the first element is that it has to be compelling. It has to have so many twists and turns and surprises that it stimulates your curiosity. It has to be a ride that you want to get on so badly that when you see it, you feel yourself right there, riding it. Seeing, hearing, and feeling, what you would see, hear, and feel, if you were actually riding that roller coaster. You just feel like you are drawn to this ride. You must take this ride.

"He said, the second element is that it has to be exciting. It has to be so exciting, that as soon as you get off, you want to climb right back on again. You want to take this ride multiple times.

"You know how when you are sitting there, and you start to make that long, slow, climb, up to the top? And you can hear and feel that *click*, *click*, *click* as you go higher.

"The anticipation keeps building. Your breathing gets harder, your heart begins to pound as you get closer and closer to the peak. You get to the top and the adrenaline is flowing. As you hit that first big drop, you come screaming down with a rush of that sweet, sweet flow of life energy.

"Then, he said, the third element is that it has to be safe. You have to know that you will not be hurt. They have to have insurance to operate the ride, and no insurance company will cover them if it isn't safe.

"They have strict safety standards. And people getting hurt is bad for business. So, you know you are going to be safe. You know you can really let yourself go."

Truly: "Good story, bro. That was interesting and stimulating, but when are we going to get to the seduction part?"

Anders: "Soon. What do you think seduction is?"

Truly: "I don't know. When I think of seduction, I think about the old movies, with Rudolph Valentino giving women that googly-eye stare."

Anders: "That's Hollywood. Seduction is not a matter of tricking someone into doing something against their will. It's more like orchestrating elements into a symphony. You know how you can get really pumped up when you hear a great song?"

Truly: "Yeah. What do you mean, elements? Are elements the same as qualities?"

Anders: "Yes, by elements, I just mean component parts. The individual qualities that make up a state of mind could be considered its component parts, or elements.

"Every state of body is a result of a state of mind. A thought sends a vibration at specific frequency. You feel it in your body."

Truly: "Like what, for example?"

Anders: "Well, for example, can you remember a time when you felt really horny? Maybe a time when you just wanted it so bad, that you said to yourself, 'I gotta get some, right now.'

"As your mind starts to shift in consciousness, remembering how that feels, your body begins to change its vibration, to tune in to the frequency of wanton desire. You store those memories together in a compartment of your mind.

"The elements of that state are the mental representations and the physical sensations you feel in your body. You may find that the more you think about feeling horny, the more that feeling grows, and intensifies in your body. Can you feel your body starting to shift, as we sit here talking?"

Truly: "Uh huh."

Anders: "When you notice your body beginning to feel that way, it's almost as if the rest of the world has disappeared. Imagining feelings of pleasure creates more feelings of pleasure.

"It's interesting how a change in awareness can change the way your body feels. However, just helping you move into that mental, physical, and emotional state is not enough.

"I wonder if you can associate that state of desire with me. What do you imagine it would be like for you to think of me while you are feeling that deep passionate urge to satisfy that burning desire. Sex for the pure pleasure of sex.

"Can you imagine what it would be like to spend hours making love to someone you feel those strong feelings toward?"

Truly: "I don't know what it is, but I was wondering if you'd like to continue this discussion more privately?"

Anders: "Katie, can we get our check, please?"

A Shot of What?

XIII

Mrs. B: "Elias, have you had all your shots?"

Elias: "Grammie sometimes has a shot, but she says I'm too young."

Mrs. B: "No, I mean have you had your vaccinations?"

Elias: "Vaccinations are for people who are mana'ole. They run counter to my beliefs. I don't need them."

Mrs. B: "But you could get sick. Don't you worry about catching a disease? Vaccinations are proven to help eradicate diseases."

Elias: "Fear of disease brings disease. A needle in your arm won't change your beliefs. It only reinforces bad ones."

Mrs. K: "What do you mean bad ones?"

Elias: "'To each, unto him as he believeth.' I believe I have divine immunity from disease. You get what you expect. All dis-ease begins in the mind and is expressed in the body.

"inā mana'o 'oe he pono ka nila, pono 'oe i ka nila.
If you believe you need the needle, you need the needle."

Mrs. K: "Most vaccines are ninety to ninety-eight percent effective in preventing spread of disease."

Elias: "I am one hundred percent effective in preventing disease. You want me to have a higher handicap?"

Mrs. K: "A vaccine won't make you weaker, it will make you stronger. They just put a little bit into your system so your body can identify it when there is more."

Elias: "I understand the theory. My mind is programmed for health. It can already identify it. My body is not polluted, so my immune system works perfectly. I am stronger than any disease. ho'omana is more powerful against ho'oma'i than lapa'au."

Mrs. K: "Don't you think you should listen to what the science tells us?"

Elias: "I love science. Have you read *Quantum Healing*, or *Ageless Mind, Timeless Body*? Quantum physics and mental science prove to me the mind creates the body.

"The average age of cells in our bodies is seven years. But our atoms exchange with our environment to give us a whole new body every 11 months.

"I choose not to accept mental disease. It will not appear in my body. I have no fear.

"*Mens sana in corpore sano*; healthy mind in a healthy body."

Mrs. B: "So, you do speak Latin. Do you think you can control your health with your mind?"

Elias: "We always do. I believe it in my heart. 'As a man thinketh in his heart, so is he.'"

Day 2

XIV

Walking to the classroom door, Anders said to Truly, "You look pretty chipper for someone who has been up all night."

Truly: "I am not tired at all. That was amazing. I didn't even know that was possible."

Anders: "All things are possible."

Truly: "You have dried blood on your sleeve. Are those the same clothes you had on yesterday?"

Anders: "Yeah. I didn't get a chance to go home. Something came up."

Truly: "You can wash it at my house after class. Then you'll have a clean shirt for tomorrow."

Anders: "Didn't we have an agreement? Besides, I have to go home to take care of my cat. I usually take her into the woods to climb trees. She's probably mad at me for not coming home. She thought we were going to play."

Truly: "I know how she feels."

Anders: "I tried to tell you this part wouldn't be easy."

Truly: "There is no try. The word *tried* implies failure."

Anders: "Let's give it a couple of days. At least until this module is complete."

He pulled out his speaker. As *The Grand Illusion* played, the cadets took their seats.

Starkstrom: "Cadet Coyote will not be joining us this morning because he made some bad decisions yesterday afternoon that resulted in his having to spend the night in the hospital. He is fine and getting better as we speak.

"We're going to talk a little about our unconscious minds and how we can use that part of our minds to enrich our lives on a daily basis. How does that sound to you?

"Have you ever wondered how it is that some people just seem to get all the breaks, while others seem to struggle all their lives? What do you think is the causal relationship between success and struggle?

"Do you think we are subject to God's will? Or, do you think we're just random bits of debris, floating on an ocean, tossed about, drifting wherever the tides of life take us?

"Let me offer a more empowering thought. We create the world we live in."

Alonzo: "We create all of it? Then, why don't we just create good stuff? Somebody else must be creating wars and disease."

Starkstrom: "You don't have a hard time believing man creates wars, do you?"

Alonzo: "No. Man does create wars, but not this man. I don't get how I create wars between other people or make other people sick.

"I mean, I have seen people make themselves sick, but most of the time, we don't have control over our health. I'm allergic to peanuts. There is no way for me to control that, so I don't let them in my world. Is that what you mean?"

Starkstrom: "That is an interesting topic, that you believe you don't have complete control over the health of your body. There is a lot to unpack there. So, let's narrow down to allergies. You believe you are allergic to peanuts, yeah?"

Alonzo: "I *know* I'm allergic to peanuts. One time, I didn't have my pen, and I almost died from it."

Starkstrom: "Glad to see you made it through. How long have you believed you were allergic to peanuts?"

Alonzo: "My mom said I've been allergic since I was a baby."

Starkstrom: "And you believed her. Listen. Your immune system is designed to protect your healthy cells from pathogens.

"Pathogens are microorganisms that can reproduce themselves in your body and produce symptoms of disease. Allergens do not reproduce."

Alonzo: "Well, whatever is going on, all I know is that if I eat anything with peanuts, my nose starts running, my skin gets all itchy, and my throat starts tightening up, even if I don't know they're in there."

Starkstrom: "You give your subconscious too little credit. Your subconscious recognizes the substance, even if you're not consciously aware of it.

"An allergic reaction is your immune system overreacting to an otherwise harmless substance. It is treating an allergen as though it were a pathogen. Your immune system is sending an army to deal with a jaywalker."

Alonzo: "You mean sending Space Force, don't you?"

Starkstrom: "Right. By sending Space Force to *destroy* a jaywalker, it blocks traffic for miles."

Alonzo: "But peanuts aren't a harmless substance. It's not just me. I have friends who can't eat that poison. More than a couple of us have had close calls. You can't tell me that's just our imagination."

Starkstrom: "The symptoms are very real and potentially deadly. That shows how powerful your subconscious is.

"Not everyone responds to allergens that way. Most people, and by *most* I mean over ninety-eight percent of people, do not have an allergic reaction to peanuts. A fact, by itself, that tells you peanuts are not poisonous. It is not the peanuts that cause the symptoms. It is your own individual immune system overresponding to a nonthreat."

Alonzo: "Then, how come my body responds that way? If I could get rid of my allergies, I'd do it in a heartbeat."

Starkstrom: "Come on up."

Alonzo: "You mean right now?"

Starkstrom: "You said you'd do it in a heartbeat. A few heartbeats have passed. Come on up. Have a seat."

Alonzo: "What are you going to do?"

Starkstrom: "Yesterday we talked about the programming we get from our environment that we accept before the critical factor is developed.

"Food allergies are a product of incorrect programming. At some point, from whatever source, you learned to believe you are allergic to peanuts. Your software has a bug in it. We can debug you."

Alonzo: "How is it a bug? If I've been allergic since I was a baby, that's my whole life. Isn't that just the way I am?"

Starkstrom: "It's the way you have been. Before we learn languages, we sense vibrations. Somehow, a line of code that identifies peanuts as a threat was written into your immunity app. You can open up that directory tree and edit the code. It's easier than you believe."

Alonzo: "Let me think about it for a while."

Starkstrom: "Whenever you're ready.

"We were talking about how the beliefs we have formed, through the programming we have received, are the foundation of the environment we create.

"We see the world through our beliefs. Our beliefs are what have gotten us to where we are today. Good and bad. Each of us has our own unique combination of thoughts and beliefs known as a paradigm.

"Some of those beliefs still serve you. Some of them do not. Some of your beliefs move you away from what you want. All of them are your limits.

"While we are using our imagination, let's do something unusual. It's not really too unusual for what we've been doing here; it's unusual compared to what you usually do.

"Aka is a substance that is formed of i'o, the formless. It is the first stage of formation, or matter.

"Aka is an invisible form of substance that is all around us. Whenever you think about someone or something in existence, and everything exists already, an invisible thread goes out connecting the two of you.

"Psychometry, finding lost objects or tracing events through objects, relies on aka as a conductor.

"Aka threads also connect when you see, hear, smell, taste, or touch someone or something. As more and more of these connections are made between the two of you, the threads begin to braid themselves into cords.

"These invisible cords connect you to everyone and everything in your world. These cords connect you to your world. At the same time, they bind you to your past.

"You are already a different person, but your friends and family still see you as the person you were before.

"It is time to cut the cords."

Cadet: "If we cut all our cords, are we going to lose touch with the people who are important to us?"

Starkstrom: "What you are doing is cutting *old* attachments. You can reconnect with the people who are important to you just by thinking about them. You send out kind loving thoughts to them that form new pure connections. Some of those people will sense the disconnect and start sending *you* new aka threads.

"Because everyone and everything, including thoughts and beliefs, has a form or it could not be, we will use the term *form* for all nouns.

"The vagus nerve, behind your solar plexus, is the yoke of the sympathetic and parasympathetic nervous systems. It forms the union between the conscious and subconscious in your body. It is also where the aka cords connect to the body.

"Imagine, from your center, millions of golden threads radiating in all directions, reaching out to all the forms you are aware of. Some of these threads have been woven, or braided, through repetition, together forming a strong cord that binds you to that form.

"Some of these cords are mutually beneficial. Those cords can be re-created easily in a purer form. So, we are going to cut all of these old aka threads with a long silver-light sword. That's right. Imagine. With your sword, you can easily cut through the cords."

Cadet: "Mine's a lightsaber."

Cadet: "Mine too."

Starkstrom: "Then, make the sound of a lightsaber. Make it real. Convince your subconscious that you mean business. *This* is what I want. No question of intention or doubt of outcome. Cut all of the cords that are feeding on your energy. Cut them close to your body. Cut them all!"

Cadet: "Mine was too."

Starkstrom: "When you have finished cutting all those cords, you can put away your lightsabers; just stand there … and notice how you feel right now. And say, 'I am free.' Say it out loud."

"I am free!" they chorused.

Starkstrom: "Let's take a break; allow your system to reboot. We'll go outside and get some air. Meditate on the ones you love. Reconnect with them in your mind. Hold a pure thought of their ideal self. Some of your phones may start ringing. Let's meet back here in twenty minutes. I'll bring the music."

Magic of Believing

XV

Mr. H: "Elias, do you believe in magic?"

Elias: "What do you mean by magic?"

Mr. H: "Spells, manifesting, voodoo hexes. Things like that."

Elias: "Things like what? Those are different things."

Mr. H: "Things that are inexplicable. Things that seem to have a supernatural cause."

Elias: "All things are explained by science. Mind science is natural science. We cast spells every day around here."

Mrs. B: "What kind of spells do you cast every day?"

Elias: "At the end of each day, we make a list of what we want tomorrow."

Mrs. B: "Isn't that just a to-do list?"

Elias: "It's a might-do list if you don't write it down. Also, to begin each season, we write down our big goals.

"To transmute goals from ideas into form requires daily persistent faith.

"There's magic in writing down what you want. Why do you think they call it a spell?"

Mr. H: "What about lucky charms, voodoo hexes, and faith healing?"

Elias: "Charms have exactly as much power as you believe they do. Voodoo is like a Catholic sect. Grammie says we're not Catholic anymore. But I have seen healing in many faiths."

Mrs. K: "Yeah. So, is there a force, or power, or science behind all that?"

Elias: "The one thing they all have in common is belief. All things work for the people who believe they will.

"Dumbo was fooled into believing by faulty reasoning. 'If birds have feathers, and birds can fly, then if you have a feather, you can fly.' We all know it was his ears."

Mrs. K: "He believed the feather helped him fly, so he flew."

Elias: "They gave Napoleon the *Star Saphire* when he was young and told him it would make him emperor. He *believed* he would be emperor. Voodoo is also a form of suggestion that can be used for good or evil. The same is true for faith healing."

Mrs. K: "I'm not sure I understand how faith healing can work."

Elias: "It is done unto him as he believeth. Whatever you believe is true must be true for you. Whether you believe you will be healed or not, you are right.

"If you believe I have the power to heal, you will be healed. People who believe crystals contain magic healing power will be healed by their faith. People who believe in the medical paradigm *need* medical practitioners. That is their form of faith."

God Exists

XVI

Starkstrom: "Welcome back everyone, including you, Coyote. Good to see you back in class. God has blessed us with another beautiful day!"

Coyote: "God doesn't exist."

Starkstrom: "You certainly are a ray of sunshine. Tell me what you mean by that."

Coyote: "I hate to tell you this padre, but there is no God. There isn't anyone out there watching over us to see if we're being naughty or nice. They try to tell us, if you're really good, you get to go to Heaven. If you do *anything* wrong, you will burn in Hell for eternity. It's all just a fairytale for ignorant people.

"If there is a God out there, why is there so much suffering and sickness in the world? Oh, 'It's just God's will.' No. It's just bullshit. Y'all can believe whatever you want. I'm not buying it.

"Religion is just a bunch of people trying to control other people, using fear tactics to keep them in line. Those people actually get paid to lie to children. They tell them to behave, or God will get them. He's watching you."

Starkstrom: "I have found, when people argue about God, what they are really arguing about is their *concept* of God. The worst atrocities in history have been done in the name of God by *people*."

Coyote: "Yeah. The bomber on the bus is always someone who was 'told by God' to kill these random people. Wars, fighting, and killing, all kinds of death and destruction for God. That doesn't match up with the 'God Is Love' mantra. They're all manmade rules used to control people.

"God is another one of man's creations. We created him in our likeness and image, not the other way around. On your way out, make sure you leave some money for God in the basket."

Starkstrom: "I choose to believe the money put in the baskets helps many people. I agree with most of what you're saying, but not the sentiment behind it. I understand your point of view because I was there at one time too. I've studied for decades to acquire this level of awareness. This is a topic that we could spend hours on.

"I'm not going to try to persuade you one way or another, but I will briefly state my opinion. Keep in mind two things. One, we have an agenda to fulfill here that doesn't allow time for this discussion. And two, the government doesn't want me talking about religion."

"What we are talking about is the *concept* of God. I agree that the Christian concept of God, shared by most of the major religions, as a separate being outside of us, does not exist. When you look at your beliefs, you may find that it is religion, and religious doctrines, that you cannot accept.

"The Bible is not a history book. It's an esoteric book of human psychology and a book of the deepest occult about *you*. If you want, at another time we can discuss it. For now, let's get back to our syllabus."

Coyote: "Ho-old up. You can't just drop a bomb like that and move on. What do you mean, 'The Bible is a book of the *occult*'? Why would they burn witches if their main book is occult?"

Starkstrom: "That is another one of the perplexing puzzles of religions and the human condition. So, quickly, I will say that God never instructed anyone to kill, not even thine enemies. Man has thought all evil into existence. People kill people."

Griffin: "Didn't he tell Abraham to kill his son? That's so brutal."

Starkstrom: "Not literally. 'God told Abraham' means Abraham became aware. Where it says, 'to kill his son,' it means to release old ideas which no longer serve. Ideas are children. Which is metaphor, and which is material?

"The Bible, even with the challenges of translations, is a map of the human experience told metaphorically. Each of the characters represents a stage of development, awareness, or a personality trait. That is the code.

"It doesn't matter if your physical gender matches up with the gender of the character. We all have male and female qualities. The Virgin Mary gives birth to a new idea. Meaning, from a blank slate, we conceive of an idea and give birth to it.

"Study the stories of Jesus and the twelve disciplines; the twelve aspects of mind to be mastered.

"When Simon proved himself to be a good disciple by his works, Jesus gave him the surname Peter. Petros, the stone. Simon Peter is the discipline of unwavering faith; the first state of mind to be mastered; the gateway to heaven.

"Israel is a pure state of mind with no deceit. We are all David, the son of Jesus the father, when we are born. If you want to become wealthy, study King Solomon. Take on that aspect of personality. Become a wealthy person in your mind first."

Cadet: "But doesn't it also say poverty is a virtue? Monks take a vow of poverty. A rich man can't get through the eye of a needle, or whatever. Which way are we supposed to go on this one?"

Starkstrom: "We're going to run way over time, if we don't get back to our schedule. We can talk about these other things, but I have to deliver on the syllabus I presented. Let's focus on the task at hand."

Coyote: "You were the one who brought up God. Then you said the Bible is like a grimoire or something. You can't just leave us hanging like this."

Starkstrom: "Okay. Look, there is no inherent virtue in poverty on its own. There is virtue in making a strong commitment, like sharing your blessings with those who are coming out of poverty. But none in being impoverished.

"Poverty is a mental disease that can be eradicated with the right approach. Study the principles of King Solomon.

"Jesus said the people who call themselves religious don't even know God. He also said that, if you believe, all these miracles and more will you do. It is all spelled out in great detail in the Bible. You need to study it in a certain way to learn it.

"First, understand that the Bible is a book about you, now. And then repetition, repetition, repetition, with the proper mind set.

"Those religious scholars didn't know how to study it. So, they deeply embedded incorrect information through repetition. They weren't aware of the difference between witchcraft and higher faculties.

"I understand that you don't believe in what they're selling. I don't believe them either. Are we good?"

Coyote: "For now. We'll talk more later."

Starkstrom: "Now, this actually provides a decent segue back into our topic. We are going to talk a little bit about paradigms.

"Yesterday, we talked about how our paradigms are the autopilots of our lives. Today we are going to talk about how they are formed. Why do you believe what you believe?" Long pause.

"We touched on this already. Remember, when we are born, our critical factor does not kick in until we are about seven or eight.

"Our subjective mind is wide open and taking in everything its physical sensors can pick up. It doesn't know how to sift through all that data to verify anything. We are blessed with the ability to learn quickly, so we accept it all.

"At this point in life, we don't know how to sort the information. The subconscious then starts to group things by vibrational frequency. Things that resonate with each other begin to move together.

"I just told you how the Law of Attraction works. I hope you got that in your notes."

Griffin: "Wait. If it's that important, can you repeat it?"

Starkstrom: "You will hear it many times. The question is, when will you get it?

"Everything vibrates. The subconscious mind sorts things according to their vibrational frequency.

"Things that resonate with each other begin to move together. That is the Law of Attraction powered by the Law of Vibration. Got it?

"When we are babies, we take in all the information we can pick up. We sense the vibrational frequencies of the people around us. We hear the music of the language spoken. We may not know what each lyric means, but the volume, tone, and cadence become familiar.

"Familiar means having to do with family. For something to become familiar to us, it is to become like family, or the things we learned from our family.

"Along with learning the language spoken around us, we also sense the emotions with which those words are delivered. We learn the beliefs and behaviors of the people around us.

"Their vibrations are the ones we pick up on the strongest, because their sources are the closest to us. If only one language is spoken in the home, we will speak that language.

"People don't learn to say *ain't* at school.

"Yesterday, we talked about the mental state of hypnosis. A question was raised regarding suggestibility.

"The subconscious mind is *highly amenable* to suggestion. That means the subconscious *wants* suggestion, or guidance. Like a child, it doesn't know the difference between the material world and the fantasy world of imagination.

"If it receives a suggestion from a perceived authority, and that suggestion doesn't go against its established beliefs, it will accept the suggestion. Babies perceive everything as authority. They absorb information.

"Who is teaching our babies? We plop them down in front of the TV while we take care of a few things. Televisions broadcast at a frequency that hypnotizes people of all ages. Corporate sponsors deeply embed their messages into wide-open minds.

"What are the messages they are absorbing? Stories that are woven to push agendas. Stories made from misunderstanding the world, some of them attempting to explain this or that. Bad information, presented convincingly and repeatedly, becomes belief.

"Earlier, Alonzo shared with us that he believes he has a peanut allergy."

Alonzo: "I do."

Starkstrom: "And you will as long as you believe that. Can anyone tell me how allergies, diseases, and even cancer are created in your body according to your subconscious beliefs?"

Alonzo: "Why would anyone create an allergy? I can tell you from experience, it isn't fun."

Starkstrom: "No disease is fun. There is always a positive intention behind every action of the subconscious mind. Regardless of the results, it is always trying to help. It is your inner child."

Alonzo: "How does this kid think a peanut allergy is helpful?"

Starkstrom: "Only you know for sure. There is no love like a mother's love. When you were a baby, your mom was, as most mothers are, concerned about your welfare. She opened her awareness to possible dangers in order to protect you. This takes us back to the Law of Vibration.

"The mother's antennae are tuned to the frequency of potential dangers. She even has an app that notifies her when new ones show up. She reacts to the news that more and more kids are suffering from peanut allergies.

"She thinks about her child getting an allergy. The thought can be dismissed or repeated. Most people don't accept that possibility for their child, so the thought is given no more energy.

"Some people start to run the message in their heads. Fretting and worrying and amplifying those fears. Those fears vibrate at a specific frequency and attract other thoughtforms that resonate with them. More thoughts and fears gather to form a massive belief.

"There are no time or space restrictions on thoughts. We are always projecting thoughtforms. You also have sensors that pick up those thought forms. And you, having no counterexample, accepted 'peanut allergy' as true for you. Over the years, that belief was reinforced. And now you believe you have an allergy."

Alonzo: "I'm telling you, it's real."

Starkstrom: "Come on up here Alonzo. Have a seat in the rearranger."

Alonzo slow walked to the chair and sat down.

Starkstrom: "What is it like when you are exposed to peanuts?"

Starkstrom noted the physiological changes in Alonzo's body and breathing.

Alonzo: "Well, like I said, my nose starts running, my eyes start watering, I get itchy all over, and I can hardly breathe 'cause my throat gets so tight. I'm even starting to feel it right now."

Starkstrom: "Yes. You are talking yourself into it. There aren't any peanuts here. Take a breath. As you let it out, you can begin to relax, even further.

"Remember earlier when I said allergies are a mistake of the immune system? It's treating peanuts as though they are harmful when they are not. The role of the immune system is to protect the body from parasites, pathogens, and carcinogens.

"Your immune system has the wrong guys. The allergens are harmless. It is your own immune system that is the problem. Without that response of the immune system, there is no problem. Don't start none, won't be none.

"How do you imagine your life would be different, if you were not allergic to anything?"

Alonzo: "Man. Honestly, I never thought about it. I have always been allergic to peanuts. It's something I've accepted. I take my meds, keep a pen handy, and stay the hell away from peanuts."

Starkstrom: "Would it be okay for you to not have any allergies at all, or do you have some hidden reason to keep them?"

Alonzo: "I can't think of any reason to keep them. I don't see any way they help me. It's just who I am."

Starkstrom: "Okay. You can't think of any reason to keep them, and you don't see any way they help you. You are willing to change that part of you.

"Now, can you imagine yourself healthy, with none of the restrictions of allergies? What would that be like?"

Alonzo: "I feel like it's easier to breathe already. And I wouldn't have to keep track of all that stuff."

Starkstrom: "Imagine yourself going to a friend's house, or a restaurant, and not have to worry about your food. Feel how much more relaxed you are. That's right. Breathe it in. Feel the freedom."

Starkstrom placed his hand on Alonzo's shoulder, like a soft Vulcan nerve pinch.

"Now, you know it is your own body that was operating from a mistaken identity. Peanuts have no power to harm you. Remember, your body knows the difference."

Alonzo: "Yeah, now it does."

Starkstrom: "You have a rational understanding. You are now operating from choice. From this moment, forward, you are healed. I think He said something like that."

Alonzo: "So, can I just go out and eat a Snickers bar, or something, after this?"

Starkstrom: "You have shifted your perception, but your subconscious may need more convincing. Before you do anything like that, I want you to do something. I want you to use your imagination again.

"Imagine, right now, that there is a plexiglass wall across the room. We are on one side, and everyone else is on the other. Can you see that? It goes all the way across the room, and it's airtight."

Alonzo: "Yes, I see it now."

Starkstrom: "Now I want you to imagine that you see yourself, right over there, back in your seat. Notice there is something different about you now."

He placed his hand on Alonzo's shoulder as before to fire the anchor. "You have new resources and understandings about your body that the old you was not aware of.

"This new you, that you have decided to be, knows that peanuts are not harmful to you. Your immune system operates perfectly."

He lifted his hand and put it back in place to fire the anchor again. "Breathe."

"A few minutes ago, you produced symptoms by calling them out. You know your subconscious is powerful enough to do that. You are in complete control of your body right now.

"Your immune system is working in perfect harmony.

"How would the new you, over there in the chair, respond if the person sitting next to you pulled out a bag of trail mix? You know the kind, with almonds, cashews, candy, and peanuts. What would happen now?"

Alonzo: "At first, he jumped and took a quick breath. Then, he realized it wasn't a threat. It's not a problem."

Starkstrom: "And how do you feel?"

Alonzo: "I'm good. Calm and relaxed."

Starkstrom: "Can you imagine that other you enjoying some of that trail mix?"

Alonzo: "Sure. He's curious about that, and this process."

Alonzo appeared to watch himself eat a handful. "He seems to like them okay, I guess."

Starkstrom: "Would you, on this side of the wall, like to try some trail mix? The other you seemed to like them."

Alonzo: "I don't know if I want to do that."

Starkstrom: "This is an imaginary bag of peanuts. It's just your imagination."

Alonzo: "You said my imagination was the one that made me respond that way."

Starkstrom: "Exactly, your imagination controls your response. You can direct your imagination.

"This is a safe environment for you to enjoy some peanuts. Take a deep breath. Pretend you, like me, don't have any allergies.

"As you let it out, you can release all attachments to allergies. Just let them go."

Alonzo: "Okay. I'll try some. Let me see that bag. I don't know what y'all see in these things anyway. They look like wooden pebbles. Here goes nothing. They're okay, I guess. You know, I don't think this is working."

Starkstrom: "Why is that?"

Alonzo: "I thought you were going to make me like peanuts, but I still can't imagine myself liking them."

Starkstrom: "Yeah, well, I guess we didn't get you to like peanuts. Was that the goal? Sometimes suggestions just don't take right away. You might find you like other products that are made with peanuts."

Alonzo: "Maybe I just don't like them plain like that."

Starkstrom: “Could you do me a favor? Do a quick scan of your body and tell me how you feel.”

Alonzo: “I feel pretty good. Actually, now that I think about it, I feel great.”

Starkstrom: “Okay. Go ahead, collapse the plexiglass wall, and come back over into your own body.” He reapplied the shoulder pinch anchor to reinforce the state. "Do you still feel neutral about eating peanuts?”

Alonzo: “Pssh. I’m fine with peanuts. I feel like … I don’t think I have any allergies.”

Starkstrom: “You can allow that feeling to grow stronger as you sleep. Stronger each day.

“Think of a time in the future, when you are around peanuts that used to create an allergic response for you. You may even find yourself beginning to like peanuts.”

Alonzo: “I think I’ll take it slow at first, but I feel like I’m okay with peanuts now.”

Starkstrom: “I can see that your eye accessing and breathing have changed from what they were before.

“You look like you could be ready to test with a real live peanut.”

Alonzo: “Do I have to eat one now?”

Griffin: “I have a peanut butter cup. Wanna try that?”

Alonzo: “I like chocolate.”

Griffin: “Who doesn’t? Here. I think you’ll like it.”

Alonzo: “Damn. That’s good. Why did I ever hide from you?”

Starkstrom: “Does anyone have any questions about this process?”

Cadet: “How long will this last? Is he going to put down his pen, only to have the allergy come up again?”

Starkstrom: “He has made a permanent change. Once he understood his immune system was the problem, and not the allergen, he was able to reprogram his system to a new, more empowering response.

“His conscious and subconscious have a new agreement. It’s not likely that he will revert to a state of ignorance from this state of awareness. He sees himself as a different person, and he is.”

Cadet: "You said the subconscious creates allergies, disease, and even cancer. That doesn't make sense. Why would people create disease in their own bodies? I don't get that."

Starkstrom: "It doesn't seem to make sense, does it? If our mind creates our body, and our cells are continuously renewing, why does anyone have chronic disease?

"The simple truth is people believe they have limited control over their health. They are not aware of the power of their own minds to regenerate their bodies. Your body, your entire world, is a reflection of the thoughts and beliefs that you entertain."

Cadet: "How and why would a person create cancer in their body?"

Starkstrom: "First, remember we're talking about the subconscious, which has control of cell replacement. One of the qualities of the subconscious is that it always acts with a positive intention. No matter the results, there is always a positive intention behind it."

Cadet: "How can there be a positive intention behind getting cancer?"

Starkstrom: "You are asking a rational question about an irrational behavior. If you look at it from an emotional point of view, it may make more sense.

"For some people, disease can be an excuse from one or more responsibilities. It can also be a way of getting sympathy and attention. People start coming over to see you and bring you stuff."

Coyote: "Come on. People don't get cancer just to get attention."

Starkstrom: "People do not make a conscious decision to get cancer. But I have seen lonely people do desperate things. It's more complex than simple attention seeking, but loneliness and isolation play a major role. It's never obvious.

"People with cancer want the same thing every human being on the planet wants. It is what drives us to do the things we do."

Cadet: "What is that?"

Starkstrom: "Acknowledgement. To every human being, he or she is the most important person on Earth. It can be no other way.

"When people are berated by those with authority in their lives, they come to believe what they are told about themselves repeatedly. Every person knows, somewhere inside of them, that they are valuable as human beings. Praise helps increase that awareness."

Cadet: "So, do you make up a little chart with gold stars to help cure people of cancer?"

Starkstrom: "That is an interesting idea. That could work as a method of reinforcement. When a person gets a bump of endorphins, that moves them in the direction of health. I don't cure anyone of anything."

Murphy: "Then why would someone come to see you if they had cancer?"

Starkstrom: "People must heal themselves. I can add my healing energy to their fields. I can help them process the jumbled information in their minds and shift their focus from challenges to the results they want. I can help them create a tapestry of beautiful images to drape across their minds."

Cadet: "Still, there has to be more to it than that. If you could just think cancer away, wouldn't we have discovered that already?"

Starkstrom: "We have. There's no money in a cure. Cancer treatment is big business. Where would the medical industry be if everyone believed we each have the power of God to be healthy?"

Cadet: "There have to be other factors though, right? I mean, like cigarettes cause lung cancer, we all know that."

Starkstrom: "Cigarette smoke clogs the lungs. The lymphatic system collects all the garbage from the body and deposits it in the lungs. Healthy lungs expel the toxins.

"Smokers not only add carcinogens into their bodies, but they also block the release of processed waste. Their bodies are polluted with overeating, smoking, and negative thinking."

Alonzo: "My uncle smoked right up until he died at 82. He never got cancer."

Starkstrom: "The environment of the mind creates the environment of the body. There is an emotional aspect to every disease.

"Studies have found that six months to a year before a person is diagnosed with cancer, they have experienced a *significant emotional event.*

"They become obsessed with their perception of that trauma to the point where it actually damages the brain. The brain then sends a disharmonious signal to the corresponding body part."

Coyote: "Everybody has trauma and drama in their lives. Not everybody gets cancer."

Starkstrom: "No two people process information in exactly the same way. If there is no prior trauma, or unresolved prior event for the event to attach to, the person won't tend to obsess over it.

"Remember yesterday, when we went back into your past to reveal unresolved events and reexamine them with the wisdom you have now? That fulfilled one of the primary objectives of this training.

"All of you now have an awareness of how significant events from the past affect our view of the world. We removed the anchor points from your psyche. We actually went back, in our imaginations, and changed how we reimagine those events.

"We changed the frequency of those events. We demagnetized them. Think of it as emotional immunization."

Cadet: "Is that because the government doesn't want to pay for cancer treatment for us?"

Starkstrom: "We weren't actually supposed to spend this much time on cancer specifically, but it is a good vehicle to help you understand the higher concepts that your subconscious mind has complete control over your body, and your emotions amplify your vibrations."

Cadet: "So, what does emotional immunization do for us? It hasn't kept Coyote from crying about his bike."

Starkstrom: "By clearing up the way you relate to the past, you deal more intelligently with the future. Old liabilities become new resources.

"Now, when you are presented with challenges, you are aware of more options. 'What you believe and say about yourself is the word of God to you.'"

Coyote: "There is no scientific evidence of God, or that the Bible is true. There are so many contradictions, inconsistencies, and errors it is literally unbelievable.

"If He can and won't help people, He is cruel. If He can't help, He is impotent.

"Why is there so much misogyny, murder, and mayhem? I just can't accept the whole concept of God."

Starkstrom: "I get what you are saying. Organized religions insist on a concept of God that's hard for many of us to accept. This is the one fundamental idea that I think they all got wrong.

"You see, there is no God … out there. The Kingdom of Heaven is within. If you are looking out there for evidence of God, it is no wonder you can't find it. God is not out there.

"God is hidden within you. What makes that so hard to believe?"

Murphy: "One thing that I have a problem with is how it's possible for God to know all, hear all, and see all? And then, how do people expect Him to answer all their prayers, requests, and bargains?"

Starkstrom: "They will tell you to have faith. They will say, 'We're not capable of understanding, but God knows.'"

Cadet: "What do you say?"

Starkstrom: "I believe that God is not separate from us, but that God is hidden within us, and collectively, we form God.

"Therefore, He sees all because He sees through our eyes; He hears through our ears; He feels what we feel; He knows what we know."

Murphy: "How do we know God is a man?"

Starkstrom: "God is both male and female. Use whatever pronoun you want. If you are God, then God must be a woman."

Murphy: "She must be."

Starkstrom: "She also doesn't take requests or bargain with people. That's not how it works. She will respond to well-defined commands. You can see how misinterpretation of fundamental beliefs leads to all sorts of problems with communicating them to people.

"Theologians never *really* understood, but they were convinced that the people they learned from were telling them the Truth.

"The Bible is incomplete, but it contains enough information in one place to keep anyone studying for a lifetime. The books that weren't originally included are readily available now. Since it's a book of coded information, it must be studied in a certain way."

Murphy: "You've said the Bible is a user's guide for the human mind, and a book of magic and healing. No wonder everybody is so messed up.

"Why did they put it in a code even they don't understand? Why isn't it in simple language that everyone can understand? It sounds like the damned blind leading the damned blind."

Starkstrom: "Don't say that. Nothing is damned. God does not condemn or punish. When you condemn things, you get more condemned things in your life. Bless the change you want into the things you want to change.

"One of the great mysteries of life is the wisdom that disappears at the end of a generation, then is rediscovered by a future generation.

"Human beings are so resistant to change that every time some enlightened individual speaks up about a rediscovered truth, we kill them.

"If someone says, 'Hey, I was just thinking about this whole God thing. And I was thinking they interpreted some things wrong in the Bible.' We make them take it back, and if they don't, we lock them up. If they persist in their heresy, we kill them. At least, we used to."

Murphy: "Where is the key for this code? We do have a key, yeah?"

Starkstrom: "It isn't the kind of code you need a decoder ring for. The secret is in the *way* the Bible is studied. It isn't a history book. The Bible is taking place right now. Studied incorrectly, the Bible doesn't make sense. There are contradictions and inconsistencies all over the place."

Coyote: "Some of it just flat doesn't make sense."

Starkstrom: "I've listened to many debates about the existence of God. Both sides have valid and interesting points. Some atheists say they're not denying God, but they have no reason to believe in God. They put up the challenge to anyone who can prove the existence of God. Then they receive lists of all the incredible beauties and intricacies that we find in the world.

"From my perspective, those things add to the evidence, but I agree with the atheist that data alone is not proof of God."

Coyote: "It's not really. It's circumstantial at best."

Starkstrom: "Correct. It's not proof of a God outside of us. Nor does it provide any support for the belief that if we accept our struggles in life now, we will be rewarded in the afterlife."

Coyote: "How else were they going to get people to accept class structure? 'Poverty is so virtuous; you will get your reward in Heaven. God bless you.' Then they tell them the devil will drag them into Hell if they get out of line. And the little sheeple nod their heads."

Starkstrom: "I heard Reverend Ike say, 'There is no lie like a religious lie, because it invokes God to sanction it, and a devil in Hell to frighten those who do not accept its domination.'

"No debate ever changes the mind of either principal. Whenever I watch these debates, I want to reach into the TV to just turn their heads a little. It seems like they are arguing past each other.

"They seem to be talking *around* the same subject. The audience is there for the battle, looking forward to that one little zinger, from either side; it doesn't matter which. They're there to see some blood.

"Some of the audience may be persuaded to see things differently. The speakers never say, 'Huh. I never thought of it *that* way before. You know, you're right. I see it all now. Thank you so much for enlightening me.'"

Alonzo: "If anything, they seem to be more convinced of themselves."

Starkstrom: "That is the power of repetition at work. For days, they bathe their beliefs in energy, thinking about what they are going to say. They think about it some more before they speak.

"They keep those thoughts in mind while they are speaking. Then, they think about it some more on the way home, all the time reinforcing those thought forms.

"Strong opponents' arguments energize their own positions. Opposing forces strengthen each other. In their minds, they have already made the decision that the other point of view is incorrect."

Griffin: "What is the point of having a debate if their minds are already made up?"

Starkstrom: "Each presenter is expressing their voice, singing their song. Debates are shows for the audience. And a chance for the master debaters to peddle their books.

"Even though I believe in the teachings of Christ, I don't call myself a Christian because the people who call themselves Christian have appropriated that name.

"It seems to mean people who worship Christ. I don't worship Christ because that is part of His teachings. He taught that each of us is His equal."

Griffin: "Who is equal?"

Starkstrom: "He taught us that you, me, and Jesus are the same. It's in the scriptures."

Griffin: "Jesus is the son of God. You're saying *I'm* God? And *you're* God? Where does it say that in the Bible?"

Starkstrom: "Using a clever marketing technique, the New Testament quotes the Old. John 10:34 tells us Jesus quoted Psalm 82:6 when he said, 'You are Gods, and all of you are sons of the Most High.'

"John 14:12 also tells us that if we believe, we will do the works He has done, and greater. I know that goes against what they taught you in Sunday school."

Griffin: "That goes against almost everything I believe about God. Of course, I've heard those verses before, but I don't think it's been presented that way. I'm going to have to think about that for a while."

Starkstrom: "Yes, think about it."

A cadet from the back: "I didn't finish reading that book you gave us yesterday. Are we going to be tested on that?"

Starkstrom: "Every day of your life. That little book, *As a Man Thinketh,* when understood, is an essential key to unlocking one of the greatest treasures of life. I suggest you read it many times."

Coyote: "Once you've read it, why would you want to read it again?"

Starkstrom: "The first time you read a book, your mind gets distracted by the ideas presented. You continue to read while your mind goes off on a little journey.

"Have you ever read something but were so focused on a new concept, you don't remember the next line? Pretty soon, you get to the end of a paragraph, but you weren't paying attention to those words.

"The next time you read it, you are a different person. You see things in yourself you didn't see before."

Coyote: "How many times do we have to read it?"

Starkstrom: "As many as it takes. I've read some books a dozen times, and I learn something new each time. Yesterday, we cleaned up the past. Today, we learned the power of now.

"Tomorrow, we are going to create the future. Think about the changes you want in your life. God bless you. Class dismissed."

Murphy waited for the other cadets to leave, so she could secure the room.

Truly: "Are you sure you don't want to come over?"

Anders: "I'm sure I do want to. It takes all of my focus to shift my attention."

Truly: "I don't see the harm."

Anders: "I'm asking you to have faith in me. This for something better."

Truly: "You should probably go take care of your cat."

MSIs

XVII

Mrs. K: "Elias, do you get an allowance yet?"

Elias: "What do you mean by allowance?"

Mrs. K: "Do you receive money from your father on a regular basis? You know, so you can learn how to save and manage your money."

Elias: "I receive money on a regular basis for the value I create. The money doesn't come from Papa, but it is a blessing from our Father."

Mrs. K: "What sort of things do you create to receive this money?"

Elias: "Besides my books, I have a podcast, and on my blog, I sell books and other information products. People want to hear my song. I use the internet to sing to them."

Mr. H: "What kind of information products do you sell?"

Elias: "Papa has books and courses to help people find their true selves. He teaches the Word on Sundays. Oh, yeah, he's also licensed out a couple of inventions.

"We have set up multiple sources of income. They provide us with resources to help people. We keep generating more resources to share with those who are still finding their way."

Goals

XVIII

While Styx's *The Grand Illusion* is playing louder than on any of the previous days, Starkstrom dances more expressively than on any of the previous days. This time he plays the song through to its finish.

Starkstrom: "Good morning everybody. Welcome to the third and final day of this training module, *Past, Present, and Future.*

"On day one, we learned how to use our imaginations to control the way we reimagine the past. Yesterday, we learned how we use conscious intention to direct our subconscious to rebuild the body daily in amazing health.

"Today you will learn how to direct your subconscious to create your future. You have been doing it since before you were born, but from now on, you will do it on purpose."

Cadet: "Can I object to you saying we've been creating our future since before we were born?"

Starkstrom: "Thank you, I appreciate your honesty, and your objection is duly noted. If I am to teach you what I know, it doesn't make sense for me to tell you what you believe.

"My responsibility is to share my perspective. Your responsibility is to discern what you will accept and what you will reject."

Cadet: "Well, right now, I reject the concept that I've been planning my future since before I was born. You don't plan for this in the womb. You didn't see where I grew up. I worked hard to get where I am."

Starkstrom: "I'm confident you did. I can only speak my truth. He that has ears to hear, let him hear.

"Today, we are going to learn how to define and decide what we want and the specific steps to achieve that.

"Further, we are going to learn how to use our minds to accelerate the accomplishment of our objectives.

"You have all done some sort of goal setting in the past, and it's likely that you have had success in the achievement of those goals."

Cadet: "Not all of 'em. Some of 'em never even got off the ground."

Starkstrom: "There are specific reasons you did not achieve some of them. You may not have had a well-formed outcome. You may have become discouraged and abandoned the idea.

"You may not have believed in it. Maybe you didn't believe in yourself. Your goal may not have been in harmony with Divine Purpose."

Cadet: "You're not going to tell us it's because God didn't want us to have them, are you?"

Starkstrom: "Not at all. When I say *Divine Purpose*, I'm speaking in general terms of advancing everyone rather than gaining at the expense of someone else.

"God wants you to have everything you want. 'It is your father's good pleasure to give you the kingdom.'"

Coyote: "I thought you weren't supposed to talk about God."

Starkstrom: "Yeah. That cat jumped out of the bag yesterday. Last night, while meditating on today's class, this quote was presented to me, 'If you always do what you've always done, you will always get what you have always gotten.'

"Do you want to be told what you are *supposed* to be told, or do you want to hear the Truth? At least, as I see it. I may have it all wrong too.

"Look, I can teach you guys what's in the syllabus. It is highly advanced mental training. The sciences of NLP and hypnosis are grossly misunderstood by the masses.

"If you just learn and mechanically apply these techniques, that will set you in a class of distinction undreamed of by 99% of people."

Cadet: "Hey, that makes us one-percenters."

Starkstrom: "Yes. You are one-percenters, but if you want to understand the Laws *behind* the techniques, the principles by which the principles operate, you must become aware that your imagination is God."

Griffin: "Say that again."

Starkstrom: "'Your own human imagination is the creative power of God within you.'

"Is that the first time you've heard that? Neville Goddard said that before I was born. They won't teach you that in school, or church, or anywhere else. Jesus taught it.

"I'm not supposed to be teaching it to you now, but I've been studying human potential all my life. The One Great Truth that was always so elusive, that finally brought everything together into harmony, are three simple words. You are God. Say it in first-person: 'I am God.'"

Coyote: "If I was God, I wouldn't be living in this state."

Starkstrom: "That has Truth on more levels than you think. Remember yesterday, I said the Bible is an esoteric book about *you*. If you read the first commandment in first person, it says, 'I shall have no other gods before me.' That's gods, plural.

"The only difference between you and Jesus is your awareness of who you are. He was aware that He is one with the Father. Right now, your awareness is that He is one with the Father.

"Change your awareness. Stop praying to a false God. YOU are one with the Father.

"There is no God out there, watching over you. The kingdom of God is within you. 'Have I not told you that you are gods?'

"Now, do I have your attention? I don't expect you to accept this immediately. You didn't believe Jesus when He told you. Why would I expect you to believe me?"

Cadet: "Is this going to be on the test?"

Starkstrom: "What I'm going to teach you today does not require you to believe any of the previous statements. Having heard what I said will help bring your awareness to the truth of it.

"With these NLP techniques, going through the exercises and processing the information in a new way will still get results for you. The techniques are mechanical in nature. Step 1, 2, 3, and so on. Follow the procedure to get the result. Bing, boom, bam.

"I'm going to show you a program, developed by some of the pioneers of NLP, that will help you achieve any goal you want. It is a 21-day program, but don't worry. We'll do some time distortion, and you'll get it all in one day."

Cadet: "Time distortion? Are you serious?"

Starkstrom: "Yes, time distortion is real. But I'm rarely serious. Actually, I have condensed some of it into one day. The rest you will do in self-study.

"The techniques we are going to do today are the same ones I use for myself at the beginning of each season, winter, spring, summer, and fall."

Cadet: "Why? Is the magic stronger at the beginning of a season?"

Starkstrom: "I don't know if there's anything magical about it. The seasons change with the phases of the sun. Each one begins with a solstice or an equinox.

"I just wanted to do a three-day fast, four times a year. It seemed like an easy way to make it a habit. We are all quite aware of the first day of each season. Makes it easy to remember."

Cadet: "You *wanted* to stop eating for three days? Four times a year? Again, why?"

Starkstrom: "For the tremendous physical and mental health benefits. Fasting is the fountain of youth. Another one of those things they don't teach in school or anywhere else.

"I fast for 72 hours during the first weekend of each season. I begin Thursday at 2 PM, and go until Sunday at 2 PM. I also take this time to sit down with a pen and a piece of paper to assess my current coordinates and set my next destination. That is what we will be doing."

Cadet: "I'm not starving myself. I'm one of those people who gets real hangry when I don't have something to eat. You don't want to be around me then."

Starkstrom: "We don't have time to do a 72 hour fast today. Although, one day, I didn't eat for a week."

Cadet: "Did you hear that one at the county fair?"

Starkstrom: "I meant we are going to sit down with pen and paper to sort out where we are now, and where we want to be. We are going to decide on one goal. A plan for its accomplishment will be revealed to you.

"Since I do this four times a year, and because I wanted to share my discovery with others, I produced a workbook with a three-month journal for each season. Journaling is one of the best ways to clarify your thinking."

Cadet: "'Writing causes thinking'; I heard that somewhere before."

Starkstrom: "Yes. Pass these workbooks back. These are yours to keep. Write your name in them."

Cadet: "*Spring Forward*. Nice flowers."

Starkstrom: "This is the spring cover. Each one has a different theme. On page one, you will find an introduction to the process.

"Summarized like this, to find the path to where you want to go, you must identify where you are now.

"What are your current coordinates? On what frequency are you now, and on what frequency is the person that you want to be?

"Find the section with the heading, 'Have & Want.' Right now, I want you to write down everything you have and want in your life."

Cadet: "Like a gratitude list?"

Starkstrom: "Yes, exactly. Make a list of all the people and things you have in your life that you are grateful for. Get your pens moving. You created your environment. You must have attracted a few things you wanted."

After a few minutes, "Okay, now in the section, 'Have & Don't Want,' make a list of the things you have and don't want.

"What are the things in your life that bug you? You know what they are. Write them down."

Another pause while they write.

"The third list is going to be an acknowledgement of the people and things you are grateful NOT to have in your life. We don't want to spend too much time on this, because we don't want our minds to operate on those frequencies.

"We just want to clarify the contrast as a point of reference. I am happy I don't have crushing debt or terminal illness.

"Acknowledge them, cross them out, and move on.

"Now this next list is the most fun. This is the list of the things you don't have but do want. This is your wish list.

"Write down everything you want, or have ever wanted, in your life. If you could have *anything* you want, no limits, what would that be? Kids have no limits on their wishes. Do you want a rocket ship with a swimming pool?"

Murphy: "I want to be the first *captain* of a starship."

Starkstrom: "Write it down. There are no limits. Raise your imagination out of poverty.

"Now, take a moment to notice which list draws your attention, which one was the hardest or easiest? The longest or shortest? Let your mind wander over how things are and how you want them to be.

"Now, notice, which of the two lists, Want & Don't Have, or Have & Don't Want, occupies more of your attention?

"Want & Don't Have is a list of *toward* motivations.

"Have & Don't Want is a list of *away from* motivations.

"Which ones are more important to you?

"Now, look at each of the lists and prioritize the items. Just put a number next to the item in order of importance to you.

"After you have prioritized both lists, consider what change, if you were to get it, would make the most difference in your life? It might be on top, or it might at first seem minor. Look through your priorities again for those items that will be the most likely to produce the most change when they change, and put a star next to them.

"Here is where we are going to rearrange part of our minds. Look at your list of things you Have & Don't Want in your life. Think of a positive phrase for each item that means the same thing to you.

"For example: 'Have and don't want a few extra pounds' could also mean 'want and don't have a slimmer, more muscular body.' 'Don't want this dead-end job' could also mean 'want a job with more pay and opportunity.' Or maybe you want your own business.

"Create a transformative statement for each item that is satisfying to you.

"You have two prioritized lists now: your original wish list, and the *away from* list you have transformed into a *toward* list.

"Now, take a few minutes to combine them into one prioritized master list in their new order. It's okay to add to the list if something else pops up.

"Look at your new list of wants. If you have prioritized them properly, you will have the things you want the most at the top. Pick one. Circle the item you want the most. Don't impose any limits or restrictions on it. This process does not recognize lack of resources.

"We are going to take one of your top-priority goals all the way through the Well-Formed Goal Conditions.

"At the top of the next page is the question, 'What Do You Want?' Write your positively phrased goal in present tense, preferably beginning with the words, 'I AM.'

"Make sure it is something that can be initiated and maintained by you. In other words, does this goal result from your own actions, or does it rely on outside circumstances?"

Cadet: "Can you clarify what you mean? What is the difference?"

Starkstrom: "An example would be wanting a certain person to fall in love with you. You can do things you believe will make yourself more attractive to that person, but you can't make them fall in love with you.

"You can become a different person. You cannot change another person. The change you seek is within you.

"If you want more money, how can you provide more service? What can *you* do?

"State it in the present-tense, positive form. For example: 'I AM so happy and grateful now that I AM a wealthy and successful business owner.' Can you feel the power in that statement? Say that about your own goals.

"I AM so happy and grateful now that I AM … (fill in the blank). Write it down now. Be more specific than my example.

"With your goal clearly stated, in positive form, you can let go of the random, half-formed thoughts that clutter the back of your mind. Release them now. Pay the price to achieve your goal by letting go of nonessential thoughtforms.

"Here's an interesting question: How will you know when you have achieved it? Will there be an awards ceremony? What evidence is there that you have achieved your goal?

"Think about that.

"What will you see, hear, smell, taste, and touch on achievement?

"When, where, and with whom will you experience this accomplishment?

"What effect will this change have on the rest of your life, your work, and family?

"See what comes up for you. Write it down.

"You have done something already this morning that most people will never do in their entire lives. You wrote down a clearly defined goal. And now we're going to push it to another level.

"We are drawn to what we find attractive, yeah? You can make your goals so compelling that you will naturally be drawn to them.

"Once you set your conscious mind on the path to the achievement of your goals, your subconscious mind will continue in that direction unconsciously.

"I wonder if you can begin to imagine what it would be like to be the person who has achieved that goal of yours. Imagine you are that person.

"How does that make you feel? Can you feel that, right now? It must give you a tremendous sense of confidence knowing the challenges you have overcome to become who you are today.

"Call up your control center with the heads-up display. If your goal isn't in the form of a movie already, have it take the form of a movie now.

"And then, increase the size and brightness of these images, adding vivid colors and dimensions.

"Continue to increase the size, brightness, and colors as long as the feelings increase and then hold them there.

"Add rich, upbeat music coming at you from all directions. Hear strong, supportive, encouraging voices cheering you on to your future.

"Enjoy it! Allow those feelings to flow and increase.

"Now, let's set some anchors. Pick or create a symbolic image of your chosen one, your number one priority goal.

"What image can you flash on the screen of your mind's eye that represents your accomplished goal? See that in your mind's eye now. This image is your visual anchor.

"Now, I want you to hear, in your mind's ear, a word, a phrase, or a sound that you will hear when you have achieved your goal. This is your auditory anchor. Pick a sound.

"Now, I want you to touch yourself in a unique way, like tugging on an ear lobe, pinching the back of your hand, or whatever."

"You are creating a kinesthetic anchor. You want it to mean something. You want a distinct sensation."

"You can tap on a lymphatic point. That always gets things moving. Do something that your body will specifically associate with the wish fulfilled.

"Moments ago, you were the person you wanted to be, with the goal you wanted to achieve.

"Remember *that* with all of its richness and flavor now. And feeling that, exactly the way you want to feel it, you can see your visual anchor and hear your auditory anchor, and as you fire your kinesthetic anchor, you orchestrate everything into one harmonious song.

"Now, I'm going to ask you to do something you have probably never even heard of before. It is a variation of a technique Richard Bandler used with his audiences.

"Everybody, please stand up while you are feeling excited about everything you have accomplished. Now, I want you to notice where you *feel that* in your body. That's right.

"Notice where it begins, where it flows, and where it goes.

"With your hands, take hold of the stream as it leaves your body, and direct it into that place where the feeling begins, creating an energy loop.

"For me, the energy flows into the top of my head, down through my spine. However you do that is fine. You can increase the speed and flow of that energy using a combination of mind and body.

"Hold your hands in front of you, palms facing you, elbows up, like you are hugging a tree."

Griffin: "Hippy."

Starkstrom: "It's just a starting posture. Feel the energy ball that is beginning to form between your hands. Raise your hands up above your head and bring that energy into your crown, or wherever it begins in your body.

"Add that power to the flow of your good feelings and increase the speed by pushing it all through your body. Pretend your hands are collecting energy from infinite space and increasing the flow to and through you. Increase the speed and power of the flow.

"Let your hands relax and use only your mind. Spin it faster and faster.

"Allow that feeling to energize every cell of your body. Fire off your anchors now.

"See your image. Hear your sound. Feel the touch. Feel the flow. You can continue to allow that program to run in the background while you take your seats.

"Notice what we have done here.

"What you just did, in a small space of time, is reorganize the thoughtforms in your mind into alignment with what you desire. You have clarified your most important goals and cut off that which you do not want.

"You know what you want and how it feels be that person. Then, we amplified that feeling. You already have what you want."

Alonzo: "So, is my Ferrari out there in the parking lot now, or how long does this take?"

Starkstrom: "Your Ferrari is wherever you believe it is. The length of time it takes for it to get from where it is, to where you want it to be, depends entirely on your beliefs.

"Where did you see it? Did you see yourself driving it? Did you take ownership of it in your mind?

"Other people's beliefs will affect your outcome as well. That is why you must tell no one. Their doubts can have a negative impact on your results.

"Herod will kill the young child. TELL NO ONE.

"There is a gestation period for everything. We know a human baby takes nine months. I don't know how long a Ferrari takes for you.

"When you plant an apple orchard from seeds, you don't expect to harvest apples the first year. Plant vegetables for your daily bread, but also plant your orchards. What you want is on its way to you.

"Persist in your tasks and persevere in your faith."

"The difference between an ordinary bar of steel and one that has been magnetized is not in the composition, but in the arrangement, of its molecules.

"You have rearranged your mind to concentrate your energies toward accomplishment of your goal. You were able to amplify that feeling. Would you believe we can still make that even more compelling?

"I'd like for you to call up your heads-up display, again, and notice where your future is. Now, I want you to imagine you have a picture frame in your hands. You are holding it by the sides, and inside the frame is a still image of you being the person you want to be.

"We are going to charge that image with mana. Take a deep breath in and blow life into that image. Notice how the image gets clearer and brighter.

"Again. Another deep breath in and, as you exhale, charge your image with goodness. A third time. Take a deep breath in and blow the mana into the image.

"Four is a magic number. Take in a fourth deep breath and feel the energy flowing into that image of you having already accomplished your goal.

"Take your mana-charged image out into your future and drop it like a slide into one of those old carousel projectors, in the time slot of its fulfillment. You'll know when you get there. Trust yourself.

"Now that you've gone into the future to become the person who has what you want, you can look back on your path to see what you did to accomplish your goals. 'You can connect the dots looking back,' as Steve Jobs said.

"You now have the confidence to move forward, knowing the resources you need will reveal themselves as you need them.

"How does it feel to have the good you desire already manifest? What would you do if you knew there were no limits?

"Do you guys have any questions about this process?"

Griffin: "Can we do this to get anything we want? I mean, I want a whole bunch of things."

Starkstrom: "Yes, you can use this process to achieve any goal you want. You should have all those things written down on your list.

"By identifying them, you have raised their frequency, energized them, and magnetized your mind toward them. You are moving toward them, and they are moving toward you.

"Use your willpower to focus on one goal and see it all the way through to completion. That is one of the great secrets to success.

"Prioritize your tasks, start at the top, complete each task to the best of your ability, and then move on to the next. There is no more efficient way to get things done."

Griffin: "What if two of them are in conflict with each other?"

Starkstrom: "Unresolved conflicts are like having two tugboats pulling your ship in opposite directions. The only way to go anywhere is to make a decision and disconnect one of them."

Griffin: "How do I know which one to let go?"

Starkstrom: "Nobody can decide that for you. You are the captain of your ship. You decide your destination. If you still have conflict, you are not clear on what you want. Trust your intuition.

"Take another look at those items. The reason they may be in apparent conflict is that they may be different paths to the same ultimate goal. The same people who gave us today's exercise have developed another process, called Core Transformation.

"Basically, you have wants that you think will give you something that is even more important than what that wanted thing will bring you directly. At the heart of what all our parts want for us are five core states.

"If you ask enough questions, wants always boil down to these five states. All the weird things you see people do are usually an attempt to achieve one or more of these states. They are: Being, Inner Peace, Love, OKness, and Oneness."

Coyote: "What did you mean, 'what all our parts want for us'?"

Starkstrom: "The science of NLP includes so much more than we can cover in a few days. When the people who control the purse strings open them up a little more, I can expand this program to include more concepts and techniques.

"Bridges take time to build, and you, my friends, are the foundation stones."

Griffin: "Do we have time for you to tell us more about parts, now that you brought it up?"

Starkstrom: "Of course. Parts therapy is fundamental. If I had included it before we defined our goals, no one would have goals in conflict with each other. I'm always learning something. Next time.

"Parts are entities, or demons, or thoughtforms in the subconscious mind that are usually born from trauma, with their own values and belief systems, and a positive intention.

"Have you ever heard someone say something like, 'Part of me wants to go to Europe to see the castles, but another part of me wants to lie on the beach in the sun'? Those are literally parts of your subconscious mind, thoughtforms, that are in apparent conflict."

Murphy: "Why do you say *apparent* conflict? If one part wants one thing and the other part wants something that excludes the possibility of the first one, then isn't it just a conflict?"

Starkstrom: "Right. I say apparent because they may be different ways of achieving the same core state. Think about it. One part wants to see castles and one part wants to go to the beach. Aside from the obvious fact that they both involve travel, what do these two trips have in common?"

Murphy: "They're vacations. Pleasure trips."

Starkstrom: "Exactly. She imagines each journey will be pleasurable, and that will make her feel good. Both ideas are on frequencies that resonate with her desires for pleasure.

"Once she becomes aware that she can be just as happy with either choice, the two parts can integrate and get both tugboats pulling in the same direction."

Griffin: "What if the conflict isn't that simple? Now that I prioritized my list, they are both at the top. These tugboats are pulling my stern apart."

Starkstrom: "That brings up one more thing that I will want to add back into the syllabus for yesterday's lessons on mind and body, that is, secondary gain. I think I might have touched on it when the question came up about why anyone would create a disease, like cancer, in their own body.

"Why *would* anyone choose sickness? Think about what *possible* gain there could be."

Alonzo: "People will take care of you."

Starkstrom: "That is a powerful motivator for some people. What else?"

Alonzo: "You can shirk responsibility. When my uncle was staying with us, man, he didn't do anything."

Starkstrom: "That could be another motivation, especially for someone who has gotten overwhelmed. We are all conceived in perfection. As we go through life, we meet challenges.

"Sometimes challenges hit us hard, and a part may splinter off. That part will detach itself from the conscious mind, but it's still operating at an unconscious level. The tricky thing about these little demons is that they are like hurt and confused children.

"Parts generate behaviors that they believe will benefit your being as a whole, and they believe it is their duty to protect and continue that behavior. Secondary gain is whatever benefit it gets as a result of a behavior."

Coyote: "Even if what they are doing gets them the opposite of what they want?"

Starkstrom: "Right. Remember the distinctions between conscious and subconscious minds. We are talking about a *part* of the subconscious that has detached itself from the rational, thinking, conscious mind.

"It operates from emotional energy and does not have the ability to think rationally. Secondary gain is entirely subjective. It may not make any sense to us. It doesn't have to."

Griffin: "So, you're saying there are shards of me, in me, that are cutting me up for my own good? And that's why I have conflicting goals?"

Starkstrom: "Come on up here."

Griffin: "I'd rather not share, thanks."

Starkstrom: "Don't worry. Sharing is not part of this. We are working with structure and process. Only you will know the content. This is the last day, and you're getting good at this. So, come on up.

"The full Core Transformation process takes more time than we have here. But we *can* go through a simple Parts Integration exercise.

"Now, one part of you wants something, and another part of you wants something else, correct?"

Griffin: "Yes."

Starkstrom: "Keeping your elbows bent, hold your hands out in front of you with the palms facing up. Now in one hand, you have something that symbolizes the thoughtform of the first part. In your other hand, you have something that symbolizes the opposing thoughtform.

"Take a moment, close your eyes, and just allow each of them to reveal themselves to you. Ask them if they are willing to communicate with you. They usually are. It would make them happiest to reunite with the rest of you."

Griffin: "They both said yes."

Starkstrom: "Focusing on one at a time, you can ask the first part, if you had exactly what you want, exactly the way you want it, what does that get you that is even more important than that?"

Griffin: "Respect."

Starkstrom: "Okay. Respect. Now, ask the other part the same question. If you had exactly what you want, exactly the way you want it, what does that get you that is even more important than that?"

Griffin: "Sense of freedom."

Starkstrom: "Sense of freedom. Now, ask that part if you had a sense of freedom, exactly the way you want it, what would that give you that is even more important than that?"

Griffin: "Inner Peace."

Starkstrom: "Inner Peace. Now, turn to the other part and ask it if you had respect, exactly the way you want it, what would that give you that is even more important than that?"

Griffin: "Huh. It said Inner Peace too."

Starkstrom: "As you recognize that both of these parts want the same core state for you, you may begin to notice how they are naturally bringing your hands closer together. As the two parts recognize their common desire, they begin to merge into one entity with a singular purpose. They take on a new form.

"When you are ready, you can bring the two in agreement as one back into your body through your solar plexus. That's right. Hold your hands there while it reintegrates itself."

Griffin: "That is so weird. I don't know whether I'm going to fall over or float away."

Starkstrom: "Neither. It's an unusual but natural sensation. As you all become more aware of your states of consciousness, you will begin to recognize their qualities as you go through them.

"It looks like we've gone past our time. Let's wrap things. Thank you. You can finish your prioritizing at home. Please return to your seat.

"You have already found the cards I tucked into your journals. These are not my business cards. They are your goal cards. Write your goal down on this card and carry it with you every day. Touch it. Read it out loud. Put a drop of essential oil on it if you like. Engage your senses.

"Over the past three days, you have gone through various levels of mind, used your imaginations to release past trauma, learned how the mind creates the body, and learned how to decide on, and envision, a new future on purpose.

"I understand that you may not be able to tell someone else what hypnosis is, but you now have an awareness of mental states that you did not have before. Discard all those old images of hypnosis. This was a good start, but there is so much more for you to learn, grasshoppers.

"Giving me a good review will help keep me on par for my *Performance Assessment Report*. Your results in the field will speak for themselves, but your words on paper will help build this program into a new way of training for all recruits, commissioned and enlisted.

"One last thought I would like to leave you with is this: The old version of you came here three days ago. That version of you no longer exists.

"You have been transformed by the renewing of your minds. Tomorrow morning, a new version of you will arise. Happy Easter. God bless you. Class dismissed."

Griffin: "Easter is *next* month."

Starkstrom: "Is it?"

After the rest of the class had cleared out, Cadet Murphy secured the classroom.

Together, Truly and Anders walked to the parking lot.

"How much longer are you going to be here?" she asked him.

Anders: "Until the end of September. I usually only stay here for about three months, but I came early this year for this class."

Truly: "Maybe we can get together again before you leave."

Anders: "I'd like that."

Truly: "What are the rules of this cooling-off period?"

Anders: "I have no idea. I'm not even sure it's necessary, but my inner voice is telling me to let you be free."

Truly: "Free to choose what I want?"

Anders: "Yes, of course, but addicts don't operate from choice."

Truly: "I'm not an addict."

Anders: "I've heard that's what addicts say. Detachment is an act of love. We have both gone through a powerful shift. I need a little time to adjust. This isn't over."

Truly: "I don't want a boyfriend; I just want to spend some time together. You are an unusual man, Anders Starkstrom."

Anders: "And you are Truly unique, Murphy. In a few weeks, we can start a new segment."

Naya

XIX

Mrs. B: "Elias, when you said you sell your books, did you mean ones *you* have written?"

Elias: "Papa helped me. I've published two books. The first one didn't do too well. The second one is a best seller. I ran a killer book launch. Reviews are important. I only have it translated into Spanish, so far.

"My friend, Naya, did the watercolors. Excuse me. I meant my *best* friend. She has tons of paintings at her house."

Mrs. B: "Are they all this amazing?"

Elias: "Most of them."

Mrs. B: "How did she paint so many beautiful images?"

Elias: "You just do what you can, the best you can, with what you have, every day."

Mrs. B: "What are these, over here, in the frames? Are these hers?"

Elias: "She sold those for book covers. The right one is mine. The other one is for a children's book. I have a copy, if you want to see it."

Mrs. B: "It sounds like she is quite accomplished. How old is Naya?"

Elias: "Oh, she is way older than me. She's twelve."

I'M LATE!

XX

DARREL: "NICE SHOT."

Anders: "Thank you. Those are the ones I come out here for. Sometimes, when everything comes into alignment, you feel the true gravity in the golf swing and hit that pure shot."

Caden: "There you go again, Andy. Talking about all that mind stuff. How do you get so lucky all the time? If you sink that putt, you get two bucks from each of us. If you miss, it costs you nothing."

Anders: "We all have the same opportunity. The last few times we've played this hole, you've said, 'I hope I don't hit it in the water again.' And where did your ball go?"

Caden: "Right into the drink."

Anders: "Your core swing thought was 'hit it in the water.' You gave your subconscious a command, and it obeyed."

Darrel: "Stop trying to spread your false beliefs around here."

George: "You had to poke the bear, didn't you? I'll see you guys down on the green."

Anders: "How do you know which beliefs are true and which are false? You're convinced your beliefs are true. That's why you believe them. But how do you know what *you* believe is *the* truth? True Gravity is pure harmony and balance of the inner and outer bodies.

"Even if you play the same course every day, every round is different."

Darrel: "That is true. Now, let's go down and see if you can convert it to cash."

Anders: "You know, I just feel aligned with the golf course today; in harmony with the universe. Let's head down."

Overhanging branches concealed the identity of the person walking down the path. The clunking sound of boots on the paved cart path, at first dim, got louder as they got closer to the green. Although Anders heard the approaching march, he did not look up but, instead, kept his attention focused on the task at hand.

He was in the moment, feeling the joy of sinking the putt before sinking the putt.

Anders was talking while getting ready. "You guys know I never play against you. It's not about the two bucks. I play with the intention of commanding my mind and the golf course, not taking a competitive attitude with my buddies. The Zen of golf is in bringing the mind, body, and environment into harmony."

Darrel: "Come on, while we're young."

The clunking of the boots softened to a squishing sound as they transitioned from the pavement to the grass. *Squish, squish, squish* could be heard in the otherwise silence before the putt. His buddies didn't want to break his concentration, but danger was approaching rapidly as heels of cowboy boots left a trail of deep craters on the green.

As the ball rolled into the cup, he turned to see Truly Murphy, not more than two feet from his face, hands in fists on her hips, eyes fixed, "I'm *late,*" she said very deliberately.

Anders: "If you're late, I'm late. I thought we were meeting at six. If you want to hang out with us, we can all have a beer in the café when we're done. You're going to have to stay off the greens though."

Truly: "NO. I won't be drinking any beer for a while, because I'm *late.*" She emphasized with a little forward nod of her head, as if asking for acknowledgement.

Realizing this was a discussion that could not be put off, he turned to his friends and said, "Looks like I'm going to have to leave you gentlemen."

George: "You can't collect if you don't finish."

Anders: "George, you're worth millions. Dollars are like toothpicks to you. Thank you, though. You guys go ahead. Just leave my clubs on my cart. I'll get them later."

George: "I like my toothpicks."

Anders: "Truly, let's walk back this way along the service road. If you're telling me what I think you are telling me, I agree, it's definitely important enough to interrupt a game of golf."

Truly: "There is no question who the father is."

Anders: "Have you done a pregnancy test?"

Truly: "I thought I wasn't going to hear from you again. After you finally called, I started tidying up around the place. I've been so busy with my training, I kind of let things go. Then, for some reason, I suddenly realized I was late. So, I got a test. Two lines."

Anders: "That's wonderful news. Are you sure? Thank you for brightening my day. How do you feel?"

Truly: "Bordering on panic."

Anders: "No entres en pánico."

Truly: "What does that mean?" She giggled.

Anders: "It means don't panic."

Truly: "I can't help it. I can't be pregnant. No way. I can't raise a kid. I'm not done growing up myself. I don't know the first thing about having a kid."

Anders: "Nobody does really. They don't give you an owner's manual for the little darlings either."

Truly: "I don't want to mess up somebody else's life just because I don't know what I am doing."

Anders: "What makes you think you would mess up the child's life?"

Truly: "When you do something, and you don't know what you're doing, you usually mess it up somehow."

Anders: "The world is full of people whose parents didn't know what they were doing."

Truly: "Thank you for making my point. Look at how many people around the world are messed up."

Anders: "The past does not equal the future."

Truly: "Duh."

Anders: "What I mean is just because things have gone a certain way before, or conditions show what has been, that doesn't mean things will always be that way."

Truly: "The definition of insanity is doing the same thing over and over while expecting different results. The world is insane."

Anders: "And that is why we don't do the *same* thing. We do a different thing, or we do the same thing in a different way.

"Creative thinking begets creative people. When we make a decision and move forward, even if we don't know all the steps to get where we want, we just take the *next* step, and the rest of the steps will be revealed.

"Go as far as you can see. Then you'll see the next steps on the path. Aside from parenting, you have other concerns, don't you?"

Truly: "Well, besides the fact that having a baby will sink my career and destroy my life's plans, there is having a human being growing inside of you, pushing and squeezing your guts so they can't function properly.

"Then, it grows until it is too big to come out the same way it came in, but there is no way to unlaunch that rocket. Also, I don't want to push out a bowling ball."

Anders: "That is a pretty big stack of cons, but nothing is all bad. You must have some positive associations with kids. What are your pros?"

Truly: "Oh, I love babies … as long as someone else takes care of them. My nieces are adorable. I just don't want to bring another human into this world and mess them up. That kind of normal isn't good."

Anders: "Billions and billions of people have been raised by parents who did not know what they were doing; most of them weren't mature enough to take care of themselves.

"Still the human race expands and marches on.

"If I were to raise another child, I would take more control over what they learn."

Truly: "How can you control what they learn?"

Anders: "The number one thing I would do is completely eliminate television, radio, and internet."

Truly: "All internet?"

Anders: "For the first nine years, yes, I would eliminate advertising. Advertisers know how to control people's thoughts and feelings.

"Probably, the worst thing they do is give people suggestions that start, or increase, negative conditions. Suddenly, subconscious minds accept the suggestions of disease.

"Ads point to a problem that affects about two percent of people and offer their product as a solution. People who didn't have a problem suddenly feel the need to correct it.

"Whether you have the problem or not, ads elicit an emotional response, then magnify the feeling. The increased vibration motivates you to act."

Truly: "No electronics seems extreme."

Anders: "The first nine years of a child's life is when they are the most open to suggestion. It's not the electronics that are the problem; it's some of the information coming from them.

"Telephones, TVs, and computers are fundamental. So, it's important to know how they work, and the best ways to use them.

"I would just block advertising. I'd rather not have that input going into a child's mind."

Truly: "You're saying you want to be in control of the programming."

Anders: "What if you could? What if you could keep out, or at least minimize, negative thoughts and limiting beliefs? What kind of person would develop from an environment of positive input without all the false disempowering beliefs?"

Truly: "How would you determine what is positive and what is negative? Do you have all the answers, and if so, why aren't you perfect?"

Anders: "Nobody is. I have been studying Mental Science most of my life. I have a leg up on more than 99.99% of the people on this planet, so I have a lot of *good* answers, but I don't have all the answers.

"Knowledge is infinite, and we can tune in to that. There is no way for anyone to have all the answers—ever.

"My theory is that a person who was raised under those conditions would be able to get closer to the Truth than a person with the limiting beliefs of the world.

"Like a rocket shot out of the nose of another rocket that's already at maximum velocity."

Truly: "You are talking about mind control, but in a positive way?"

Anders: "Yes. I'm talking about raising a child, using the best methods I know, as well as the ones I intend to learn along the way, giving that child the best tools and developing their mind to the highest human potential. At least, to the best of my ability."

Truly: "An ubermensch? You can't make a perfect human, Dr. Frankenstein. Things always go sideways when people try that."

Anders: "Everybody is already perfect. False beliefs hide that from us.

"The world isn't nearly as bad as Newspeak would have us believe."

Truly: "What's Newspeak?"

Anders: "It's the negative form of mind control from Orwell's *1984.* It's a language, meant to dumb everybody down and reduce thinking."

Truly: "People really don't need to think less."

Anders: "The term is new, but the technique is ancient. Emotionally charged words manipulate people to believe, on a subconscious level, the narrative du jour.

"People have their TVs running in the background. They aren't filtering the information. They're not deciding whether the information is true or false. Their *conscious* mind is busy focusing on other things.

"If they're staring at their phones, they're still engaging their conscious mind, while their subconscious mind accepts the suggestions directed at it from the TV."

Truly: "So, that's why people believe all that crap?"

Anders: "If you don't control your own mind, someone else will.

"The subconscious mind is only capable of *deductive* reasoning. If a premise is *believable*, whether true or not, the subconscious mind will come to a logically perfect conclusion. It doesn't have the ability to determine if a premise is true.

"That, and repetition are why people believe all that crap.

"People have been conditioned to let others control their minds. They act on their beliefs. They believe they're 'doing the right thing.' They're not at all aware that most of their thoughts and beliefs are implanted by others."

Truly: "They're being controlled by fear."

Anders: "Raise a specter. People get scared. Scaring people has always been a tool used by those in power to control the masses. Do this, or you're endangering society. Do that, or you won't go to heaven. 'Join us, or you're doomed … forever!'"

Truly: "I'm a Catholic, so I'm doomed anyway. Sometimes it seems like I can't do anything right."

Anders: "That's exactly what I'm talking about. Those are incredibly limiting beliefs based on specific religious teachings.

"You are not doomed, and you can and do, do things right."

Truly: "How do you know which philosophy to follow?"

Anders: "Certain empowering beliefs and applications of Mental Science, using Natural Laws, applied in a certain way, can produce results not previously experienced by common man.

"All the great advances of society have come from people who do not conform to groupthink."

Truly: "You can't just pick and choose what you want to believe."

Anders: "I've heard that before, from one of those pastors who think their way is the only way. I still reject that."

Truly: "Can you? I mean, if you take one thing from here and another thing from there, what do you have?"

Anders: "You have something entirely new. Taking what works from different disciplines and creating something new, is the *inductive* reasoning of the conscious mind."

Truly: "Then it's not any of those religions. It's a whole new religion. What would you call it? What faith is it, if it isn't one already?"

Anders: "Labels aren't important to me. I don't feel any need to name my set of beliefs and put them in a box. Labels impose limits."

Truly: "Maybe you could write it down, so other people can follow your example. You may not need to put it in a box, but the rest of us could use a little guidance.

"I know Jesus and Buddha didn't call their followers Christians and Buddhists, but their teachings were written down."

Anders: "Neither one of them wrote down their philosophies. In fact, their teachings weren't even written down during their lifetimes."

Truly: "Maybe they should've been. It might have eliminated a lot of misunderstandings. And you are a writer. Maybe you could, I don't know, *write it down.*"

Anders: "The Gospel of Anders? I haven't achieved their level of awareness"

Truly: "What do you know?"

Anders: "I know the limitations we place on ourselves persist because we continue to impress those limitations on the Universal Subjective Mind.

"Once we change our self-image, our mind will reflect a different set of conditions, resulting from a different set of beliefs."

Truly: "Write it down. We traveled a long way from the discussion of me not wanting to have a baby. Where were we?"

Anders: "You were about to list the upside."

Truly: "The upside? I don't see much upside to being pregnant, giving birth, or raising a kid. I don't see much upside in putting my career on hold indefinitely. Once you lose that momentum, it's tough to get moving again. A couple of years has compound effects."

Anders: "What if I told you that I had alternatives to all of those conditions?"

Truly: "Are you going to carry it and give birth to it? That would be some magic, brother."

Anders: "That's not what I meant. I meant I know how to help you make your pregnancy comfortable, and childbirth painless and beautiful. I meant I will raise the child while you pursue your career."

Truly: "How can you help make pregnancy comfortable and childbirth painless and beautiful?"

Anders: "By helping you reshape your mind. You have certain beliefs about pregnancy and childbirth. Those are your expectations, and your subconscious mind will create those conditions for you.

"Believe that you can create the conditions you want. In other words, if you believe you will be uncomfortable, and it hurts like hell, then *that* will be your experience. I have counter evidence for you, so you can choose."

Truly: "All the evidence I have says it's uncomfortable and painful. Women who want to be mothers may be willing to accept that, but I'm not. What about pregnant women who don't want to be mothers? For some of us, it's equivalent to a lifetime prison sentence."

Anders: "There are always more options than you may see. An unplanned pregnancy is easier to adjust to than an unwanted pregnancy, which can be unwanted for any number of reasons."

Truly: "I have a number of reasons."

Anders: "Most beliefs are passed down through centuries of paradigms. The collective fears surrounding childbirth are based on stories that have been passed down eagerly. Bad news sells.

"Stories of complications that resulted in death strike a chord of fear in the mind.

"Once those strings start vibrating, they resonate with other fears and negative beliefs, and they attract more of that. When other people add their own energy to the collective belief, it becomes even more powerful."

Truly: "Are they making it all up, or is it because it's true? All the doctors believe it too."

Anders: "Doctors are amazing people who apply their talents to the field of medicine. The techniques they use work more often than not for those who believe in them. The error is not in questioning whether physical medicine works but in *not* questioning whether there is a *better* way."

Truly: "Are you saying the entire medical community is wrong?"

Anders: "I'm not saying they're wrong, but the current medical paradigms have evolved from incorrectly attributing everything to secondary cause.

"Doctors look to battling the malignancy. *Battling* a malignancy adds more energy to it.

"Even when they look for cause, they look at physical influences on the body. Most of them are unaware of the underlying, unseen causes that create dis-ease."

Truly: "If they are unseen, no wonder they're harder to battle."

Anders: "It might be better to think in terms of overwriting bad programming. We use unseen forces constantly, whether we know it consciously or not. Our subconscious never sleeps.

"When the body needs rest, the conscious mind sleeps and stops all conscious movement. The subconscious ceaselessly continues all the processes in your body automatically, healing and rebuilding."

Truly: "How does that apply to cancer?"

Anders: "The subconscious mind builds structure and maintains function of the body.

"Unresolved emotional conflicts resonate with each other and gather together, creating complexed thoughtforms.

"All locations in the body correspond to different kinds of emotional conflict. Someone can be a literal pain in the neck. The body is physical expression of the subconscious mind.

"People tend to obsess about emotionally charged events. Being stuck in it adds more energy to the psychic entity. Then, a last-straw event accelerates growth."

Truly: "My mom has breast cancer. What is that related to?"

Anders: "How long has she known?"

Truly: "A couple of months."

Anders: "How is she doing?"

Truly: "She's doing all right, but she doesn't want to go through any of the usual treatment options. The doctor wants to do a mastectomy, but that seems so barbaric to me. Is that the best they can do?"

Anders: "At this time, surgery, radiation, and chemo are the only treatments doctors are *allowed* to use."

Truly: "That's what they are allowed to use. What else is there?"

Anders: "Change their perception."

Truly: "The doctors?"

Anders: "Yes, the care providers too. But I meant change the way their patients see the world.

"The power in knowing that your own subconscious mind created the condition is knowing that your own subconscious mind can create a new, healthy condition to replace the old one."

Truly: "Nobody would choose to have cancer."

Anders: "Yeah, I keep hearing that. It's not a *conscious* decision. It's a response to stimulus. We can learn new responses."

Truly: "What's the difference?"

Anders: "Remember the subconscious mind needs the conscious mind to tell it what's right and what's wrong. It can't discriminate fact from fiction, true from false, on its own.

"It *does* have a set of beliefs that are based on past experience. It operates from those beliefs."

Truly: "So why would it deduce that cancer is the answer to their problem?"

Anders: "I don't know. Remember, parts have a positive intention.

"It's not usually simple mathematical reasoning. It's more like responding to uncertainty with a physical expression. Cancer is not just a physical growth.

"The physical growth is an expression of worry, doubt, and fear. It expresses an imperfection in the matrix; a malformed cell is the physical manifestation of unresolved conflict."

Truly: "Why does my mom have breast cancer, then?"

Anders: "Breast cancer usually is related to nurturing issues. It can be an issue surrounding a child, a childlike husband, or anyone else they may have a nurturing relationship with.

"How is your relationship with your mother?"

Truly: "Mine? We've always had a good relationship, but she's different since my brother died in a motorcycle accident."

Anders: "How long ago was that?"

Truly: "It's been almost a year, Christmas was rough. You think she has breast cancer because my brother died?"

Anders: "Not by itself, no. I think we can agree it was a significant emotional event. If there are similar unresolved traumas in her past, they can magnetically attract themselves to each other and form a complexed set of beliefs."

Truly: "You mean like when her brother died? Also in a motorcycle accident."

Anders: "Yes, well, that's a little on the nose, but that is exactly the kind of unresolved emotional trauma that can become the nucleus of a complex. When did that happen?"

Truly: "When my mom was pretty young. I never met him. Uncle Tommy was four years older than her."

Anders: "We don't know what previous events contributed, but these two, by themselves would not necessarily cause cancer.

"Let's assume your uncle's accident was the first trauma, and your brother's the trigger, and other events happened in her life that she didn't understand. Those events were vibrationally similar, so they all were magnetically attached to each other."

Truly: "So, Uncle Tommy gets killed, Kyle gets killed, and a bunch of other stuff happens.

"I still don't see how that adds up to cancer."

Anders: "The subconscious mind has a blueprint of the perfect physical version of you. Our bodies are continuously renewing cells. We have completely new skin cells every two weeks."

Truly: "Why do people have scars? Marcas has a big nasty scar on his shin."

Anders: "He's still holding on to the trauma. If he completely released the trauma, his shin skin would grow back without the scar."

Truly: "Why wouldn't he release it if he can get his shin back?"

Anders: "He doesn't have the awareness of that ability. Most likely he's doing what most other people do, and that is to keep the scar as a reminder to avoid doing what he did the way he did it."

Truly: "I remember how I got all my scars."

Anders: "Did you learn the lessons of those events?"

Truly: "Maybe."

Anders: "The subconscious rebuilds the body with precision. If the cell-coding is damaged, the cells will be reproduced incorrectly.

"It could be argued that the growth has a purpose, and the cell-coding isn't damaged, just different."

Truly: "That doesn't make sense. A tumor with a mind of its own?"

Anders: "Not a mind, a purpose. The tumor is there to produce a specific result.

"If there is a purpose for a tumor, it could not be misinformation; it must be the right information.

"With that in mind, we can look at the tumor as being a part with a positive purpose."

Truly: "Are we going to just stand here in the parking lot and talk?"

Anders: "We could go back to Fisherman's Alibi. That's a nice place to talk."

Truly: "Table in the Wilderness is closer."

Anders: "Does it have a view of the bay?"

Truly: "Yeah, it's right over here, at Wapato Point."

Anders: "I'll follow you there."

Dolphin Soccer

XXI

Mrs. K: "What else do you do during the day? Do you play outside?"

Elias: "I was just outside, building a village for the geckos, when you came. Sometimes, Papa and I go play golf, but we usually go fishing in the morning. Well, he goes fishing while I swim with my friends.

"When we come back, we exercise and study for a couple of hours. I have soccer practice in town on Tuesdays and Thursdays and matches on Saturdays."

Mrs. K: "You have friends who swim with you in the morning. Are they the same ones you play soccer with?"

Elias: "Dolphins can't play soccer. Maybe water polo. That's kind of like soccer. I'll ask them, though. We also have a luau on Sunday."

Mr. H: "Do you have a full luau? Like, do you roast a pig in an emu every week?"

Elias: "Nah. We have a breakfast feast every week. Sometimes it's moa, sometimes ahi."

Mrs. K: "So, you have a big feast on Sunday mornings? What do you do the rest of the day?"

Elias: "Not in the morning. We never eat in the morning. It's not good for you. We study, have services, then prepare for the feast."

Mrs. K: "Don't you get headaches when you don't eat?"

Elias: "What are headaches?"

Mrs. K: "Never mind."

His Name is Elias

XXII

"Hi. Welcome to Table in the Wilderness. My name is Sarah."

Anders: "Thank you. Do you have a booth by the window?"

Sarah: "As a matter of fact, you are very lucky."

Truly: "What, did we get the owners' table?"

Sarah: "No, but we are just clearing the table with the best view of the bay. The sun will be setting soon. If you keep an eye out as it sets, you may get to see Tatsu."

Anders: "Yes, that's perfect. Thank you. How do you know about Tatsu?"

Sarah: "Everybody around here knows about Tatsu. I thought that was why you were here. What can I get started for you?"

Truly: "I'll just have a chef's salad and a glass of water."

Anders: "Same for me."

Sarah: "Coming right up."

Truly: "Would you be willing to talk to my mom? I don't know if she'd be open to it. I'd have to talk to her first."

Anders: "Of course. I am happy to talk to her anytime she likes."

Truly: "Now, what are we going to do about *this*?"

Anders: "His name is Elias."

Truly: "That's not fair. I haven't even decided if I'm going to have it. You can't name it."

Anders: "I didn't name him. He told me."

Truly: “How is that possible? He can’t talk; he isn’t even born yet.”

Anders: “He said, ‘I am Elias.’ Thought transference isn’t limited by our physical senses.”

Truly: “A cluster of cells can’t have thoughts, can it?”

Anders: “I’m a cluster of cells. I think I can have thoughts.”

Truly: “I wasn’t talking about you. You’re a full-grown person. I’m talking about this thing inside me. How can it have thoughts? How can it communicate telepathically?”

Anders: “At the moment of conception, a unique DNA chain is formed. At the end of the first month, we've already begun to form blood cells and facial characteristics.

“At this point, two months, we're only an inch long, but we have limbs with fingers and toes. The spinal cord, nervous system, and Internal organs are forming. Cartilage is turning into bone, and the head makes up about one third of the baby.”

Truly: “You mean fetus.”

Anders: “Do I? To me, the terms are interchangeable. A unique individual begins at conception.”

Truly: “To me, it isn’t a baby until it’s born.”

Anders: “You can use whatever terms you like. Is it okay if I do too?”

Truly: “Of course. But that doesn’t mean I have to like it. I’m only two months along. I can’t call it a baby yet.”

Anders: “In another month, he'll be a fully formed baby, with fingernails and teeth starting to grow. He will open and close his mouth and his fists. His circulatory and urinary systems begin working.”

Truly: “Are you saying it’s too late for me to end this? Aren’t there other modes of contraception?”

Anders: “It *is* too late for contraception. Contraception, by definition, means to prevent conception. There is no way to prevent conception after conception. He got around contraception.”

Truly: “Words again. There are ways to terminate a pregnancy up until birth. I should be able to decide what I want to do with *my* body.”

Anders: "We are not talking about just your body. We are talking about a unique human being at its most vulnerable stage of development growing inside your body. Your body is a host."

Truly: "How are we *not* talking about my body? You aren't carrying it. You aren't blowing up and throwing up. *My* body is going through all that. My whole life is changing.

"Everything I ever wanted gone, vanished. No career. No space travel. I don't want to give all that up because of one night."

Sarah: "Pardon me folks. Here you go, two chef's salads, two waters."

Anders: "Thank you, Sarah.

"There are always more than just two options. I want you to make your own decisions, but they should be based on facts, not illusions."

Truly: "This is not an illusion. You can't think this away. I really am pregnant and facing a huge life-changing decision."

Anders: "Consider the possibility that some of your beliefs are illusions created by ignorant people."

Truly: "There are plenty of ignorant people around. I hope you aren't going to try to tell me everything I know is wrong and everything you know is right. I had enough of that growing up."

Anders: "I'm saying that my studies of human potential have included prenatal development. As with most of my studies, I found an incredible amount of misinformation being promoted by so-called experts. It's good practice to question what *they* say.

"Have you ever wondered why it is that people only believe in science when it supports what they want to believe? "

Truly: "It makes them feel good to have confirmation."

Anders: "People want to show everybody how smart they are by stating they believe in science, but when you question them, or show them evidence that goes against their beliefs, they reject what you say."

Truly: "Don't confuse me with the facts."

Anders: "Exactly. According to embryonic scientists, life begins at conception.

"It is true that your egg has only your DNA. When your egg accepted one of my sperm, an entirely new and unique DNA chain was formed.

"More than just your cells and my cells, the combination of the two is the conception of a new human being. Fun fact: one teaspoon of semen carries enough sperm to repopulate most of the planet."

Truly: "That's a scary thought. Good thing they don't all survive. But two cells, or even a blob of cells, is *potentially* a human being. It isn't a boy or a girl."

Anders: "The immediate product of fertilization is a human being with two X, or with one X and one Y, creating characteristics and a gender."

Truly: "Philosophically speaking, it doesn't become a person until it starts thinking and having feelings."

Anders: "When someone goes into a coma, and they don't appear to be thinking or feeling, are they no longer a person? Are people with Alzheimer's, Parkinson's, or drug addictions still considered human beings, but not persons? That's a pretty shady line."

Truly: "Of course they are people. They have already been born. The supreme court said life doesn't begin until live birth."

Anders: "They said it was not up to the judiciary to decide. The closest they got was saying there has always been strong support for the view that life doesn't begin until live birth.

"There is no branch of science that says life begins at any other time than conception. That's what the word conception means."

Truly: "It sounds like I don't have any choice in this matter."

Anders: "You always have choice regardless of government approval. I've found I make better choices when I know my options and possible consequences."

Truly: "I know we have choices. Remember those lines of bad code you said were etched into our brains? Well, I have the Catholic code etched in mine. They're not in favor of abortion.

"I know we didn't have to spend that night together, but it seemed like a good idea at the time. Those choices had unexpected consequences. Now I have new choices to make."

Anders: "*We* have choices to make."

Truly: "It's still my body."

Anders: "Your body, as host to a brand-new person, will go through many new experiences. Your body will feel sensations you've never felt before. Hormones will be released that will amplify your emotions.

"You can make it an ordeal or an adventure. It all depends on your expectations."

Truly: "I haven't heard very many good stories about being pregnant, giving birth, or raising a kid."

Anders: "It's tough to make an informed decision if you're misinformed. We compartmentalize information to keep it organized.

"In your compartment for those states, you have mostly negative video clips, audio clips, and vibrational memories. Other people's real and imagined experiences are all you have to go by."

Truly: "Yeah. Definitely my first time with all this. I don't have any of my own experiences with it."

Anders: "You can accept the old paradigm of pain, agony, and sorrow, 'even though it's worth it,' set up your belief system based on that, and you will get what you expect."

Truly: "That is what I expect."

Anders: "Or you can make new choices, set up the belief system that you want, and you will still get what you expect. You want to make your choices based on facts, not someone else's illusions."

Truly: "Either way, I get what I expect. I expect what I believe. So, how do I change what I believe?"

Anders: "You change your beliefs by reevaluating them."

Truly: "What if I don't believe in telepathy?"

Anders: "Then you won't be aware of telepathic communications. The communication is still there, you just won't be aware of it.

"Your mind sends thoughts out. Your thoughts don't just stay inside your head. Thoughts are energy forms that emanate from you constantly."

Truly: "Every thought I think goes out into the world?"

Anders: "Like a little broadcasting tower. Your attitude determines your thoughts. Your thoughts are broadcast to the universe. Your feelings are based on your beliefs, which draw to you what you focus on. Your world reflects your mind."

Truly: "I don't know whether I feel empowered or scared."

Anders: "It's probably a little of both, isn't it?"

Truly: "Can you read *my* mind? Can you hear what I'm thinking?"

Anders: "Sometimes. I'm usually busy listening to my own thinking, but I also pick up on thought vibrations from people I interact with. Sometimes, I receive specific thoughts. Most of the time, I get a general sense of their mood.

"I don't worry too much about what other people are thinking."

Truly: "Aren't you worried that someone *would* know what you are thinking?"

Anders: "I'm not perfect, but most of my thoughts are harmonious. I don't have any agenda for other people, other than to teach what I've learned. I offer knowledge for people to consider. It's up to them to determine how relevant it is for them.

"Anyone is free to accept or reject anything I say. So, I'm happy to share my thoughts with the world."

Truly: "You're okay with people knowing your secrets? You can't tell me you never did, said, or thought anything that you don't want people to know."

Anders: "Without a doubt, I've said stupid things and made plenty of mistakes. Life would be boring without mistakes. How would you ever learn how the Laws of the Universe work if you were always in fear of what other people might think?

"I like to test theories. I mean no harm to anybody. I use my will power to focus my thoughts in the direction of my ideals. I still have occasional unkind thoughts toward people, but it keeps getting easier to replace those with blessings, praise, and gratitude."

Truly: "I don't know. I can't see myself turning the other cheek to someone who hits me. Sometimes, I can just feel when someone is thinking bad thoughts about me. That really bugs me."

Anders: "That impression of what they're thinking about you is your intuition. You are subconsciously aware of your own vibratory frequency resonating with the thought vibration the other person is sending out. When it senses disharmony, your subconscious puts up its shields."

Truly: "One thing Marcas taught me was, if someone hits you, you have the right to hit them back, and when you hit them back, give it everything you've got."

Anders: "Is Marcas your ideal of a human being?"

Truly: "That pile of garbage? Hardly, but he is my dad. He knows how life goes for a Murphy."

Anders: "Turning the other cheek isn't about letting people take advantage of you. Some people misinterpret forgiveness and tolerance for weakness.

"The point of that parable is that you don't want to allow another person to pull you off your track and away from your purpose. If you engage with them, you're adding emotional energy to their errant thoughts.

"When you add electrical current to a magnet, making an electromagnet, you amplify its strength. Emotions are the amplifiers of thought vibrations."

Truly: "Also, if you hit them back hard enough, they won't do it again."

Kapu

XXIII

Mrs. K: "Elias, you said you were born in the bay. I thought they passed a law preventing that."

Elias: "It was okay when I was born. It's only kapu to give birth in the bays now, auntie."

Mrs. K: "Yes, it seems there were too many sharks coming in."

Elias: "Too many babies in small bays. Too much blood attracted sharks. The dolphins kept most of them out. You haffa go out to the point now. It flushes better."

Mrs. K: "Are women still having babies in the ocean?"

Elias: "Some. Auntie Gracie has a birthing pool at her house. She says she has more control that way. She is closer to the hospital, too. Just in case."

Mrs. K: "In case of what?"

Elias: "Sometimes doubt and fear creep back in. Negative frequencies create negative conditions."

Mrs. K: "Can a woman be fearless and believe, but still fall back into old fears?"

Elias: "It happens. Fear and tension cause pain. If they could only trust themselves." Shaking his head, "I find their lack of faith disturbing."

HypnoBirthing®

XXIV

Truly: "Tell me about hypnosis birth. Do you just put me to sleep so I don't feel anything, like you did with Benjamin?"

Anders: "I still think you misunderstand what hypnosis is. There's so much bad information out there about hypnosis that very few people really understand it. It's simply a state of mind, and everybody is suggestible.

"With hypnosis, you bypass the critical faculty and communicate directly with the subconscious mind. The subconscious mind is a follower.

"It will accept any suggestion given that doesn't violate what it believes to be moral and comes from a source of perceived authority."

Truly: "So, you're going to hypnotize me and suggest that I won't feel any pain? If it's that easy, why doesn't everybody do it?"

Anders: "That's a small part of the process. Like I said, most people don't understand it. They don't know that they are already under the influence of bad hypnosis.

"Most people live under the beliefs of the collective paradigms. They put their faith in the consensus of experts."

Truly: "They are the experts. Who else are we supposed to listen to? If everyone is doing it, it must be the right way."

Anders: "Consensus is not science; it's following the herd. Science is testing new theories to find new outcomes. I love science. I love to test theories.

"A bunch of people nodding their heads in agreement is not science. Any dolt can look at a report and confirm, according to their limited knowledge, that the report is true. It takes a real scientist to ask if the details are accurate.

"The subconscious mind doesn't question whether a premise is correct. It can only deduce from a given set of facts a logical outcome. It doesn't concern itself with whether the facts are true."

Truly: "How can the facts not be true?"

Anders: "It may accept a false statement as a fact and combine it with other beliefs to create a new belief that's built on a swamp. The public is relentlessly bombarded with false statements presented as facts."

Truly: "You can't help but hear it. How do you know what's fact and what is false?"

Anders: "I don't watch much TV, and when I do, I definitely don't watch the news. News programs are designed to present and perpetuate specific narratives."

Truly: "I know not everything they say is true, but some of it is. Do you think they are intentionally misinforming people?"

Anders: "Unfortunately, bad news sells, and they are in business to make a profit. They use scare tactics to keep people in line and sell their sponsors' products. They control public belief through coordinated repetition of the same message.

"Only about five or six huge conglomerates own all the news outlets. They sit in corporate offices and decide what narratives they want to push. Then they send that out to all their affiliates to use those guidelines to select the stories and the angles they will be told from."

Truly: "That sounds like a conspiracy theory. Are you sure there aren't any false facts in there?"

Anders: "It's not a theory. Do a search across the networks. It is a fact that the news outlets are controlled by a handful of corporations. It is also a fact that they use exactly the same phrases across their networks.

"When they want people to believe a certain thing, they hammer the message out repeatedly. Tap, tap, tap."

Truly: "Tap, tap, tap?"

Anders: "That is one of the techniques for embedding a belief in the subconscious. Repeat a suggestion enough times and people will accept an outright lie as fact.

"In Claude Bristol's *The Magic of Believing*, he wrote about the techniques the National Socialists used in the 1930s to influence the minds of the German people. Similar techniques are being used again around the world. The media are their bullhorns.

"For example, science and due consideration reveal the masks don't protect from viruses, but the politicians tell us we have to wear them, and the media blasts the message."

Truly: "That's all you hear. 'You must wear a mask to protect yourself and those around you. You must wear a mask.' Then, you see someone walking down the road, with no one else around, wearing a mask. What's the point of that?"

Anders: "It's a suggestibility test to see who will comply. It's no coincidence that they all voted for the same party.

"Have you ever noticed how some people are always so grateful when an election year is over? Election-year news cycles are emotionally disturbing for some.

"People become convinced of a narrative, and there's no way they'll believe they've been fooled. Anything you are convinced of must become real for you."

Truly: "I love how Mark Twain said, 'It's easier to fool a person than it is to convince them that they have been fooled.' I've seen that firsthand."

Anders: "Epidemiology tells us one thing and the media and politicians tell us another. As more people accept the narrative as a belief, they start repeating the mantra.

"Advertisers play along. They gear their commercials to amplifying the fear of the virus. They want to sell more of their products.

"The next thing you know, the TV shows themselves are writing the narrative into their storylines. Repetition is the key."

Truly: "They definitely keep saying the same thing over and over. Maybe you should take a couple of deep breaths. You seem a little amped up. They're not all lying though, are they?"

Anders: "When I hear people parroting false narratives they've heard on the news, I get frustrated. It's especially disturbing when I hear it from members of my own family.

"I can usually tell when someone has been influenced by propaganda. They get highly emotional when challenged. Totalitarians appeal to people's sense of the greater good to implement social control. They are intentionally inducing mass psychosis. It's nothing less than mind rape."

Truly: "That sounds diabolical. The world is insane right now. You're saying that's the plan?"

Anders: "It's an ancient plan. Menticide *is* diabolical. Ignorant people are pliable people. Pot and liquor stores are apparently essential, so people can get their *Soma.* It keeps them sedated, complacent, and compliant. People eagerly self-medicate.

"Fear, isolation, distraction with mindless programming, and repetition are tactics used to condition people to follow commands.

"I have to believe most reporters started as good people with good intentions. Some truth, some lies, all mixed together. Some believe they are telling the truth. Some know they are being told to lie but don't want to upset their own apple cart.

"To keep their jobs, they do what their bosses tell them to do."

Truly: "No wonder the world is so messed up."

Anders: "Things aren't really as bad as they make it sound. Many of our global crises are fabricated narratives magnified by emotions and ingrained through repetition. Inducing fear is part of the process of getting the attention of the collective subconscious.

"Once they have that attention, people will more easily accept almost any suggestion. Unfortunately, the public doesn't get accurate numbers in their proper perspective. They believe the false narrative."

Truly: "Do you think labor pains are a false narrative? I mean, obviously, women have been having babies since there have been people; long before there was ever any news. Did those women give birth in pain?"

Anders: "I can't say for sure because I wasn't there, and giving birth pre-dates talking. Have you ever seen a cat give birth to a litter of kittens? What was her state of mind? Did she wail and scream?"

Truly: "No. She was just lying there calmly, and the baby kitties kept coming out. I even heard her purring."

Anders: "You can find that calmness in most mammals during delivery. You might say they don't know any different."

Truly: "Like they don't know it is supposed to be painful, so it's not?"

Anders: "Right. Animals operate only from the animal self. They live in the here and now. They're not aware of any history of previous childbirths and, thus, do not have any expectations about the experience."

Truly: "Still, how can you push out a bowling ball without it hurting?"

Anders: "I doubt that anybody could. Whatever gave you the idea that giving birth to a baby was like pushing out a bowling ball?"

Truly: "That's just what I heard. It's easy enough to imagine how painful that would be. Makes sense, doesn't it?"

Anders: "Not to me. There are a lot of differences between a baby at birth and a bowling ball. First, there's the weight. Professional women bowlers roll a ball that weighs, about 14 – 15 lbs. The average baby weighs between 7, and 7 ½ lbs., half the weight."

Truly: "Okay, but what about pushing that big head through? That can't be easy."

Anders: "Again, the difference is huge. Bowling balls are over 26 inches in circumference, while a baby's head is more like 14 inches."

Truly: "I've seen some babies with pretty big heads."

Anders: "We don't usually see babies out in public when they're newborn. Even when people take their newborns out, they usually keep them bundled up. Their heads grow rapidly in the first couple of months. You know how a newborn has a soft spot on the top of their head?"

Truly: "Yeah. It's so delicate."

Anders: "That's the last part to fill in as the skull hardens. Babies' heads are phenomenally engineered for birth. Until we're born, the skull isn't a ball. It's a combination of plates that can move independently and overlap each other, making the head even smaller.

"After we're born, the plates move into their normal positions and begin knitting themselves together."

Truly: "Really? The skull folds up, then grows together? That's badass."

Anders: "Women have everything they need to give birth to their babies, and babies are designed to be birthed by their human mothers. You can say it's a result of evolution if you like, or you can call it divine design.

"Either way, one of the myths of childbirth is the incompatibility of the birth canal in relation to the size of the baby. Babies are squishy … even their heads."

Truly: "But even with big childbearing hips, the opening is still smaller than the thing trying to go through it. Like a bulldog stuck in a kitty door."

Anders: "That's not a good simile. A kitty door doesn't have any flexibility. It won't stretch or change its shape for the bulldog, which is another terrible representation. Human muscles, connective tissue, and skin are all elastic, and babies are smaller than you hallucinate."

Truly: "There are limits though."

Anders: "Yes. You understand that comparing childbirth to passing a bowling ball is a ridiculous, overdramatic mythology. You now have a better understanding of that part of the birth process, and probably are more relaxed about it. When you reevaluate your beliefs, you can change them.

"HypnoBirthing® is more than hypnosis for childbirth. It's a completely different approach, a change of paradigm."

Truly: "I'm not convinced it won't be painful. I feel a little bit better about it, but I'm not going to say I'm relaxed. Sorry, not sorry."

Anders: "You've seen births on television and in the movies?"

Truly: "More like heard them. They don't actually show the baby coming out. Gross."

Anders: "Yeah. You hear the cursing and screaming. You see the agonized look on the actor's face, and the horrified looks on others. *Acting*. Some of it's funny. Some of it's sad.

"All of it is designed to evoke a strong emotional response. That implants the suggestion deeply in your subconscious that *this* is what it's like to have a baby."

Truly: "There are real life examples too. I've talked to women who had babies. They all say the pain is real, but then they try to tell me it was worth it. I don't want it to be 'worth it.' I don't want to spend that much to begin with."

Anders: "They got what they expected. Growing beyond your limitations can be uncomfortable. Overcoming difficulties is one of the great pleasures of life. Challenges keep us feeling alive. You said you wanted experiences you have never had before."

Truly: "I love challenges. I'm just not a big fan of pain."

Anders: "Pain is a message from the body to central command, sounding an alarm that there's a breach of harmony. It's amazing how simple it is to turn off the alarm."

Truly: "You can just flip a switch and shut off the pain? Teach me."

Anders: "Not just shut off the signal. Your body can naturally produce painkillers to flood the area. We get the results we believe we will get. Change your beliefs; change your results. Are you ready to challenge your beliefs about childbirth?"

Truly: "Sure. As long as it's not painful."

Anders: "It's only the fear of what might happen that causes any pain in changing beliefs. The subconscious mind does not like change. It will use fear tactics to keep you where you are.

"People become passionately attached to their beliefs. To the subconscious, change is threatening, and it will do everything it can to counter an attack. It will lock itself down, put up barriers, and shut off the lights."

Truly: "Even if it's something you want?"

Anders: "It doesn't like change. After all, it's worked awfully hard to acquire the beliefs that it has. Your subconscious loves your consciousness exactly the way you are.

"It prefers the easy way. Advertisers know this. How many products are sold with the promise of making lives easier?"

Truly: "I like easy too."

Anders: "We all do. Our paradigms are the autopilots of our lives. All our habitual activities are controlled by our paradigms and most activities are habitual. We mostly go around in autopilot throughout the day. Mental activity is not the same as thinking."

Truly: "People don't think."

Anders: "When you think about childbirth, since you haven't experienced it yourself, you rely on the wisdom of those who have gone before. You have a folder in your mental file cabinet where you store all the information you have gathered about childbirth and raising a child.

"You have a set of beliefs that say childbirth is painful and potentially life-threatening.

"You have stories and reports full of supporting evidence, including stories that say yeah, it hurt, but it is a badge of honor. We have generations of women passing down a tradition of painful childbirth.

"Fear creates tension; tension magnifies pain. The three physical responses to fear that cause pain are muscle tension, lack of blood flow to the area, and toxic hormones released into the body.

"Your birthing muscles were designed to work in harmony. Your body even emits lubricant into the canal during delivery. You can condition your mind and the physical area over the next seven months.

"When you are hopeful and in a good mood, your body produces chemicals that make you feel excellent. And on the contrary, when you are fearful and doubtful, your body produces chemicals that are toxic to your systems.

"It is simple, really. Condition your mind and body, and you will have a childbirth that empowers you and your baby."

Truly: "I still have to complete my initial training. That's three more months."

Anders: "You have plenty of time. Your baby grows a little each day, and that's all you have to do, a little each day. There are different roads you can take. It's up to you."

You Pushed Out

XXV

Mrs. B: "Elias, what did you mean when you said negative frequencies create negative conditions?"

Elias: "The mind brings good and evil through the same power. When you tune into the frequencies of doubt and fear, you attract those conditions. Perception is projection. Everything you see is a reflection of your mind."

Mrs. B: "Is that true with people too? Even the people who irritate us?"

Elias: "Everyone is you, pushed out. The people you are aware of in your world are aspects of yourself that your subconscious wants your conscious to deal with.

"We attract those people into our lives to help us address inner conflicts and unresolved issues."

Mrs. B: "But I'm still not them, and they're not me."

Elias: "Every material thing is made of energy. Every person is an energy mass, yeah? The way they appear to you is the way you perceive them. You filter your reality through your paradigm. Your imagination fills in the details."

Mrs. B: "Don't we appear to people the way we present ourselves? We see people the way they are. I see you as a little boy sitting here in front of me. Isn't that what you are?"

Elias: "I am that to you. You see me in the state I am from your level of awareness. Uncle and auntie see me from their levels of awareness. You all agree I am me, but I appear differently to each of you."

Awaiku

XXVI

Anders: "Truly, do you believe in angels?"

Truly: "Yeah. I suppose I do. Let's say I believe in the possibility that angels exist, but I also believe they could be entirely made up by ignorant people who want to blame their lives on outside influences."

Anders: "Most people feel the need to place responsibility for their lives on someone or something outside of themselves. They've been conditioned to believe they're too weak to influence their worlds. They just can't believe that they create the world they live in through the choices they make."

Truly: "It's hard for me to accept that someone would choose to be sick or poor. I still can't believe anybody would choose to have cancer."

Anders: "I think you may be confusing conscious choice with the actions of the subconscious. I agree that people do not make a conscious decision to have cancer. You can, however, make a conscious decision *not* to have cancer."

Truly: "Yeah. You can decide not to have cancer, but that doesn't stop it."

Anders: "A committed decision is the first step. It takes more than just saying the words."

Truly: "So, my mom can just decide not to have cancer, and it will go away? If that were true, why wouldn't *that* be the headline of every medical journal on the planet?"

Anders: "I may be wrong about this, but if everyone knew they could heal themselves, the entire medical industry, with its sub-industries, would collapse. It would be the end of the world for those people.

"Think about what that means. Not just doctors, nurses, and their books would be affected. Hospitals, pharmaceuticals, devices, equipment, research, advertising, universities, fund raising, insurance, lawyers, and salespeople of all sorts, all have built their castles upon the current medical paradigm.

"That is a massive mountain of belief to move. All those people would have to find other creative ways to earn wealth. Cancer treatment, alone, is a $150 billion entity. There is no money in the cure; the money is in the treatment."

Truly: "That's a lot of people. Probably way more than the number of people who get sick and die. Does that justify letting people die like that? If I knew how to cure cancer, I would shout it from the rooftops. I would tell everyone I meet."

Anders: "When they heard what you had to say, they would probably call you a crackpot. If you persisted, they would probably throw your ass in jail.

"Historically, that is what people have done to anyone who dares to tell the Truth. The masses won't tolerate anyone who challenges their beliefs."

Truly: "People are so stupid."

Anders: "People are ignorant. Stupid implies an inability to learn. I just think people are misinformed and unaware, which is the state of ignorance. States are changeable."

Truly: "Leopards don't change their spots and people don't change. So, I guess they'll stay ignorant."

Anders: "That's an extremely limiting belief. I have seen many people assume the moment of power and permanently change the course of their life in an instant."

Truly: "You mean like instant healing?"

Anders: "Healing comes in many forms, but it can come in an instant."

Truly: "That sounds like a miracle. Marcas said only the Apostles did miracles, and they're all dead now. He said God doesn't do miracles anymore."

Anders: "I know Marcas is never wrong, but he may be mistaken about that. The men may be dead, but God lives. In the book of Luke, Jesus sent out 72 *ordinary* people to work miracles.

"Miracles are divinely natural. We just aren't aware of it.

"Saint Augustine said, 'Miracles are not contrary to nature, they are only contrary to what we know about nature.'

"The twelve apostles, or disciples, are actually twelve qualities, or disciplines, of your mind. Remember, the Bible is a psychological map of the human mind. Through disciplined action of the twelve aspects of mind, God works miracles through you.

"If you think of each of the disciples as a center of energy…"

Truly: "Wait. The twelve disciples were not men? They're energy centers?"

Anders: "Yeah. Those men may have lived, but their stories are about us and how to use our minds."

Truly: "What is Judas all about then, look out for people who betray you?"

Anders: "Sure. It can represent that. I think of Judas as representing undisciplined aspects of your mind that will betray you every time. Judas is the quality of detachment. His greatest gift was to detach himself from Jesus.

"You have to let go of the old you to become the new you. Detach yourself from your past and your past betrayals in both directions. Until you let go of who you think you are, you won't become what you desire to be."

Truly: "That's not the way I remember Judas."

Anders: "I know. It's an old way of thinking that's new to most people."

Truly: "Funny how that works. All right, so … the disciples are aspects of the mind, and *energy centers*?"

Anders: "Right. Every thought form has a nucleus, which attracts to itself the energy and particles it needs for expansion. Many of these thoughtforms have grown into gods and demons. Powerful shared beliefs can seem to take on a life of their own."

Truly: "Thoughts become gods and demons? Is that true with things like dragons and unicorns? People just thought them up, but not enough people believe in them for them to be real?"

Anders: "I've never studied unicorns, but I know a little bit about dragons and angels."

Truly: "I'm sure it's not what 'everybody knows' about them, is it?"

Anders: "Not exactly. I think of dragons as guardian spirits of locations, and angels as guardian spirits of people."

Truly: "Dragons are watchdogs, and angels are bodyguards. Got it."

Anders: "I know you've heard the word *genius* before, but I want to give you another way of thinking about it."

Truly: "Of course you do."

Anders: "The ancient Romans believed we were each assigned a guardian spirit at birth, which is your genius. The parallel to that, in ancient Hawaiian beliefs, is called aumakua. New Agers call it the Christ Consciousness or Higher Self."

Truly: "I've heard of the Higher Self, but I'm not sure what that really means. You're saying it's my genius? Tell me more about my genius."

Anders: "I'm getting there. The Romans also believed that there was a spirit guarding every location, which they called genius loci. Different cultures call the genius loci by other names, like dragon, or god, or spirit.

"For example, this bay is a location separate and distinct from all other locations. It also has a spirit, which Sam told me, when we were over there on the other side, they call Tatsu. The area vibrates at a specific frequency in resonance with that spirit.

"Not all dragons are monsters like in fairy tales. Water dragons—the Japanese call them tatsu—are mostly benevolent spirits that protect their area from discord."

Truly: "They're geniuses of harmony."

Anders: "Genii. The plural of genius is genii."

Truly: "Is my genius a genie?"

Anders: "Your genius can be joined with another genius to form genii. Where two or more gather ..."

Truly: "Do I get three wishes with my genie?"

Anders: "You can have as many wishes as you want. If you work with the Laws, there is no limit. You don't think you can break God's bank, do you? No matter how much you receive, you will not deprive God of anything."

Truly: "What about the poor people? Shouldn't we leave some for them?"

Anders: "The Father's kingdom is infinite. God wants you to be rich. Can you help more poor people if you have lots of money, or if you have rabbit ears?"

Truly: "What are rabbit ears?"

Anders: "You know, when your pockets are so empty, if you pull them out, they look like rabbit ears. The best way to help the poor is to become rich."

Truly: "What do I have to do to get my wishes? That's what I want to know. You said I have a genie with unlimited wishes. Now, where is my stuff?"

Anders: "Wherever you believe it is. It's not like in the movies or TV, but it does work like magic. Really, it's more like a science, an exact science like geometry or arithmetic. Science always seems like magic to the unaware."

Truly: "I would rather just twitch my nose or polish a lamp. I don't want to do a bunch of work."

Anders: "How easy do you want it to be? Everything has a price. You can have anything you want, but you have to give value in return. The secret is to give more use value than you receive in cash value."

Truly: "All the stories say you tell the genie your wish and, *poof*, there it is."

Anders: "That may be fun for a while, but there is no growth in that. It would get boring quickly. And you don't want to manifest negative thoughts instantly.

"It's so much more satisfying to go through the process of becoming the person who has what you desire."

Truly: "What if I don't know how to do that? How am I supposed to know how to become a person who owns a helicopter? I don't even know anybody who owns a helicopter."

Anders: "Is that what you want, a helicopter?"

Truly: "Yeah? I guess so. Sure, why not? Yes. I want a helicopter … eventually."

Anders: "You said you don't even know anybody who owns a helicopter. That doesn't sound like a desire. It sounds more like a daydream of maybe.

"There is something you want though. Something you have wanted for a long time, but you haven't gotten it because you doubt your ability to get it. What is that?"

Truly: "I thought you were supposed to be some kind of psychic. I don't know. What?"

Anders: "You know better than anyone else. If you could have anything you want, no limits, what would that be?"

Truly: "Hmm. Tell me more about the water dragon while I think about it."

Anders: "I mentioned the tatsu as a reference to spirit entities who are genius loci. We each have a guardian angel genius as a part of ourselves. Angels are genii. They all operate on the spirit plane. There is no competition on that level, only creativity."

Truly: "You mean our guardian angel is a genius and a genie? That's what I'm talking about."

Anders: "The Hawaiians call our guardian spirit aumakua. Our aumakua know each other and the other aumakua, whether they are attached to a person or not. Those genii who are not aumakua are called awaiku. We call them angels.

"They all work together to help those of us in mortal garments with our desires here on Earth. We all have aumakua and a number of awaiku."

Truly: "How many angels do we have?"

Anders: "I don't know how many you have. I have three. At least, I am aware of three."

Truly: "How do you know you have three?"

Anders: "I met them when I was in Kona. About 20 years ago, in a training, we went into trance and met our awaiku. We learned their names and where they live in our bodies."

Truly: "Where do they live in your body?"

Anders: "The number of awaiku, and where they live, is different for everyone. It's entirely subjective. For me, the locations are consistent with the metaphoric qualities they represent.

"I have an awaiku of masculine energy, who introduced himself as Maximus, who resides in my right arm. I also have an awaiku of feminine energy that I know as Avril, who is surprisingly like the singer. She resides in my left arm. Avril is extremely selective. For whatever reason, she sure seems to like you.

"The third awaiku, who was the most reluctant to reveal itself, is balanced masculine and feminine energies. His name is Thoth, and he resides in my pineal gland."

Truly: "Why was he reluctant?"

Anders: "He wasn't reluctant to reveal himself to me. He just wasn't sure that I would be able to understand what his name meant. He didn't think I'd get it, I guess. The ancient Egyptians believed Thoth had no parents but was self-produced.

"To me, that represents my nucleus from which my world is created. Thoth was the great magician who knew all that was hidden under the heavenly vault. The subconscious also knows all that is hidden."

Truly: "So, you have a gladiator, a skateboard punk chick, and an all-knowing Egyptian god as angels who live in your body?"

Anders: "Their names and locations represent the qualities they possess. They revealed themselves to me in a way I could comprehend."

Truly: "If you were in a trance, how do you know you weren't hypnotized to *think* you were meeting your angels?"

Anders: "That is a great question. I wondered about that myself. I also considered that maybe I wasn't ready to accept just how powerful I really am. Maybe that was why I ignored them for almost 20 years."

Truly: "Why the hell would you ignore angels who are with you all the time? If I knew angels had my back, I'd be balls to the wall 24/7."

Anders: "An interesting phenomenon occurs when people come back from seminars. When most people attend a seminar, they usually have friends and family who have a fixed idea of who that person is and what they do.

"Someone goes to a seminar, learns new and exciting ideas, and comes home ready to implement these life-changing principles, but they fall back into their old habits.

"Their friends and family still see the person who left, not the person who came back. Sometimes, we let other people's perception of us pull us back into the old habits."

Truly: "Not me. I don't care what people think of me. I've got power. Bow down bitches."

Anders: "Not everyone is as certain of themselves as you. It is also easier when you're young and have fewer attachments. Many people have deeply ingrained relationships that pull them back into old ways of thinking, feeling, and acting.

"Collective consciousness also has a gravitational or magnetic force that pulls them back."

Truly: "They have to be somewhat different though, right? What is the point of taking time out of your life and spending all that money if everything stays the same?"

Anders: "People do learn and grow during seminars. Even when they go home with their new awareness and gradually fall back into old habits, they have still grown.

"I thought when I came back with an effective way of treating cancer from within that everyone would be excited about it. So, I started talking to people about it."

Truly: "Were they excited?"

Anders: "You would think so. Instead, most people thought I was crazy. They couldn't believe that a construction contractor could have an answer when the entire medical profession couldn't beat it. They didn't understand what I was saying to them."

Truly: "Did you talk to doctors about it?"

Anders: "Yes. I also went to a meeting put on by a couple of oncology nurses. When I spoke, they looked at me as though I were the devil incarnate. What I was saying was a direct threat to their beliefs and their industry. Needless to say, I didn't get any referrals from them."

Truly: "I always thought the truth will prevail against all resistance. Did you just give up?"

Anders: "No, I didn't give up, but I did stop trying to re-educate the misinformed."

Truly: "Never try to teach a pig to sing. You only get frustrated, and it annoys the pig."

Anders: "I continued studying and started looking for better ways to get the message accepted."

Truly: "Hmm. I wonder what you could have done if only you had some powerful angels working with you."

Anders: "Right? What good does it do to have power that you don't put to work? We humans are reluctant to change, even when it's in our best interest.

"Basically, as an independent type, I ignored my angel guides and became an improved version of who I was before. Not yet the person I wanted to be."

Truly: "They are *angels* who live in your body. They are always with you. How can you ignore that?"

Anders: "Through my own acts of ignorance. Angels, like your higher self, are always with you. If you want their help, all you have to do is ask, but you do have to ask.

"They are in direct communication with your subconscious and produce the results it calls for. Without conscious direction, the results can seem random."

Truly: "My life is full of random stuff."

Anders: "It can appear that way sometimes."

Truly: "Wasn't it random that we met in a training session, some other stuff happened, and now we're here, dealing with this." She pointed to her belly with both index fingers.

Anders: "I don't believe anything is entirely random. Every effect has a cause."

Truly: "Well, random is the best way I can describe the things that happen to me."

Anders: "It's a good word for describing how some things appear. The truth is there is always an underlying cause for everything. I don't believe our meeting was random. I think angelic intervention helped bring us together."

Truly: "You think angels brought us together? What, do you think this baby is some kind of new messiah? Like the second coming?"

Anders: "I don't know anything about a new messiah. That is a lot of pressure for everyone. I'm not making that claim. Can you imagine?"

Truly: "Well, that's a relief. Thank God."

Anders: "A few months ago, I was not in a very good place, emotionally. I was trudging along, in my rut, putting one foot in front of the other, just to keep going. Then I met you. The catalyst.

"As we talked, I began to feel different. You talked about doing things that reminded me of my life at your age. I started to feel younger. You talked about your time in Kona, where I met my awaiku, which refreshed my awareness of their presence.

"There were other bits of information that made me consider that the awaiku had played a role in our meeting each other, especially Avril.

"It may even be possible that Elias chose us to execute his plan."

Truly: "Dude, if you had told me *that*, while we were still at the bar, this would probably *have* to have been an immaculate conception. Because I don't know if I would have taken you home."

Anders: "I'm glad you did. I am in Heaven right now. I guess I shouldn't tell you about the rainbow I saw a couple of days later."

Truly: "You probably shouldn't, but you might as well tell me now."

Anders: "When I was at the golf course the following Saturday, I saw a rainbow that went from where I was, directly over to Bowman Bay. I don't even know if you were over there that day."

Truly: "I'm there every weekend. Why is a rainbow significant?"

Anders: "I had to look it up. It's generally considered an omen of good luck. Of course, there's the old Irish folklore about the metaphoric pot of gold at the other end. Some say it's a bridge to Heaven. My concept of Heaven is happiness here on Earth."

Truly: "But you're not saying it's magical, right?"

Anders: "I'm not going to say it's not."

GET INTO THE SPIRIT OF THE THING

XXVII

MRS. K: "ELIAS, YOU seem to be happy about everything you do. Joy just flows out from within you. How do you do that all the time?"

Elias: "Everything is easier and more fun when you get into the spirit of the thing."

Mr. H: "What does that mean, to get into the spirit of the thing?"

Elias: "It means you focus all of your attention on it. Put your heart into it. Every activity has a spirit. A story, a song, or a game has a spirit that vibrates at specific frequencies.

"When you set your intention to enjoy something, your mind will tune to that frequency, and the thing will be in harmony with you. Put joy into the thing, and the thing will give you joy in return."

Mrs. B: "How do you get into the spirit of dull, boring chores, like washing dishes?"

Elias: "You live from choice. Okay, say you have dirty dishes in the sink. You could neglect them, leave them for someone else to do, or you could take control of the circumstance.

"If you approach the task, expecting it to be dull and boring, it will be. If you take control with the intention of having fun, it will be fun. You add life to the spirit and the spirit adds life to you."

Mrs. B: "What a wonderful philosophy. I wish I could get myself to enjoy my commute. I know I have to do it. I just dread sitting in traffic. It's so counterproductive."

Elias: "Make it productive."

Mrs. B: "How can I make *that* productive? I can't talk on the phone, it's too distracting."

Elias: "The easiest way is to set your intention for that segment of time. If you focus on dread, you will get dreadful results. Decide to enjoy the journey. Papa and I usually listen to audiobooks or other programs when we drive somewhere."

Mrs. B: "It seems like every morning, I start out happy, but then, like I knew it would happen, some jerk does something stupid, and I'm angry the rest of the way. Then it usually gets worse."

Elias: "You get what you expect. You knew it would happen, and it did. Then, negative feeling attracts more negative circumstance."

Mrs. B: "I can't control other people."

Elias: "Did you ever hear the one about the little girl who was afraid to ride with her mother to the store? Her mama said, 'Don't worry honey, the dumb bastards only come out when Daddy's driving.'"

Marcas Murphy

XXVIII

Anders: "If you don't mind me asking, what's up between you and Coyote? You don't seem to like him much. Are you masking other feelings?"

Truly: "Benjamin is a narcissist, a covert narcissist. You know, the kind who everybody thinks is so great. But they're really devils in sheep's clothing."

Anders: "Don't you mean wolves in sheep's clothing?"

Truly: "At least with a wolf, you know what to expect. With a narcissist, you never know. They can say things to you that sound like love on the surface, but what they are really trying to do is get you to follow their agenda.

"They always have an agenda, and they always have to get their little barbs in that make them feel superior to you. That's important to them."

Anders: "Coyote is arrogant, and he certainly has narcissistic traits. You're not saying it in a casual way though, you sound like you mean it clinically. Having the traits of a narcissist doesn't necessarily mean a person has NPD."

Truly: "True, but how many do you have to have to qualify? Even though he's always tearing people down, everybody still thinks he's this awesome dude. That devil doesn't fool me. He thinks he's smarter than everybody else; that he can do anything better than anybody else."

Anders: "There's a lot to be said for being self-confident."

Truly: "Of course, there is. If you don't believe in yourself, who will? You have to sell yourself first.

"But I'm talking beyond someone who thinks highly of themselves. I'm talking about someone with low self-esteem who can only feel better about themselves by downgrading everyone around them.

"*Especially* when they say they are only trying to help."

Anders: "Maybe they are trying to help."

Truly: "Maybe I don't want their help. Maybe it costs too much. Maybe their way *isn't* the best way. Maybe there is nothing wrong with my way."

Anders: "Maybe it's their way of reaching out to show they care."

Truly: "Maybe. I'm sure that's part of it. They do want to be connected, and they do care, but they are also pulling strings to get you to conform to their idea of the world, which is the only truth, because they are so perfect."

Anders: "How do you know so much about it? Most people think narcissists are just clowns who are conceited and want a lot of attention."

Truly: "I grew up with Marcas Murphy for a father. Everybody always said I must be the luckiest girl in the world to have a father like Marcas. 'He's so funny.' 'He was the first person to welcome me to the docks.' 'Such a nice guy.'

"He sure had them fooled. Mom too. I don't know why she stayed with him so long. Sometimes, he was just downright cruel to her. He was always trying to make her feel like she was crazy or stupid."

Anders: "Was it the same for you and your brother?"

Truly: "He loved Kyle. Kyle could do no wrong. Even if Kyle did something wrong, it was never his fault. It was always the school, or the coach, or the other kid.

"If anybody said otherwise, Marcas would give them a piece of his mind. He was so small-minded; I don't know why he felt like he had to keep giving out pieces. But everyone was entitled to Marcas' opinion."

Anders: "None shout so loud as the ignorant. How about you? Were you daddy's little princess?"

Truly: "Princess? No. Well, sometimes he would act that way if he thought someone was watching. He thought I was going to be a boy too. He tolerated me. It was like he was thinking 'girls aren't as good as boys, but at least this one is part me.'

"He seemed disappointed that I couldn't throw a ball as far as Kyle. He was always comparing me to him. In his eyes, I always came up short. I did learn to shoot though. Kyle was never as good at shooting as I was. Marcas gave me that much credit."

Anders: "You call your father by his first name; you don't call him Dad?"

Truly: "I haven't called that son of a bitch Dad since the night he walked out on my mom. That was the same night Kyle got killed. Then, everything changed."

Anders: "That must have been some night for your mother. How is she doing?"

Truly: "She's doing about as well as can be expected, I guess. At least she was until she got cancer. Now she has that to deal with too.

"Marcas just came home from the bar one night and told Mom he was leaving her. He hooked up with this chick, Jeanine, and said they were in love. He just came by to pick up a few things, and would be back later to get the rest.

"Mom called Kyle, and he came over on his bike. When he found out what Marcas said, he went into a rage, like he tended to do, and headed over to Jeanine's. He knew where she lived because he went to school with the little tramp. They even dated for a while.

"He wasn't thinking straight; didn't see the car turning left in front of him. He got killed on his way to see Marcas."

Anders: "Do you hold Marcas responsible for Kyle's death?"

Truly: "He played major a role. If he wasn't such a douche, Kyle wouldn't have been driving while blind. At least not about that. I loved my brother, but he was a bit of a hothead.

"It wasn't the first time he jumped on a bike to go right a wrong. It was one of his things. He was in a club. They didn't have jackets or anything like that; they just hung out together. They were part of a network.

"You know how clubs have chapters in different parts of the country? Some smaller clubs associate with the bigger ones for strength. The ally clubs reach out for favors when they have problems in distant neighborhoods.

"Underneath this invisible network of clubs that wear colors is an even more invisible network of clubs who do not wear colors. Kyle was one of the guys who got called when someone needed special attention. He could be very persuasive."

Anders: "I've heard of Dial-a-Punch."

Truly: "Yeah. If they want to get to you, they will. Kyle was one of *those* guys. Y'know, some people thought he was an outlaw, but to us, he was more like a hero. He hated it when anyone tried to get away with stupid stuff."

Anders: "There are a lot of people trying to get away with stupid stuff. Ignorance is the biggest problem in the world."

Truly: "Kyle made it his mission in life to teach stupid people lessons they wouldn't forget."

Anders: "Sounds like he had his own strong moral code that didn't always match up with what everybody else thought. It takes courage to walk in your own direction, to do what you believe is right, even when that means going against the herd."

Truly: "Who gets to call what is right? If a majority of us agree that something is right, then everyone else will have to abide by that. That's how societies work."

Anders: "Do you trust that the people who write our laws really have the best interest of the public in the front of their minds?"

Truly: "Not always, but I think most of them *want* to do what's best for the public. Then, when they get into office, they do what they're told."

Anders: "Some, maybe. Do you think those people *know* what is best for anyone? We've all been taught that the world is a certain way.

"People study existing ways and become experts to teach the rest of us what they learned. Then *everybody knows* that the Sun God pulls the Sun across the sky, in his golden chariot, to warm this flat land and give us light."

Truly: "Ha ha. There are people out there, *right now*, who believe the Earth is flat!"

Anders: "More evidence that you can get some people to believe anything. Did you know that some people in social media development put that theory out as a test to see how powerful their influence could be?"

Truly: "No way. It started out as a joke?"

Anders: "I am sure they got a good laugh out of it. They were trying to see if they could get an absurd thought balloon to float. You know how you can look something up on the internet and for the next three weeks you get ads for that product or something related to it?"

Truly: "That is so creepy. Sometimes I was just looking to see what something was. That doesn't mean I want to buy a stupid anti-distraction helmet."

Anders: "They use that same technology to feed people stories that support what they show interest in. You can go down any rabbit hole you choose, and you will find stories and articles that support any belief. The more people who share a belief, the more energy it has and the stronger the stance."

Truly: "It's a gameshow. I'll try door number three this time."

Anders: "The point is that the information may be false, but it's all presented as fact. Sometimes the presenter just wants attention. Sometimes they believe what they are saying. And sometimes, they are presenting a false narrative intentionally.

"They keep repeating a lie until it is believed as truth. Just because something is believed to be true, that does not make it the Truth."

Truly: "Isn't it the truth if enough people believe it?"

Anders: "Consensus is not truth. The number of people who share a common belief has never been a convincer for me. Truth with a capital T has never been dependent on people believing it.

"The Truth is still the Truth whether anyone believes it or not. For example, the world has over 4200 religions. Most of those are sects of major religions with variations of the same sets of beliefs. Yet, they kill each other over who is more right.

"If one of our primitive ancestors mistakenly thought they had it all figured out and taught their students those ways, and they taught *their* students those ways, that means about 100 billion people, going back through the history of mankind, missed the mark. Beliefs built upon beliefs built upon sand."

Truly: "That would explain why *every* generation rebels against their parents. Because the kids are always right. What the previous generations had been teaching wasn't really True."

Anders: "Right. We may not know the Truth, but that ain't it. At some point, people finally give up, go along with the masses, and become part of the machine. Or get eaten by it."

Truly: "How many people do you think ever figured it out?"

Anders: "You know what they did to Jesus when he showed people what they were capable of. Most of the great men and women who tried to show us great truths were demonized, imprisoned, shunned, and/or killed.

"When you think about how many were burned at the stake, you wonder how many more just kept to themselves."

Truly: "Kyle wasn't one of the great ones. He just had his own sense of what was right."

Anders: "How did Marcas take all of this? Does he blame himself?"

Truly: "Marcas doesn't take responsibility for anything in his *or* our lives. Whenever something goes wrong, it is because someone took advantage of his trusting personality. He never does anything wrong.

"It must be 'whoever it is' trying to destroy him. He is always the great guy who has been victimized, but he won't ever call himself a victim. He just gets mad at people and accuses them of *his* faults."

Anders: "They call that projecting when you attribute your way of thinking to someone else's mind."

Truly: "Like liars and thieves who think everybody is lying or stealing? And racists seeing racism everywhere?"

Anders: "The world is what you think it is. Everybody is *you* pushed out."

Truly: "What do you mean?"

Anders: "If you think of every material thing as made of energy, you may be able to think of every person as an energy mass. The way they appear to you is determined by the way you think about them. Your paradigm filters your perception and your imagination fills in the details."

Truly: "You see what you want to see?"

Anders: "You see what you believe you will see. What you see may not be what you want, but it may be something that you need to learn. Sometimes, we do see things the way we want them to be regardless of evidence to the contrary."

Truly: "Like wearing beer goggles? No offense intended, but you seemed a lot younger that night. Don't get me wrong. You're still very handsome and look way younger than your age. If you had lied to me about it, I would have believed you."

Anders: "I must admit I *felt* a lot younger then. You still make me feel like a kid. It's those love chemicals we were talking about."

Truly: "Rein in those horses, buddy. That part of the journey is over. Your thirty-day cool-off period was effective. Besides, remember what happened last time."

Anders: "The road ahead is paved in gold. To be clear, this door remains open to you."

Truly: "I know."

Anders: "So, did your father ever own up to being the creator of his world?"

Truly: "Never. Oh, well, if it was something good, it did not matter one bit if it was his work or luck, he always patted himself on the back and wanted everyone else to pat him too.

"If he was missing his keys, it was always because Mom put them somewhere. When he lost his truck, it was because the bank lied to him."

Anders: "The dirty bastards."

Truly: “Always someone else to blame. Nothing was ever his fault.”

Anders: “Well, we’re done eating. Do you want to finish this up at my house?”

Truly: “What do you have in mind?”

Anders: “Just talk.”

Truly: “Be careful with it.”

God-In-You

XXIX

Elias: "Auntie, the God-in-me blesses the God-in-you."

Mrs. B: "Thank you, Elias. I'm not sure what that really means. But I suppose we all have a little bit of God in each of us."

Elias: "I am God. You are God. The Lord's Prayer begins with *Our* Father. Reverend Ike said, 'There is no more God in me than there is in you. There is no more God in Jesus than there is in you.' You are the God who creates your world."

Mrs. B: "How do we create the environment we are in?"

Elias: "With your mind and emotions. 'It is not I who doeth the work, but the father within me.' Your mind is the creative center of your environment.

"Your thoughts vibrate at the frequency of the forms your mind desires. The vibration attracts the elements it needs for manifesting. Emotions amplify the vibrations."

Mrs. B: "I hope you realize this is all very difficult for us to understand. We don't think like you do."

Mrs. K: "Yes. We have our own beliefs. What you're saying doesn't make sense to us."

Elias: "The reason it doesn't make sense may be that you are not ready. If someone doesn't understand what I am saying, it doesn't mean what I'm saying is false."

Mrs. B: "I know you believe what you are saying, but it's counter to what we believe."

Elias: "You have locked yourselves into errors of thought and conforming to false beliefs."

Mrs. B: "How are you so certain what you believe is true?"

Elias: "Results speak for themselves. Do you live your life on purpose, or do you float around like a cork in the bay?"

Mrs. K: "Still, it seems blasphemous to say you are God. Aren't you afraid you'll go to Hell for that?"

Elias: "Hell is a construct of man. Have you ever wondered why God, who wants all to come to Him, would create such a thing as eternal damnation? It's counterproductive.

"Hell is a state of mind. The old churches use eternity as a fear tactic to control people."

Mr. H: "There are so many different religions. How can we ever know the truth?"

Elias: "We question our beliefs and test our theories. Believe that the mind in Jesus is the same in you. We shall do all things by the mind that is in Jesus Christ."

Resolving a Dilemma

XXX

Truly: "Your house is cute. For some reason, I was expecting something fancier."

Anders: "It's comfortable. Let's sit down at the table."

Truly: "So, what am I going to do?"

Anders: "It's not for me to tell you what you should do."

Truly: "You have responsibility too."

Anders: "Yes. I didn't mean I don't have an opinion, or desire, or responsibility. I'm with you one hundred percent. I've already set my intention and promise I will make my position clear.

"I just meant you are the one in crisis, and you have to *decide* for yourself which direction to move from here. Decision is your superpower."

Truly: "That's what I meant: How am I going to make that decision?"

Anders: "I can show you what's worked for me and a lot of other people. It might seem too easy but play along. Ask and ye shall receive. Is your question a yes or no question, or is it multiple choice?"

Truly: "What do you mean? It's definitely a yes or no question. Have it, or don't have it. That's what I see. I mean, what else is there?"

Anders: "Indeed, what else is there? The decision is binary, but the results create infinite secondary possibilities. In your awareness, there are only two choices, but in an infinite universe, the choices may be infinite."

Truly: "Well, if I'm having trouble deciding between *two*, how the hell am I ever going to make up my mind from infinite choices?"

Anders: "It's more like placing conditions on the choices. Under certain conditions, one road is preferable. Under other conditions, another one is preferred. Under what conditions would one be the better choice?

"The fastest way to get an answer is to be specific in your question. The more precise the question, the faster the answer. That's always true with man and God. Formulate your question in a way that will give you a specific answer quickly."

Truly: "Can you be more specific?"

Anders: "If you call the tire store and ask them how much a set of tires costs, you haven't given them enough information to answer your question efficiently.

"They have the information that you want, but you wouldn't understand the massive amount of data needed to answer that non-specific question. So, you would have to go through the process of sifting and sorting all that data until, at last, you arrive at some kind of an answer.

"If you spend a few moments organizing the information you *do* have into forming a specific question, like the vehicle, tire size, and the number of miles you intend to drive per year and under what conditions, and your price range, you will receive your answer instantly. The more specific the question, the faster the answer."

Truly: "Okay. How do I make my question specific?"

Anders: "The old way is to take out a sheet of paper, draw a line down the middle, put a plus sign on one column, and a minus on the other. Then you list the positive and negative aspects and weigh them against each other."

Truly: "Yeah. Do you have something better in mind?"

Anders: "Yes, a mind map. On a sheet of paper, in the middle, you write the name of the issue.

"In this case, you might write the word pregnant and circle it. Around that circle, start writing down the thoughts that pop into your mind *surrounding* that thoughtform. Circle each of those thought forms, and around each of them, write the thoughtforms that pop up around them.

"Sometimes when I do this, I have to get out more sheets of paper to unwind the stories told by the smaller thought forms."

Truly: "Well, this is a big one, so we might need to go to the office store."

Anders: "Big ones are made of little ones."

Truly: "Can we make a big one *into* a little one?"

Anders: "Divide and decide. Everything begins with pen on paper." He motioned to the paper on the table.

Truly wrote "Pregnant" on the paper. Above, she wrote "Have baby" and circled it, leaving plenty of room around it. Underneath she wrote, "Abort mission."

Truly: "What other options are there?"

Anders: "Are you asking me? Keep writing, you'll see for yourself."

By the "Have baby" balloon, she wrote "body changes," "childbirth," "Mom," "lifetime," "housewife," "school," "doctors."

By the "Abort mission" balloon, she wrote "freedom," "astronaut," "captain," "president," "adventure."

She circled each one as she went along, each balloon giving birth to another litter of balloon cubs.

She was so consumed with her work that she did not see Anders scribbling on a piece of paper himself.

Truly: "What are you doing over there?"

Anders: "I am writing my statement of intention, what I want. I've written it down so we'll both be clear."

Truly: "What do you want?"

Anders: "I want to teach you how to have a healthy, happy pregnancy and a beautiful pain-free birthing, without drugs, at my home in Kona.

"I will assume full responsibility of raising him. I want full custody, but you will have unlimited access. I have the resources to provide for his every need. His mental, physical, and spiritual training will be of the highest level I can provide and will also be in Kona."

Truly: "I'm sure you would do an excellent job raising him. But how can you promise happy and pain-free? You don't know how I feel. You don't know what my tolerances are."

Anders: "I am presenting you with *my* ideal. You have choices with that. You can see it through your own filters the way you want that future to be. If those thoughts resonate with who you want to be, then we can make magic happen by working toward the same ideal.

"When two agree on a common purpose, it shall be done."

Truly: "Like I said, I don't know what to do."

Anders: “How is your mind map coming along?”

Truly: “It’s helping me organize my thinking, and I see some other paths, but I haven’t made a decision.”

Anders: “You see this as a binary situation, but every decision creates new options. I painted one image.

"Your mind has more control over your body than you believe. Your beliefs are based on certain models of the world. The current medical model looks to outside influences.

“What if … What if the true cause of physical disease is in the emotions? There is always an emotional component to every disease, and the specific type of disease is related to a specific location in the body. Consider the possibility of emotion as cause. Different parts of the body relate to different kinds of emotional trauma.

"Your body responds physically to your emotions. You can control which emotions you experience during childbirth."

Truly: “Do you really think you can control your body with your mind?”

Anders: “I believe we do every moment of our lives. By default or design, we create the vessel and the environment around it.”

Truly: “Then logically, if you create it, you can control it.”

Anders: “We aren’t taught that concept because it isn’t in the collective consciousness yet. You know what I want. I welcome the opportunity. I consider this child to be an answer to my prayers.

“I had no idea how it would come about. I didn’t consciously direct these circumstances. Maybe I didn’t have enough clarity. I prayed for a grandson; I didn’t expect a son to be the answer.

“For me, there is no decision to make. Only receiving. You have an equal say. Now, you see that you have more options than you previously thought you had.”

Truly: “Yeah. I don’t know. If everything you say about the mind controlling the body is true, that relieves a lot of pressure, but how can I be certain it will all work out that way? That’s a huge leap of faith.”

Anders: “I know. And I understand your reservations about believing what I say. It is unconventional. Normally, I would tell a person to follow what their gut tells them, but you don’t believe in telepathy.”

Truly: "Stop that. It just seems like I'm in a binary situation where I have to give up what I want and accept something I don't want, or do something I don't feel right about to free me to pursue what I want."

Anders: "I'm saying we have a workable plan, where all three of us get what we want. Results are mathematically certain when you use your mind properly."

Truly: "I want to believe you. I mean, I get most of what you're saying. Some of that stuff though, I'll have to think about. I don't think I want to have an abortion. I never thought I'd have to make this kind of decision. I had plans for my life."

Anders: "You are still on track for those plans. Who knows, in a short time, you may look at this as a blessing in disguise. I already see it as a blessing."

Truly: "Lucky for you."

Anders: "I'm ready to step into the spirit of this thing at a nod of your head. I have a plan and the resources to accomplish it."

Truly: "You sure seem committed to making sure he has a happy, though unusual, life."

Anders: "Let's take this journey together, you, me, and Elias."

Truly: "I'm still not one hundred percent onboard, but I feel like I'm drawn into this. Be certain of this: I will hold you to your words, all of them."

Anders: "Less than one hundred percent is not a commitment. Take command of your mission, captain."

Truly: "Oka-ay. I'm all in."

Anders: "I am Truly blessed."

Truly: "You couldn't resist, could you?"

Anders: "Is it just me, or do you hear an angel choir?"

Truly: "It's just you. That's all in your head."

Anders: "Harmonious."

Dr. Murphy

XXXI

Elias: "One time we were driving to soccer practice, and we were listening to Dr. Joseph Murphy. I don't think we're related. He said in his book *All the World Believes a Lie*, 'We are here to separate the sheep from the goats; the false from the real.'

"But I thought he said separate the sheet from the ghost. Like, that's not a real ghost. It's just a sheet.

"He was quoting Quimby, 'All the world believes a lie to the point where when I tell them the truth, they think I am lying.' Boy, isn't that the truth?"

Mrs. K: "Have you read *The Power of Your Subconscious Mind*?"

Elias: "That's one of my favorites. Dr. Murphy knew how magical we are and gave us a practical guide. It's easier to understand than the Bible."

Mrs. K: "Can you tell us what you got out of the book?"

Elias: "Everyone should read it. The subconscious has complete control over our lives. We have to consciously control it or someone else will."

Mrs. K: "That's it? There has to be more to it than that."

Elias: "It's a beautiful book. A very enjoyable read, with lots of examples and convincers. Everyone should read it until they can teach it.

"The bottom line is our subconscious is all-powerful and all-knowing. Our conscious mind gives it direction, or someone else does."

Water Baby

XXXII

Truly: "How is this hypnosis thing going to work for having a baby?"

Anders: "We've already done most of the work. The biggest challenge is over. We tore down the tower of beliefs you had about childbirth. You have a much more empowering perspective. By reframing your concept of childbirth, you see choices you didn't see before.

"By eliminating false beliefs, you have changed your expectations. You know you have control over your thoughts, which control your emotions, which control your body.

"Over the next couple of weeks, I'll show you how to enter states of mind to create the states you want in your body. We'll have it easier than most people, because your birth companion is certified. After I guide you through the process, you'll practice entering these states on your own."

Truly: "Not completely on my own. We are in this together, aren't we?"

Anders: "I'll be as close as you want. You and Elias are my purpose in life right now. I have no higher priority. I just meant, when you learn the skill, you won't need me to be there, not that I wouldn't be there. You can't get rid of me that easily."

Truly: "You would know if I was trying to get rid of you."

Anders: "Have you ever heard of water birth? Babies born under water?"

Truly: "Yeah, I've heard of babies being born in pools. That sounds cool, but aren't you afraid they'll drown?"

Anders: "They don't start breathing air until they're in the air. And they're natural swimmers. For the mother, buoyancy relieves pressure and allows her to assume more comfortable postures."

Truly: "And that's what you're saying you want for this baby?"

Anders: "For both of you. With the proper mind set, mental and physical conditioning, and a welcoming environment, childbirth can be joyous for mama and baby."

Truly: "Is that why you want me to go back to Kona? Do you have a pool?"

Anders: "The pool is on its way. I have a friend, Grace, who assists in water births. Sometimes, we work together. Every once in a while, a woman gives birth in the ocean."

Truly: "Not at a crowded beach, I hope."

Anders: "That has happened. But usually, moms prefer solitude and sanctuary. I have a place like that at my house. It's a dock built on a lava formation in the bay. The overhanging trees keep it mostly secret. The pop-up shade provides total privacy."

Truly: "So, you want me to have a baby in the ocean with you and your friend Grace? And it's going to be some glorious painless birth. Do I have to go through aquatic training too?"

Anders: "You don't even have to swim. Just float. You can do that."

Truly: "I can swim. And he'll be baptized at birth. Is he going to have a christening too?"

Anders: "I don't believe in scheduled baptism. I think you can be baptized every time you release the old you. Baptism should be based on a change not a calendar.

"The shock of the water is a physical stimulus to convince the subconscious mind that a change has taken place. The water also symbolizes washing away of the past or, more specifically, past sins.

"Since the moment of power is NOW, and a person can *decide* to be a different person, they can move forward in any direction from wherever they are.

"Whatever the motivation is, a person can change in an instant. A person *can* instantly become a different person and be born again."

Truly: "Born-agains bug me. But a baptism is a ritual for accepting God into your heart. Are you saying a person can go back to old ways, then come back and start all over, get a fresh baptism and be good with Jesus again?"

Anders: "As often as time will allow. People who say they are saved, but have not forgiven themselves, have not made the change they need to be harmonious."

Truly: "What if God doesn't want to take them back again?"

Anders: "God doesn't have a personality and cannot express emotions. The Universal cannot be the Individual. God never turns anyone away."

Truly: "Even if they *kill* somebody?"

Anders: "Yep. It doesn't matter what the deed, or how gruesome it was, the path from here is all there is. There is no punishment from on high, only results of actions. Sin no more and all is good."

Truly: "I am all for murderers burning in Hell for eternity. How can God forgive someone for killing one of His children?"

Anders: "God forgives everyone who forgives themselves. Do they carry guilt or any other negative emotion about the situation, or can they completely release all attachment to the event? How do they think other people see them?

"The instant you forgive yourself is the instant God forgives you. If a person has no emotional attachment to a past event, they are freed from attracting more emotions of that specific frequency."

Truly: "Sure, a sociopath has no emotional attachment to anything, but God *still* forgives him?"

Anders: "God doesn't care either way. The law of gravity doesn't care how many times a person has fallen before they figure out how to balance. The law of flotation doesn't care how many balls of steel have sunk before one is flattened into a vessel.

"Sociopaths may not appear to have emotions, because they mask them well. It's not likely, but even a sociopath can transform instantly and become harmonious. Harmony is heavenly."

Truly: "That can't be right."

Anders: "Not according to your beliefs."

Truly: "What about living a good life on Earth to be able to make it into Heaven?"

Anders: "That is more mythology and another one of the great misconceptions. Heaven, Hell, and all frequencies in between, are your choices for how you live your life on Earth."

Truly: "Who would choose Hell? Nobody, that's who."

Anders: "Ah. This is another issue of awareness. It's a question of the subconscious mind's role and responsibilities as opposed to the role and responsibilities of the conscious mind.

"We speak with our conscious mind, but we *act* with our subconscious mind. A person may say they believe in a thing, but when they act, you will know what is in their heart. People don't choose Hell.

"We are creatures of habit. People with habits that cause hellish results live in Hell on Earth. People with habits that are in harmony with God's purpose live in Heaven on Earth."

Truly: "What exactly is God's purpose?"

Anders: "For you to be the uniquely creative person you are and multiply the good in everyone you meet. There is nobody like you. Go forth and multiply."

Truly: "What, have a bunch of babies? Are you saying God wants me to have this baby? Oh, come on. I thought you said God doesn't care."

Anders laughed. "God doesn't take a personal interest in individual lives. But God's purpose is to experience *everything*, including the things we don't like. God's purpose is to expand and grow. Every individual is a unique expression of God with unique talents.

"Go forth and multiply your talents. Those talents, however they are used, attract more of the same. That means thoughts, feelings, and actions that take life force away are on the Hell fork of the road, whereas thoughts, feelings, and actions that add life force energy are on the Heaven fork."

Truly: "So even the way we think determines whether we go to Heaven or go to Hell?"

Anders: "Especially the way we think. 'As a man thinketh in his heart, so is he.'"

Truly: "I didn't think you were going to be such a Bible thumper."

Anders: "I'm not usually. But certain passages are self-supporting."

Truly: "Right. So, how does a man thinketh with his *heart*?"

Anders: "The subconscious mind is the heart that thinks. It's the part of us that makes subconscious choices, automatically, in the background. We have programs running in the background 24/7. 'What you believe and say about yourself is the word of God to you,' as Rev. Ike says."

Truly: "I know it's real for you, because you believe it."

Anders: "There is plenty of evidence."

True Gravity

XXXIII

Mr. H: "Elias, I'm interested in hearing more about your golf game. How often do you play?"

Elias: "We play two or three times a week."

Mrs. K: "My husband plays, but I don't think he really likes it. He always comes home angry. At least it gets him out of the house into fresh air. He keeps saying he's going to quit, but he goes whenever they call. Do you get angry when you play?"

Elias: "It's not as easy as it looks on TV. Sometimes, I get frustrated, but Papa usually gets me to re-center. If I focus on my inner body instead of the results, my results get better."

Mrs. B: "What do you mean by inner body?"

Elias: "The movement of the outer body is directed by the movement of the inner body. If the two are not in harmony, you sin. You miss the target and pay Hell. Harmony comes from within."

Mrs. B: "I'm still not sure I understand what the inner body is."

Elias: "Unihipili is the spirit of the body. Everything that operates automatically is the inner body.

"Uhane is the spirit of the mind and conscious movement. I use my mind to direct my inner being to create the shot I want.

"Uhane must decide what it wants, and unihipili will perform."

Mr. H: "When I'm on the golf course, I usually know what I want to do, but it doesn't always go where I want it to go."

Elias: "Those are moments of disharmony. Something is out of synch. If the two are in alignment, you feel the true gravity of the golf swing, and it is harmonious."

Mr. H: "You just did it again, Elias. Now, what is the true gravity of the golf swing?"

Elias: "In his book, *Golf in the Kingdom*, Michael Murphy, I don't think I'm related to him either, wrote, 'When ye swing, put all yer attention on the feelin' o' yer inner body.' And then he wrote, 'True gravity is the deeper lines of force, the deeper structure of the universe.' When you align with true gravity, you are in total alignment."

Mr. H: "Can you tell me how to get into that kind of alignment?"

Elias: "I can tell you, uncle, but the only way to know true gravity is to feel it. To know the truth, you must live the truth."

GRAMMA CHRIS

XXXIV

THIS WAS THE FIRST time Anders had been to Truly's childhood home. It was a quiet older neighborhood, with streets so narrow there was barely enough room for one lane when cars were parked on both sides. The house was in need of repair, but it was clean. The rain caused the low-maintenance landscaping to glisten.

Anders: "This is where you grew up?"

Truly: "Yep. Right there is where I fell off my skateboard, landed on my chin, and pushed my teeth clean through my lip. Still have a scar there.
"Hi Mom."

Chris: "Hello. Come inside where it's warm."

Truly: "This is my mom, Christine. Mom, this is Dr. Anders Starkstrom."

Anders: "Please call me Andy. It's good to meet you."

Chris: "It's good to meet you too, Andy. You can call me Chris. Would you like some coffee or maybe tea?"

Anders: "Yes, thank you. I can't stay long, but I have time for a cup of tea. I prefer a green tea if you have it."

Chris: "I think I have some. I put the kettle on earlier."

After a couple of minutes, Chris returns with the tea.

Chris: "Truly tells me you wrote a book on alternative cancer treatment."

Anders: "I'm still working on that one. My wife and my mother both had cancer at the same time."

Chris: "That sounds like a terrible time for you. How are they now?"

Anders: "My wife had emergency surgery and survived that bout with cancer, but while she was recovering from her surgery, my mom died."

Chris: "Oh my gosh. So, you were able to save your wife, but not your mother?"

Anders: "No, I didn't have the awareness to help anyone at the time. Regardless of my skills, people heal themselves based on their beliefs. You can't actually change another person. The best you can do is help them understand themselves better. My wife died five years ago.

"I'll tell you a little about my background. My mom was a Christian Scientist. She turned away from that belief system when my younger brother was born. She had contracted German measles while she was pregnant with him, and it almost killed him."

Chris: "Rubella? I thought everyone was vaccinated for that."

Anders: "This was a few years before the vaccine was introduced. Although she probably would not have had the vaccine anyway. More important, that was an emotionally charged time for her, and it caused her to reevaluate her beliefs."

Chris: "Do you have all your shots?"

Anders: "I've had some of them. I acquired some of my mom's religious paradigm. Personally, I believe in Divine Immunity."

Chris: "You think you are divinely blessed by God?"

Anders: "We all are, but that's not what Divine Immunity means. Divine Immunity is the naturally perfect mental and physical state of being. It's a state of belief that doesn't acknowledge the *ill*usion of *ill*ness."

Chris: "You think I'm making this up, that it's all in my head?"

Anders: "No. No. No. Of course not. Both my mom and her sister were Christian Scientists, and both died of cancer. That created cognitive dissonance for me. I wondered what they did wrong. Why didn't the system work for them?"

Chris: "Did you figure it out?"

Anders: "One technique they both used was to refuse to acknowledge the existence of cancer by not allowing anyone to talk about it.

"There is a difference between *resisting* evil and *renouncing* it. When you resist evil, you give it your attention; you continue to make it real. You add more energy to that psychic entity, giving it more power.

"When you renounce evil, you take your attention from it; you give your attention to what you want. You turn your back on the concept of cancer and focus on health. I get the feeling that they wanted to renounce but were caught up in resistance.

"It's not enough to ignore a problem. Ignoring is the negative aspect. To overwrite the program of cancer, you must have a clear image of perfect health. Since they wouldn't talk about it, I don't know if they used healthy imaging."

Chris: "What else did they do?"

Anders: "Other than denial, I don't know what else they were doing, except that I know my mother had a closet full of dietary supplements and herbal remedies."

Chris: "I've gotten a lot of ads for that kind of stuff lately. How do *they* know? Just ignoring cancer doesn't seem like it would work, though. I tried ignoring a bill once. It just got bigger."

Anders: "Thought is energy. When you think about a thing, it adds energy to that thing, and the opposite is also true. If you do not think about that thing, you will not add thought-energy to that thing. It's the same principle applied in different directions.

"You can think of your subconscious like one of those old grain mills. The stream flows, which turns the waterwheel, which turns the millstones. Whatever type of grain you put in will produce a flour of its kind. Without the flow of water, the waterwheel has no power."

Chris: "If there is no power, why does it keep growing?"

Anders: "There may not be enough flow to turn the wheel—conscious thought—but the stream continues.

"The subconscious processes continue in the background. Your subconscious stream continues to flow. All of your beliefs, the stuff you think is real, everything your mind has accepted as true, holds your world in its present form.

"There is still water in the stream, just not enough to turn the wheel. Water continues to flow. Even without conscious thought, there is still awareness. Water attracts water.

"Talking about a thing adds more vibrational currents, sending more energy to the formation of that thing. Talking about it, in good terms or bad, adds flow to the stream, turning the wheel."

Chris: "How do you stop the stream?"

Anders: "You don't *want* to stop the stream. The stream and the waterwheel are your assets. The flow provides power. You want to change what the mill is producing.

"Change the image from what you don't want to what you do want. The same thought energy that creates dis-ease will also create a new healthy body.

"The question is: What are you putting into your mill that is pouring out as your life?"

Chris: "How do you know all this stuff?"

Anders: "I have been fascinated by the extraordinary abilities of humans since I was a kid. In my early teens, I started to study mind power. It was the mid-seventies, so I dabbled with various techniques and hallucinogens."

Chris: "Damn, hippy. Sounds like you let your freak flag fly."

Anders: "Blowin' in the wind. After Mom's estate was settled, I had a little money to travel to trainings that I otherwise believed I couldn't afford. I trained in Sedona, Seattle, and Kona and even flew out to New Hampshire for a hypnotists' convention. I was on a mission to learn everything I could about how the human mind and body interacted."

Chris: "That sounds like an awesome adventure. So, now you know everything there is to know about all of that? Wrote the book on it."

Anders: "I've written a couple of books, but I definitely don't know everything. As a race, humans don't even know themselves and are far from knowing everything. The more I learn, the more I know how little I know. Knowledge is infinite, and there is no single container large enough to hold infinity."

Chris: "But you still claim to know how to cure cancer."

Anders: "I do not cure anyone. People have beliefs that create an environment for the thoughtform of cancer to grow. The *idea* of cancer is given emotional energy charged by other beliefs.

"Other people in their lives have their own beliefs, many of them are shared, and all of those thoughtforms and emotions affect the cancer thoughtform."

Chris: "Cancer is a thoughtform?"

Anders: "Everything in existence began as a thoughtform, an idea, which solidified into physical form.

"Thoughts become things."

Chris: "Let me get this straight. Are you saying I only *think* I have cancer, or are you saying I got cancer because I thought of cancer?"

Anders: "Thinking about a thing is not the same as the thoughtform of the thing. The map is not the territory. What you think of a thing is not the thing itself.

"If you focus on your *perception* of conditions, you create new conditions based on old conditions. If you want different conditions, impress upon your subconscious mind the image of the way you want things to be. Imagine better than you know."

Chris: "I can just *imagine* myself well, and I'll be healthy? That doesn't fit in with my beliefs at all. You can't just pretend everything is all right."

Anders: "If you can believe that *you* somehow created this condition of dis-ease, you can understand that that gives you the power to create a condition of health. I can guide you safely through the process."

Chris: "I don't want to get my hopes up. False hopes are the biggest heartbreakers."

Anders: "With your current set of beliefs, you are already set up for failure. It's not false hope. False hope is a literary device, not an emotion. You don't have to write false hope into your story. Write yourself a good story. Cast a good spell.

"There is a difference between having a hopeful approach and sitting around hoping for something. Hope is a positive emotion, with positive vibrations and health-generating chemicals.

"Hope, even false hope, is better than dread, even false dread. Each is as true as you believe, one with a positive vibration, the other a negative.

"Thoughts and feelings of hope attract more thoughts and feelings of hope." Thoughts and feelings of dread attract more thoughts and feelings of dread.

"Those thoughts and feelings vibrate at certain frequencies. Our emotions are vibrational sensors; they tell us which frequency we are on. Like a GPS, you look at the screen to see where you are. Your emotions tell you which frequency you are on."

Chris: "Yeah, but can you guarantee it will work. What if it doesn't work?"

Anders: "This isn't an infomercial. I guarantee you it will work. No one can guarantee you a result. The results are entirely in your control. But let me ask you, what does 'if it doesn't work' mean to you?"

Chris: "I mean, what if I go through all of this, and I still die from cancer?"

Anders: "I want to make sure we are clear on what we are about to do. What do you think this process involves that makes you think of it in terms of what you will have to go through? Do you think it will be an ordeal that you will have to suffer through?"

Chris: "I guess I'm just afraid of digging up the past. I don't want to go through all that pain again. I don't want to relive all that crap and die anyway."

Anders: "That is where I come in. I will keep you focused as you process the information safely on your own. The only known side effects are deep relaxation and a general feeling of well-being.

"I'll warn you though. I am a tough taskmaster. We aren't going to just flip through old photo albums; we are going to go through the closets, shelves, and shoeboxes and get rid of the junk that no longer serves you. When would now be a good time to clear out the junk?"

Chris: "Don't you have to believe in this for it to work?"

Anders: "It is done unto her as she believeth. The basis for all healing is a change in belief.

"Let me ask you. Are there people who go through various forms of treatment who still die from cancer? It is safe to assume that the majority of people who have died from cancer have undergone some form of treatment, right?"

Chris: "But you're not a medical doctor."

Anders: "No. I have not had medical training. Nothing we are doing goes against medical advice. Any good doctor will tell you to take a proactive approach to health.

"Think of this as you doing your part, everything you can to be healthy. Take control of your own health. Do you have any subscriptions to medications?"

Chris: "You mean *pre*scriptions."

Anders: "If you have a subscription to a prescription, and take it regularly, your body will assume that your conscious mind has taken over that duty and surrender that duty to the conscious mind.

"Your body works perfectly. Your subconscious mind is capable of creating any chemical reaction you need in your body to perform any function. Everlasting health has never been found in a pill bottle. Maybe it's better to question what you are willing to do."

Chris: "I don't know. I don't want to get my boobs cut off, and I've seen people who have gone through radiation and chemo, but I don't believe in all this hocus pocus mumbo jumbo."

Anders: "Those words are meaningless. However, abra cadabra is a magical phrase that means, 'As I speak, so shall it be.'

"John 1:1 says, 'In the beginning was the Word.' He was talking about the beginning of each *and* every thing.

"Magic can usually be explained scientifically, and what I am talking about is science. An exact science, that acts with mathematical certainty.

"Changing the way you think will change the way you feel, and that will change the conditions you see around you. It doesn't have to be an ordeal. It's more like a deep clean of the garage."

Chris: "OK, Professor Magica, what have you got?"

Anders: "Science appears to be magic when you don't know the trick. Chris, I want to invite you to come and stay in Kona. We'll have more time to talk then. You can fly over with Truly when she comes. I'll take care of travel. We could use your help during this process. I'm going to head back earlier to prepare the place."

Chris: "I talked to her about it on the phone. I definitely want to see my grandbaby being born, and I'm curious about this other stuff. I just don't know if I'll like it there. Aren't you afraid that volcano will erupt and bury you in brimstone and ashes?"

Anders: "It's always a possibility, but no, I'm not afraid. People have been living there for centuries. It's a place of healing."

Chris: "I have heard how beautiful it is."

Anders: "Get yourself unstuck, and let's go on an adventure."

Chris: "Why the hell not? This could be good for me."

Anders: "It could be *very* good for you. See you in Kona."

One Died, One Healed Herself

XXXV

Mrs. K: "Your grandmother seems like a wonderful person. Does she live here with you?"

Elias: "Gramma Chrissy? She is *awesome*. I'm pretty sure all grammas are. Yeah, she moved here when I was born. She had cancer, and Papa wanted her to stay with us until she healed herself. Then, she just stayed."

Mr. H: "Elias, did you say she healed herself of cancer?"

Elias: "Of course she did. All healing is self-healing."

Mr. H: "Did she go to see a doctor to get treatment?"

Elias: "She had a doctor monitor her progress. Papa studied different ways of treating cancer when my other gramma died from her treatment."

Mr. H: "You mean she died from cancer."

Elias: "No. It wasn't the cancer. She died from the drugs. Papa says we all choose our time. Whatever the cause, we choose the time."

Mr. H: "But doctors are trained to treat people."

Elias: "Doctors are amazing people. If they saw people floating down a river, they would jump in to save them. They treat the problem.

"Mechanical treatment is working with results. Papa goes to find out how the people are falling in. He looks for cause.

"Everything you can name has a spirit within. Spirit is primary cause."

Mrs. B: "Can you heal a physical condition by working with spirits?"

Elias: "I guess you could. Papa doesn't call on spirits like that. He helps people rearrange and renew their minds. When their minds are in order, they heal themselves. Their minds direct their spirits."

Mr. H: "Cancer isn't just from a confused mind, is it? We know carcinogens cause cancer."

Elias: "Impurities play a part but are not cause. If you conform to false beliefs, you get false answers. Grammie said she started fasting then, too. She didn't like it at first, but now we do it all the time. She calls it her fountain of youth."

Mr. H: "Fasting? Isn't that the same as not eating?"

Elias: "It's the best thing for you."

Welcome to Heaven

XXXVI

Anders: "Welcome to Kona. I don't think you'll need that wool sweater here."

Chris: "Seattle is chilly in November."

Truly: "It was really cold when we left."

Anders: "You know what they say, always dress for your destination."

Chris: "I'm going to have to peel some of this off."

Anders: "I have the A/C on in the car. If you're ready, we can hop in and be home in a few minutes."

Chris: "Sure is warm."

Anders: "You'll get used to it. We can stop for shave ice on the way home."

The drive to Kealakekua Bay was pleasant. At the house, Anders showed them to their rooms and around the grounds. Truly was particularly interested in the music studio.

Truly: "Is that a Les Paul? I've always wanted one. Can I play it?"

Anders: "You can play anything you want, anytime you want. Let's go back in the house first."

Chris: "This is gorgeous. Right on the water … and look at that view. I feel better already."

Anders: "Welcome to Heaven."

Chris: "I didn't know I had died."

Anders: "You don't have to die to live in Heaven. Now that you've had a chance to get settled in and had the mini-tour, would you like to talk for a while?"

Chris: "Some of the things you said have been going around in my head since we talked. Like my mind made my body have cancer. That doesn't make sense."

Anders: "I know. That belief is outside of your awareness. There are physical factors as well. We can talk about that aspect also."

Chris: "I still don't get how all this works."

Anders: "You don't have to know how electricity works to turn on a light switch."

Chris: "Turn me on."

Truly: "That's my cue. I'll be in the studio."

Anders: "Have fun. Chris, let's go into my study."

Chris: "Is this place all right? Or do we need to find some holy ground?"

Anders: "Anywhere away from your home is good. A neutral place is best because it makes you more receptive than when you are in your place of power. People have a tendency to keep their emotional walls up when they are on watch in their castle."

Chris: "Oh yeah, I'm the Great and Powerful Grammie when I'm in my spacious castle."

Anders: "Here in my study is fine. We are just going to sit down and talk for a little while."

Chris: "That's it, just talk? Mind if I smoke this?"

Anders: "It's better if you don't."

Chris: "It makes me feel better."

Anders: "Wait a little bit."

Chris: "If you insist."

He softly shushed her as he slid his chair over, directly in front and facing her. He sat in an upright posture in the chair, their knees nearly in contact.

Anders: "Do you mind if we begin with a meditation?"

Chris: "I'd like that." She put her hands into his outstretched hands.

Anders: "We always begin with breathing, so let's stand up and face the same direction. The breath pushes out toxins and we don't want to blow them into each other.

"Eight deep breaths, filling your lungs deeper than a normal breath, each breath deeper than the one before. Inhale until you cannot possibly fit any more air in your lungs. Your chest, spine, and shoulders will adjust themselves for maximum intake.

"Then hold it to the mental count of three while the stagnant air gets mixed with the fresh air and blow it all out. Then push out some more.

"Get rid of the old stagnant air that has settled into your lower lungs. Push up from your belly. And again, that's right, keep breathing.

"To add some physical motion, we can push our palms out and away each time we exhale.

"Rotating the hands, pull back fresh energy with our palms facing us as we fill our lungs with clean air and energy, flushing out the old. The wind helps clear the cobwebs from your mind.

"Let's sit down." They sit leaning close enough to each other to hold hands comfortably, forearms resting on their knees.

Chris: "That is energizing. I feel jazzed."

Anders: "It is nice. And we are just getting started. You know that I have helped many people? (nodding) I want you to know that I am right here, right now, to give you my undivided attention to help you figure out what is best for you. How does that sound to you?"

Chris: "Like music. I don't think I ever heard that song in that arrangement."

Anders: "The best way for this to work is if we both agree to lower our shields. Do you trust me enough to fly open the doors for now to allow my inner being to sing to your inner being?"

Chris: "Incanta." She spread her arms wide open.

Anders: "I would like to have a conversation with your inner child, would that be okay?"

Chris: "Dang kid never listens to me, so sure. See if you can get through to her."

Anders: "She listens to you all the time. She heard that and believes it. She believes she is a dang kid that never listens to you."

Chris: "OK. Does that mean I should quit calling her a brat?"

Anders: "You can do whatever you want. It's your decision. If that behavior still serves you, hang on to it."

Chris: "So, how can you say that people create cancer in their bodies? That doesn't make sense. No one chooses to have cancer."

Anders: "You are absolutely right. It is not a conscious choice. Cancer is a product of the subconscious mind. Something may have been trying to get your attention for a long time.

"Your subconscious mind is a mix of information, some of it from sketchy sources, that has gotten jumbled in a pile. Clean up requires dedication."

Chris: "So, are you saying I'm a hot mess?"

Anders: "Messes deserve attention. They don't go away by themselves. If you don't have any pressing questions about the process, talk to me about something that has been on your mind a lot lately that isn't in the news."

Chris: "Well, the doctor says she wants me to have radiation therapy, but I don't know, they tell us radiation *causes* cancer. Then she talked to me about chemo, but I'm sure I don't want to go through that. So, she said surgery is the only other option."

Anders: "It is the only other option for her. She's limited by her framework. She has to stay within the laws and guidelines of the medical community if she wants to continue to practice medicine.

"You, on the other hand, have a number of other options. I didn't mean to interrupt, I just wanted you to know that. Please continue."

Chris: "That's what I want to know. What else can I do?"

Anders: "I will answer that for you as completely as I can, I promise. It's your turn to talk now."

Chris: "Music."

She paused a moment as she closed her eyes a little and raised her right ear into the air so the sound could fill it to overflow.

Chris: "Nothing has been the same since Kyle died. I really missed him at Christmas. I miss him all the time. I feel so sad.

"Aren't you going to say some words of wisdom to make me feel better?"

Anders: "I'm not a therapist. I know some techniques for processing information, but how you feel is entirely up to you. Do you still brag about your son?"

Chris: "What do you mean?"

Anders: "From the time he was born, you probably liked to tell stories about the cute things he did. You would tell friends and everyone else about his accomplishments and achievements, like hitting a homerun, receiving a writing award, or being selected to perform a solo in the school band. Tell me something about your son that brings a smile to your heart."

Chris: "When he was 17, he made an unassisted triple play. Do you know how rare that is? It was the top of last inning of the state championship.

"Kyle was playing shortstop. We were up by one, bases loaded, and no outs. Their big man was up. Full count. The runners started going with the pitch. He hit a line drive, right at Kyle. He caught it, ran over, stepped on second, and tagged the kid coming from first. One, two, three outs, just like that.

"Their coach tried to say the other kid scored before the third out. But the umpires had a meeting and said he didn't. Game over! We won the state championship! It was amazing. I will never forget that as long as I live."

Anders: "Happy now?"

Chris: "Yes. Every time I think of that, I just get so filled with pride and happiness for him."

Anders: "Dwell on good feelings, and you will feel good and better. I might suggest that you shift your attention away from missing him and focus on the things you love about him. Remember, I am in listening mode right now. Please continue."

Chris: "Where was I? Oh yeah. I still remember when I got the phone call from the state police. I was in the kitchen, cleaning up, when the phone rang. It was unreal. At first, I couldn't believe it. He was just here. It can't be. It felt just like when my brother died, when I was little. Why does everyone have to die?"

Anders: "Everybody does die. We know that ... don't we? The world operates in a constant cycle of renewal. Some even believe we choose our time. How do you feel right now?"

Chris: "I can't help it. I feel so sad. I feel lost ... like I don't know what to do."

Anders: "OK. Close your eyes. Take in a deep, deep breath. As you let it out, allow yourself to relax, even further. Now, become aware that each of us has a direction, away from our body, where we store our memories. If you were to know ... could you point in the direction of your past?"

She pointed her left hand over her shoulder. "I think it's over here."

Anders: "When you think about this feeling of sadness, and remember, when was the first time you experienced sadness? If you were to know … was it before, during, or after your birth? Go with whatever comes up."

Chris: "Before."

Anders: "In the womb, or before?"

Chris: "In the womb."

Anders: "At what month?"

Chris: "The number that comes up is three months. Is that right?"

Anders: "I wasn't there, but go with whatever comes up. Allow yourself to float up out of your body now. That's right. Float back along your past, staying above the images.

"And go back to the time when you were at three months in the womb. When you get there, notice what it is that is causing you to feel this way."

Chris: "Mom is crying. I don't know why she's so sad. Confused about something. I think she might be reading a book. Something about having to shoot a dog … No. He shot his friend. I remember now. We had to read that book in junior high! I cried too."

Anders: "With the awareness and understanding that you have right now, as an adult, what would you tell that earlier version of yourself to help you understand those emotions?"

Chris: "That is a tough one. Sometimes a life has to be ended for the Good. Everybody does die. We had a dog that wouldn't stop killing chickens. He didn't know any better, but we *had* to put him down. Lennie wasn't a dog, but then, he wasn't much smarter than one. Still, I think they had other options.

"Strange how a story Mom was reading didn't happen to either one of us, but we both felt sad.

"I guess I would tell that little me that everything is going to be OK. Being sad is part of life, nothing lasts forever. This too shall pass."

Anders: "Take that understanding, float down into the you that you were then, and allow yourself to have that wisdom now, when you were then, and notice how that makes you feel, now."

Chris: "Different."

Anders: "Try to feel the way you did before, when you were sad, to prove to yourself that it was your first, first experience with that feeling."

Chris: "I can't feel it."

Anders: "Now I want you to do something fun and unusual. I want you to bring that wisdom back from the past. Staying down in your timeline, bring that wisdom into each of the times in your life when you would have felt sadness. Notice how that changes your perception of that event.

"Come all the way back to now. Learn what you needed to learn from each event and release the emotion. Take as much time as you need, but know that your subconscious can do this very quickly."

Chris: "I'm stuck. There is something here that won't let me go."

Anders: "Float up above that scene. That's right. Take a deep breath. As you float above the event, you begin to realize you are completely safe right now. What age are you there?"

Chris: "Thirteen. I'm at school. They called me out of class into the office. There's a policeman here. He says there was an accident.

"It's Tommy. He got hit by a drunk driver on his way to the college, in the middle of the day. He was still in high school, but he was taking advanced classes. Now he's dead. I'm sitting on that awful hard bench crying."

Anders: "OK. Remember, you are floating above that scene. That's right. Take a deep breath. As you float, you begin to realize you are completely safe right now.

"I want you to float forward in time a little, so you can turn around, and see this event looking back on it from the future. With the understanding and awareness that you have now, what do you want to say to that little girl?"

Chris: "I just want to hug her and tell her things will be okay for her. How much can I tell her, without messing up the fabric of time?"

Anders: "You are the creator of this universe, so you can float down there and tell her anything you want."

Chris: "I told her he will always be alive in her memories and to focus on what she loved about him.

"Then I told her to buy both Apple *and* Microsoft stocks."

Anders: "Nice. If you haven't already done it, I'd like for you to turn toward your future, and come back to now, bringing the old wisdom and the new understandings through each of the subsequent events, learning what you needed to learn from those events, releasing the emotions as you go.

"Come all the way back to now."

Chris: "What if I get stuck again?"

Anders: "You have new understandings now, so you will be able to handle most of it. Just let me know if you hit a snag."

Chris: "Some of these things don't seem the same anymore. They don't bother me as much.

"All right, I'm coming up on last year. I don't *feel* like I have a lot more wisdom now than I did then."

Anders: "You do. You can go ahead and float back up above your timeline, looking down at that event. Just float there and meditate for a moment. Quiet your mind. If there was a word for how you feel right now, what would that word be?"

Chris: "Acceptance."

Anders: "Acceptance."

Chris: "Yes. I still want to cry, because I miss him, but I also accept that he is no longer with us. I know he is here in spirit, but I mean physically. You can't hug a ghost."

Anders: "Spirit can hug spirit. Besides acceptance, is there something else you have learned, or become aware of, that you want to tell that version of you back then?"

Chris: "We never know when it's our time to go. You have to make each moment the best.

"Can I tell her to cherish the moments she had with him?"

Anders: "Tell her whatever you like. Then bring yourself back to now, and tell me how you feel."

After a moment.

Chris: "I feel very different right now. Almost like my whole body is tingling, but it isn't really a tingle, it's more like a flow."

Anders: "You just released blocked energy. It's like unkinking a garden hose that was tied in knots. Sit there and enjoy the flow."

Chris: "Oooh. Snap, popple, crack. My joints are making all kinds of noise."

Anders: "That is a release of tension."

Chris: "I feel liquid. Is it okay if we take a break? I want to go outside right now.

"Are you still going to hypnotize me?"

Anders: "What do you think we have been doing?"

Chris: "I didn't see any pocket watch."

Anders: "I could use some air myself. Let's see what is going on outside of these walls."

It Takes a Child to Raise a Village

XXXVII

Mrs. B: "You said you are building a village for the geckos? I'd like to come out and see it, if you don't mind."

Elias: "Okay. You want to go right now?" He jumped down from the chair and started toward the door. He stopped, turned to Mr. Halemalia, and asked, "Or, do you want to ask me some more questions?"

Mr. H: "I think that will be enough for now. Let's go see your village."

Gecko Village was laid out on a hillside. The smaller huts surrounded the big longhouse, which was built on a flat lava rock three times its size. The details were fitting for their scale.

As the group approached, little green flashes disappeared into and behind the little huts. One large gecko lay motionless at water's edge on the lava rock.

Mrs. K: "Is he dead?"

Elias stroked the back of the lizard's head and said, "No. This is Moloa. He's just fat and lazy."

Mrs. K: "You shouldn't say things like that. The word fat makes people feel bad, and you shouldn't call people lazy."

Elias: "Moloa is a gecko. He doesn't mind. Besides, I'm not responsible for how other people feel about words. I have only aloha in my heart; no negative energy in my words.

"They are simply descriptive. I say what I mean. People hear what they want to hear."

Mrs. K: "Aren't you concerned about other people's feelings, or what they think? This is one of my concerns about lack of socialization."

Elias: "Feelings are vibrations. Everyone must discover for themselves what those vibrations mean. Whatever they hear comes from within them."

Mrs. K: "But your words can hurt other people."

Elias: "Words don't hurt anyone. People hurt themselves with their interpretation of words. When someone hurts your feelings, thank them for bringing that issue from inside you out to your conscious awareness."

Mrs. K: "Some words are hurtful."

Elias: "The energy and intention can be hurtful. Words are thoughtforms that generate an energy wave. Intention directs, and emotion amplifies the vibration. That is the sending part of communication.

"What another person hears, and how they take it, is up to them. Look at him." He nudged Moloa's flank with his finger. The gecko remained undisturbed. "He has too much earth and water element. It makes him fat and lazy. Those are facts."

On the Lanai

XXXVIII

Anders: "Maybe we'll see some whales. The season is just beginning. We could see a few early birds."

Chris: "That would be amazing. I would love to see some whales right now."

Anders: "Let's just sit over here for a while and wait."

Chris: "I don't know what it is that I'm feeling. It's weird. I feel relaxed and energized at the same time."

Anders: "You released a lot of tension that had been building up for decades. The points of friction that wasted energy have been removed. That energy is now freed up to do your bidding."

Chris: "I still don't see how my mom reading a novel gave me cancer. Do all the people who read Steinbeck get cancer? Maybe we shouldn't read those kinds of books."

Anders: "There is a lot to be said for that. Reading books is how we expand our awareness. The problem is not with reading. The problem may be more about how people interpret the writing.

"Orwell's *1984*, and Huxley's *Brave New World* were supposed to be warnings to society of the dangers of groupthink and government control. Instead, those dystopias have been expressing themselves in the world. Without awareness, people are creating that reality for themselves."

Chris: "Those books are fiction. Maybe they were able to see the future and that's how those writers get their stories."

Anders: "Sure, but another way of looking at it is that they imagined a *potential* future, wrote it down in fascinating detail, and it is solidifying into the material world.

"Every person who reads a book adds thought energy to the concepts of that book, which feeds the beast."

Chris: "How can a novel create reality?"

Anders: "Maybe fiction is only unmanifested thoughtforms.

"In 1898, fourteen years before the *Titanic sank*, an American author wrote a book called *Futility*. The story was about an enormous cruise ship called the *Titan* that hit an iceberg and sank on an April night in the North Atlantic."

Chris: "That's a pretty big coincidence."

Anders: "It gets better. There were countless similar details, like both ships were thought to be nearly unsinkable feats of modern engineering, carrying the maximum capacity of passengers with the minimum number of lifeboats."

Chris: "Oh yeah. So, he predicted the *Titanic* sinking? What if Jack had read that book? I wonder if he would've even gone."

Anders: "The details in the novel could have been written as a report of the *Titanic* disaster after the fact. The hour, month, and location were the same.

"Many people claimed Robertson was a clairvoyant who saw it all beforehand. He claimed no such thing. He said his father was a ship's captain, and he naturally acquired a love of the sea as well as of ship architecture. He just used his imagination to write a novel based on his knowledge."

Chris: "My dad was a ship's captain. So, are authors predicting the future or creating it?"

Anders: "I don't know for sure. There is power in the written word. The best way to create your own future is to write down what you want in exact detail.

"When you write something down, you bring your other senses into the awareness of that thoughtform. Where you only heard it in your head before, now you can also see it on the paper, and you physically moved the pen to form those words. That increases your connection to your desire."

Chris: "I should write down what I want?"

Anders: "In great detail. Cast a good spell."

Chris: "Still, how can a novel affect *my* body?"

Anders: "It's not the novel itself. It's the emotional reaction to the story. Your mother felt a deep sadness when reading that story. That emotion set her body vibrating at a specific frequency, which you were able to sense. That was your first experience with the sadness frequency."

Chris: "But when we were inside, and I figured out it was just a novel, it didn't bother me anymore."

Anders: "Exactly. That previously unresolved event was the nucleus that those other events of sadness attached themselves to. It's a complexed set of beliefs, or simply a complex."

Chris: "When I went through the rest of those events, it was easy. Except for Tommy and Kyle. That was a little tough, I have to tell you."

Anders: "Yeah, I know. Those were big events for you. How do you feel about them now?"

Chris: "Well, I pretty much dealt with Tommy being gone a long time ago. At least I thought I had. Now, I am at peace with it. With Kyle, the wound is still fresh. I feel a lot better now, but I still miss him so much."

Anders: "Remember when you were telling me earlier about how he made an unassisted triple play? Tell me about that again."

A big smile came across her face as she began to retell the story. "When he was seventeen … (you've heard this). I'll never forget that as long as I live. But I still don't get how all those things add up to me having breast cancer."

Anders: "Imagine your body as a hologram, with different organs and locations representing a correspondence to various types of conflict.

"For example: knee issues may be related to a fear of moving forward, stomach issues could be a result of indigestible anger, bladder problems could be related to territorial issues. Think about how a dog marks his territory."

Chris: "That's mine. That's mine. That's mine. So, what is breast cancer related to?"

Anders: "Breast cancer is usually related to issues of nurturing. It would usually be related to a child or a child-like husband."

Chris: "Or a brother?"

Anders: "They vibrate at similar, nurturing, frequencies. The loss of a child is particularly charged with powerful emotions."

Chris: "I've got the hat trick, then. How does that hook up with a book?"

Anders: "Not the book. The emotional response to reading the story struck a chord in the octave of the death of a loved one. That is an event about which people often feel confusion, with unresolved misunderstandings and a feeling of powerlessness, because you can't do a blessed thing to change the fact that they are dead."

Chris: "How does that prayer go? God grant me the serenity to accept the things I cannot change, the courage to change the things I can, and the wisdom to know the difference."

Anders: "Perfect. The first event of the sadness vibration for you was while your mother was reading *Of Mice and Men*. At the time, you had no way of understanding the powerful sensation that surrounded you.

"Chords are made of multiple notes. There are other notes within that octave that may not be 'death of a loved one' but still have attached themselves to that first event."

Chris: "Some of those things didn't seem like they were related, but *poof*, they all disappeared when I looked at them differently."

Anders: "They may not appear to be related in the objective world, but in your subjective world, they resonate with each other. In other words, it doesn't matter whether other people see the connections."

Chris: "Trauma for one person may be a minor setback for someone else?"

Anders: "Exactly. Everything is relative, and what we are talking about is as personal as it gets. Your subconscious stores and classifies memories.

"When it doesn't understand, and the conscious mind can't yet understand either, the memory gets stuffed into a black bag and shoved down deep."

Chris: "Why doesn't it stay buried?"

Anders: "Through inductive reasoning, the conscious mind determines whether it accepts a bit of information as true or false.

"The subconscious, handed a labeled belief, is able to file it properly with its links."

Chris: "Sounds like a good partnership. What could go wrong?"

Anders: "Sometimes, in our lives, we have experiences that we just don't understand."

Chris: "Things that make you go, 'Huh?'"

Anders: "Right. You can't consciously comprehend what in Hell just happened, because you don't have the awareness to process it. The subconscious, embarrassed that it can't do its job, suppresses the memory.

"That event is a specific song composed of the elements of that kind of music. There is a genre, pace, key, et cetera, to every event.

"When you hear a song that sounds like the one that is buried, your subconscious pulls it up from the depths to see if you can figure it out yet.

"Usually, you are too busy dealing with the crisis at hand to be bothered with that old junk. So you say, 'Not now. I'm dealing with *this*.'"

Chris: "Not *now*, Cato!"

Anders: "Cato?"

Chris: "Yeah, you know. Remember, in the *Pink Panther* movies, Clouseau's assistant had a standing order to surprise attack him randomly, to keep his wits sharp. But he always did it at the wrong time, and Clouseau would say, 'Not *now*, Cato!'"

Anders: "I like that analogy. It's exactly like that. The old stuff comes up when you are dealing with new stuff. Then you have two events that are similar songs, neither one of whose lyrics you understand, uncategorized and buried.

"Those songs are still playing on a loop. You are not consciously aware of them, but there they are, creating disharmony, adding to the background noise."

Chris: "So how does noise grow tumors?"

Anders: "Those songs are only part of the arrangement. They are unresolved significant emotional events, to which less-significant, unresolved events attach themselves.

"Multiple discordant songs being played at the same time by an amateur musician creates dissonance. Like a roomful of toddlers banging on metal pots with wooden spoons. Disharmony interrupts flow.

"The subconscious also oversees the building of the body. It has a blueprint of the perfect physical you that it uses to reconstruct your body around the clock.

"Quantum physics has revealed that it takes about 11 months for our bodies to exchange all the atoms, every single one. An entirely new body, at the atomic level, every 11 months. Cells are organisms with lifespans, so they take longer."

Chris: "Then why does my knee still bother me when that skiing accident was like thirty years ago?"

Anders: "Because your subconscious mind holds on to that trauma and factors it into the rebuilding of the knee. There is an NLP technique for removing the trauma from that event so the body can rebuild without the injury, but we can talk about that later."

Chris: "Is that why my body keeps growing this tumor? It's holding on to trauma?"

Anders: "Multiple complexed associations with a trauma. There are basically four expressions of breast cancer; each one is related to a variation of an unresolved nurturing conflict.

"The left breast usually represents nesting conflicts like mother–child conflicts, or a physically or emotionally invalid husband. And the right breast is related to general human conflict, like children at a distance, or conflicts with adult children.

"The left side or right side are indicators, and whether it is ductal or lobular is another indicator that narrows down our search. There is a faster, easier, and infinitely more accurate way."

Chris: "Let's go with that one, whatever it is."

Anders: "We ask. Your subconscious knows everything there is to know about your body—past, present, and future. It has a perfect blueprint and a perfect memory of the physical traumas that it uses to rebuild the body.

"It makes no judgment about the change orders. It simply forwards the information to the Department of Cartilage, Knee Division. They maintain the knee according to the new program."

Chris: "Pain must be the complaint department."

Anders: "I think you're right about that. Emotional traumas can cause a lesion on the brain in locations that correspond to the type of trauma and location in the body. It is the lesion that causes corrupted information to be sent to the building departments.

"Unresolved emotional conflicts cause lesions on the brain, which then sends incorrect information to the area related to the conflict. These cancer cells may never accumulate enough at any one time to be a problem, but when you continue to add more to the pile, and/or you amplify them with emotion, they can multiply rapidly and control the territory."

Chris: "Isn't a lesion a tear? Do I have little tears all over my brain?"

Anders: "Not all over. You likely have a small lesion in a very specific location. In your case, it will likely be found in the left side of your reptilian brain."

Chris: "Can we just fix the lesion on my brain, and it will all go away?"

Anders: "The lesion causes the brain to send incorrect information to the body, but it is a secondary cause. An earlier secondary cause, your emotional reaction to a set of circumstances, created the lesions.

“By going back and reprocessing your experiences of sadness, we have already made corrections and reprogrammed part of the engineering department. You have more than one emotion that comes up for you when you think about the death of your son. How else do you feel?”

Chris: “Sometimes I get so angry that she encouraged him to get that bike.”

Anders: “You get angry that your daughter-in-law encouraged him to get that bike?”

Chris: “Yeah. I do. He already had a bike, but that new one was way too fast.”

Anders: “Was it too fast, or was he too consumed with anger that night?”

Chris: “I loved him so much, but he was a bit of a hothead, like his father. Anger never seems to make anything better.”

Anders: “You may be angry at your daughter-in-law, but do you think she misses him as much as you do?

"We can go back inside, to your power spot, to release your anger, if you’re ready. Look. Whales! Maybe we’ll just stay out here for a little longer.”

Chris: “That’s fine with me!”

Music Studio

XXXIX

Elias: "Want to see our music studio? I could show you the guitar my mom taught me to play. When she comes back, I'm going to play her the new song I wrote."

Mrs. B: "You wrote a song?"

Elias: "I always make up new songs. This one is a special one for Mama. She's an astronaut, you know. It's called 'Phoenix Rising.' Phoenix is her call sign."

Mrs. B: "Is this the studio, here?"

Elias: "Yeah, come on in. You wanna jam?"

Mr. H: "Maybe another time, Elias."

Elias: "As you wish, uncle. She gave me her old Telecaster when she got this beautiful Gibson Byrdland. Look at that inlay.

"You should hear her *shred* 'Crazy on You.' She just goes *crazy*. I've been practicing the lead so we can jam next time she's here. But don't tell her. It's a surprise."

Mrs. K: "How often do you see your mother?"

Elias: "She's flying in space most of the time, but she comes here every change of seasons, so she's always here for my birthday. We have video calls too."

Talkin' 'Bout Sin

XL

Anders: "As long as I've lived here, I never get tired of watching the whales play."

Chris: "I'm not tired at all. This is incredible."

Anders: "Well, are you ready to go back inside and clear up some anger?"

Chris: "Do we have to? I really like it right here."

Anders: "No. We don't have to go in. We can sit right here, watch the whales, and talk about whatever you want."

Chris: "There's that song again. Whatever I want. You know, sitting here like this makes me forget about all the sins of the world."

Anders: "All those people who miss the mark."

Chris: "Miss what mark?"

Anders: "From the Greek-text Bible, the term *hamartia*, 'to miss the mark' or err, was translated to the English word sin, which means to miss in archery.

"They say it also means a transgression or error. To be off target is an error, but is it really a transgression? So, I have a bit of an issue with the interpretation of the translations that have been passed down for generations."

Chris: "Do you think they did it on purpose, to fool us?"

Anders: "Not intentionally. I just think they sinned on the translation. Sometimes, when you are translating from one language to another, there is no exact translation, and you have to go with the best fit.

"Do you think the scribes of old, sitting at desks for years like secretaries in a bullpen, were the wisest people in the history of mankind?"

Chris: "What was the average life expectancy back then, like 35? I know 50-year-olds who aren't very wise."

Anders: "Those scholars were extremely wise, relative to the rest of their community, but they were still not aware of a fraction of what we know now.

"They were human beings doing the best they could. They all deserve participation trophies. Under the conditions of the time, they did an excellent job preserving the knowledge."

Chris: "I get the feeling there is a big but coming on."

Anders: "*But* … that doesn't mean we have to accept it as unchangeable. We've had two thousand years of energetic evolution since the time of Jesus. With new perspectives, we can reexamine the old ways.

"We can think about the foundations of what we collectively believe in a fresh light. For example: If we think of sin as having missed the mark, the question of the *target* presents itself. What were we aiming at that we missed?"

Chris: "Doesn't that depend on what kind of sin we are talking about?"

Anders: "We can work back from there, sure. First, can we say that, generally speaking, what we are *aiming at* is a good life, with all the good things life can provide: love, health, wealth, and happiness? So, *that* is our target."

Chris: "Check."

Anders: "If we are aiming at health, and we have a drink of alcohol, we have missed the target of optimal health. In case you didn't know it, liquor is bad for your body."

Chris: "Still, it has its virtues."

Anders: "I won't argue against that. I enjoy my margaritas. I'm just saying that because it's off-target and moves you in the opposite direction of optimal health, it is a sin."

Chris: "That cheesecake in the kitchen is the devil."

Anders: "Overeating, smoking, or any other activity that harms the body is a miss."

Chris: "I sure missed the mark on wealth too."

Anders: "Money is energy."

Chris: "Then, why can't I pay the electric bill? Apparently, I didn't take my advice about the tech stocks."

Anders: "OK. I'll dial it back a little. Let's say you want to become wealthy, but you do not pay yourself first. SIN, that's the sound an arrow makes as it whizzes past the target."

Chris: "Pay yourself first? How do you do that? I get paid every two weeks."

Anders: "It is one of the ancient secrets for wealth building. Pay yourself ten percent of all your income. Ten dollars out of every hundred dollars you earn gets set aside for *you*.

"That is your seed money that you add to every time you earn money. You use that money to invest in you and your future. You can use it for education, investments, or business opportunities.

"George S. Clason wrote in, *The Richest Man in Babylon*, 'I found the road to wealth when I decided that a part of all I earned was mine to keep.'"

Chris: "It's usually all gone before I know what happened. I've got bills and I've gotta eat."

Anders: "Start small. You can start with a smaller amount. The important thing to remember is to be consistent. Use your willpower to make yourself do it.

"It will be tough at first, but when you make it a habit, it will be as natural to you as having a cup of coffee in the morning."

Chris: "We'll see."

Anders: "You get the point about missing the mark, though. If you smoke cigarettes and drink, you have missed both the health and the wealth marks."

Chris: "God is punishing me for having fun?"

Anders: "God does not punish anyone. You reap what you sow. You have free will to make whatever choices you want to make. Any punishment is simply a result of a cause you put in motion.

"When you think of yourself as low-income, you will have low income. When you think of yourself as wealthy, you will be wealthy. When you get angry at someone and curse them, you curse yourself. When you get angry at someone and bless them, you bless yourself."

Chris: "What goes around comes around. Oooh. That is a *fact*."

Anders: "If our target is to be healthy, wealthy, wise, and happy, and we spend our time and money on things that hurt our mind and body, then we miss the mark on all four counts. It is so simple. I often wonder why we humans make things so difficult."

Chris: "Life is already hard. I don't need to be punished too."

Anders: "Your punishment for not acting in accordance with a law is contained within the law itself.

"We are not being punished by gravity when we fall. It is not a blessing when a boat floats on water. Most boats, other than my old kayak, float because of the law of flotation. They are lighter than the amount of water they displace.

"A lump of steel will sink, but if you flatten that lump out and turn up the edges, it will sink only to the point where it displaces more water weight than it weighs itself. Then it floats.

"As my kayak fills with water, it gets heavier and starts sinking. Everything operates by law. We just aren't aware of them all yet."

Chris: "What about Hell? Is there a law that operates Hell?"

Anders: "Hell is an interesting subject. What do you think Hell is?"

Chris: "If you live a life with all those sins, you go there after you die. Down into a fiery blast furnace with all the other sinners to be tortured for eternity, which is a long friggin' time. Like forever."

Anders: "That sounds like a Christian definition. And what do you think Heaven is?"

Chris: "Oh, well, honey let me tell you about Heaven. I think I've been good *enough* to get there. I never hurt anybody. Not intentionally anyways.

"You see, after you die, you go through a *transfiguration*. Your body becomes young and healthy again, all the wrinkles and bulges disappear, and you are light as a spirit. Then you see your whole family again, and they're all young and beautiful too.

"You can be, do, or have, anything you want. And you only want good things because you are in Heaven."

Anders: "But you have to wait until you die? How do you find out which way you are going?"

Chris: "You have to answer to Saint Peter. He stands at the Gates of Heaven with his ledger. He has *everything* written down. You just hope you have more pluses than minuses when he reconciles your life. If not, you get turned away."

Anders: "So, what are your options if you get turned away?"

Chris: "You can't come back and get a do-over. There is only one other place to go. Hell. Now, a priest can give you absolution, and wash away all your sins, if you repent and accept Jesus in your heart."

Anders: "No matter how bad a person was?"

Chris: "Yep. Lying, stealing, even killing can all be absolved. God is forgiving of all. It doesn't really seem fair for me to live my life honestly when a criminal can still get into Heaven."

Anders: "It's not in your nature to be a criminal."

Chris: "Maybe not, but you know what I mean. Some of us struggle through plain old boring lives, working hard to make good decisions. While a bunch of ne'er-do-wells live it up by hurting people, but they can still get into Heaven."

Anders: "Do you know that one meaning of the word *heaven* is harmony? Those people live their lives in disharmony. Do you think they are suddenly going to find harmony?

"It is not enough to think the thoughts and mouth the words, you must *be* harmonious. They can give their confession to the priest or whoever, ask for forgiveness, and receive it, but it is already too late. Their Heaven will be brief."

Chris: "Their ledger still didn't add up?"

Anders: "They will enjoy their Heaven for a little while, until it dissipates back into the ether. Everything they ever thought they wanted will suddenly flood into their awareness because, at the moment of death, they have stopped resisting.

"Nonresistance is the state of Heaven. But it doesn't last, because at death, you become a spiritual being outside of the human experience and no longer desire those physical things.

"You become aware of the states inside you that you thought the physical stuff was going to bring you. You no longer put thought energy into the creation and maintenance of those things, so they just melt back into primal substance."

Chris: "You mean like the primordial ooze? God created us in His likeness and image. You're not going to try to push evolution on me, are you?"

Anders: "Can both be true? Maybe God created the world the way it was, with Divine Intention of it evolving into the world we see now. And who knows where we will end up.

"For the sake of discussion, let's say that the universe was created by the spirit of God. Before there was any *thing*, there was Spirit. Spirit plus no *thing* equals Spirit. X + 0 = X.

"The formless substance, the basic stuff that everything in the universe is made from, therefore must come from Spirit."

Chris: "OK. I get that."

Anders: "Do you think God is finished with His work?"

Chris: "It doesn't seem like He could be."

Anders: "Close your eyes. Wait. Open them up again. The whales are playing."

Chris: "Oh my gosh! They're so beautiful. Look at that one!"

Anders: "I love this time of year."

Chris: "This sure feels like Heaven. I am still alive, aren't I?"

Anders: "Heaven on Earth. You may not have been more alive than this in a long time, Chris. Enjoy yourself. I'll be right back. I'm going to get us some iced tea. It's a green tea infused with ginger. Very refreshing. I think you are going to like it."

Chris: "I'll be right here. I feel like I'm in the flow."

Anders: "Perfect. I'll be right back."

Chris felt more relaxed than she could ever remember feeling. The warm tropical breeze carrying the intoxicating scent of plumeria washed over her while she watched the whales frolic. A spinner dolphin pirouetting above the water's confines brought out a sense of freedom from deep within her.

Anders came out of the kitchen with two tall glasses of iced green tea wrapped in cloth napkins. He handed one of the glasses to her and asked, "Are you doing all right out here, Chris?"

Chris: "Well, I don't know how I could be doing any better."

Anders: "This is an incredibly special place. I put a sliver of papaya in there too, to sweeten it up a bit."

Chris: "That's fabulous. I think I'm going to like it here after all."

Anders: "You asked me if there were laws governing Hell."

Chris: "You said everything works by law. The law of Hell sounds like an oxymoron. Like the people there aren't really the types who follow any laws."

Anders: "They're subject to the same Laws of the Universe as everybody else, whether they're aware of it or not. Gravity always pulls to the center. Emerson said that the Law of Cause and Effect is the Law of Laws."

Chris: "The law of laws. I guess if you were interested in law, that would be the one to study, then, wouldn't it?"

Anders: "Absolutely, but it's important to know the other Laws as well. When you live your life by the Laws, you don't act contrary to them."

Chris: "Ignorance of the law is no excuse?"

Anders: "If someone steps off the back of a speeding truck because they're not aware of the laws of physics that apply to their circumstances, they're likely to get hurt.

"Just because they don't know that a body in motion tends to stay in motion, that doesn't mean momentum won't continue to carry them. Gravity will pull them to the ground, where friction will cause them to tumble."

Chris: "Who in the world would step off the back of a speeding truck? You must be kidding me."

Anders: "I heard it happened in a remote village in a third-world country."

Chris: "I guess they weren't used to riding in trucks."

Anders: "I guess not. But the laws still applied to them.

"Criminals and other people who keep missing the mark are not in harmony with the world. Remember when I said the word *heaven* means harmony?

"In Trine's book, he wrote, 'The word *hell* is an old English word meaning to build a wall around in order to separate; to be helled was to be shut off from.'

"He also wrote, 'To be in right relations with anything is to be in harmony with it.' The Law of Polarity implies to *not* be in right relations is to be in disharmony. If there is such a thing as Hell, there must be something to be shut off from."

Chris: "The Catholics say that Heaven is what you get shut off from."

Anders: "Heaven is harmony. I love Catholics. They have such positive energy. Their hearts are in the right place, even if their minds are not quite. They uplift individuals and communities as their purpose. There are a lot of amazing people doing amazing things.

"I don't want to pick on Catholics; nearly all organized religions are living in sin. They have all missed the mark."

Chris: "Some of that stuff doesn't make sense to me either, but I was raised to believe it. They must have some of it right, though."

Anders: "Right, close your eyes for a minute. Take a nice deep breath, and as you let it out, allow yourself to relax completely. That's right. Just relax, even more, while you let your imagination create images on the screen of your mind.

"As you drift in this state of relaxation, you may be able to imagine that there is a spiritual essence that flows in, through, and around all of us, through everything our physical sensors pick up. What if the color of this essence was purplish? How would that appear?

"If Spirit is in and through everything, then it must be the spirit *of* everything. And you may be able to understand that we are each an individual expression of Spirit.

"Spirit expresses itself in the physical world through each individual. Rather than thinking of God as a separate entity, that passes judgment on everything we say or do, you can think of the human race as a collective.

"Just as each cell in your body interacts with the cells around it, to form the physical vehicle, each one of us interacts with the people around us to form the collective of God. God wants to experience everything, and He does it through people.

"The difference between individual intelligence and cosmic intelligence is that the individual has free will to act on their own volition."

Chris: "If God can't do what He wants, who can?"

Anders: "Every individual has free will. One of the great sins, or misses, of organized religion is to view God as a personality with thoughts, emotions, and a will."

Chris: "Thy kingdom come; Thy will be done. Doesn't that say He has a will?"

Anders: "If God is in Heaven, and Heaven is within you, where is God?

"God's will is to expand and grow. God does not have an individual personality and therefore doesn't care about what you do or do not want. You get what you attract to you."

Chris: "Did you just say God doesn't care about me?"

Anders: "God loves you but has no personal interest in what you want. Deciding what you want is your job. You are the only one who can express your individuality.

"In the Dore Lectures on Mental Science, Troward wrote, 'My mind is a center of Divine operation. The Divine operation is always for expansion and fuller expression, and this means the production of something beyond what has gone before, something entirely new, not included in the past experience, though proceeding out of it by an orderly sequence of growth.

"Therefore, since the Divine cannot change its inherent nature, it must operate in the same manner with me; consequently, in my own special world, of which I am the center, it will move forward to produce new conditions, always in advance of any that have gone before.'

"Let your subconscious absorb those words.

"As you come back to the here and now, remember that your mind is *a* center of Divine operation; that your mind is a craft room for God's projects done with your hands.

"You direct the outcome of the projects. You define what you want and bring it into being. Whatever the outcome, it is perfect.

"Allow your eyes to open naturally as you allow these thoughts, these beliefs, to strengthen your concept that you are a creator. Your special world is a reflection of your thoughts, beliefs, and actions."

Chris slowly opened her eyes, looked out toward the area where the whales were moments ago, and said, "That is a different way of thinking about God. We always thought of God as someone who was watching over us like a father. And if you didn't do what He says in the Bible, He will strike down upon thee with great vengeance."

Anders: "That's a sin. They've missed the mark. God, being universality, has no personality, and cannot get angry or have any other emotion; therefore, God can*not* direct anger toward us.

"Religious leaders may direct *their* anger at me for saying that, but God can*not*. God does not punish or reward. If you operate in harmony with the Universal Laws, you will get favorable results. If you act contrary to the principles, you will get unfavorable results. It's as simple as that."

Chris: "How do we know if we are working with the Law, or against it?"

Anders: "It's easier than you may think. If I imagine a shelf to hold my glass, right here, along this wall, I can create it. I can go out to my workshop, select the materials, define the dimensions, cut the pieces, and assemble my shelf.

"Now, at that point, neither one of us would doubt the existence of this shelf. I have gone through the physical process of constructing that shelf, and we both believe it.

"Without the convincer of the completed object, we would not believe that it was there. We can still imagine it there, but we don't believe it. If we don't believe it is there, it isn't.

"If I place my physical glass on the imaginary shelf, it will fall to the lava rocks below and shatter into fragments."

Chris: "Of course it will. That's how gravity works. You should know that by now. If you build a real shelf, and put it up there, *then* I'll believe it. Imagination won't hold a glass."

Anders: "The physical glass is heavier than the etheric thought form of the shelf. As my glass shatters on the rocks, it sends out disharmonious vibrations. Those vibrations tell me that I have violated the law of gravity or flotation, depending on your perception, and therefore could not get the results I wanted.

"Was that a punishment from God, or was it the result of disobeying a law? Reward or punishment, success or failure, are contained within the law itself."

Chris: "Gravity is a constant, and you get instant feedback when you don't cooperate with gravity. What about the other ones we can't see the results of right away?"

Anders: "That's where faith comes in."

Chris: "I *had* faith, but now I don't know what to believe. You're telling me that God isn't God, Heaven isn't Heaven, and Hell isn't Hell."

Anders: "Those things still exist. Your *perception* of them was off target."

Chris: "They told me I was a sinner."

Anders: "In a certain respect, we *are* all sinners. We all miss the mark. But if we can change the way we view sin, everything will change.

"I don't know if you're ready to hear this, but I'll say it anyway. The greatest sin, or biggest target missed, is not accepting that *you* are God. That is the real target.

"So, if you consider we are not aware of anyone hitting that mark in present day, you could come to the conclusion that we are all sinners.

"Another definition of sin is not being who and what you want."

Chris: "I've seen people give up on themselves because they think they've committed too many sins to be redeemed. They think everything is already decided because of their past sins. So they don't even try to be good."

Anders: "Yeah. Many people in this world think they're too far along the road to Hell to ever make it back to Heaven. They don't realize that NOW is the moment of power.

"From now, you can move in any direction you want. It doesn't matter what path you were on ten seconds ago. You have the power and ability to change your path instantly."

Chris: "All is forgiven?"

Anders: "You are the one doing the forgiving. The moment you accept that you are Divine, you are saved. You clearly see the target and move toward that light. You no longer look to the deceptions of the physical world for happiness."

Chris: "There is still the matter of the ledger."

Anders: "Another false belief. You could list your past thoughts, beliefs, and actions, but they are not weighed against each other to give you a final grade in life. No entity sits in judgment of whether you have been good enough to make it to Heaven."

Chris: "Now St. Peter isn't Saint Pete? What are you trying to do to me here?"

Anders: "I'm not trying to do anything to you. I'm presenting you with alternative viewpoints that could change your life. It's up to you to accept or reject anything I say."

Chris: "It all sounds well and good, but some of it fights with my beliefs."

Anders: "Everything I've said, I can back up with the Scriptures."

Chris: "If I change what I believe, will I still be me?"

Anders: "You can't be anyone else. You always have been, and always will be, who you are. No one else has had your experiences or sees the world exactly the way you do. With every new idea and experience, you change.

"You grow when you overcome challenges. Your mind expands and takes a new shape every time you learn something new. You become a new person moment by moment, but you don't become a different individual.

"I could never tell you everything I know. Even if I could, you would still filter the information through your beliefs, making the information your own. You cannot become me or anybody else. You can only be you."

Chris: "I *gotta* be me."

Anders: "Yes! Be you. The real you. What do you want? What is the one thing you want the most?"

Chris: “The one thing I want the most? Well, I know that’s not possible, so let me think about it.”

Anders: “Whatever it is, say it anyway. What is the one thing you want the most?”

Chris: “I want to hug my son again.
"Well … that’s what I want.”

Anders: “Does it make you feel better to say it out loud?”

Chris: “Yeah. It does. That’s what I’ve wanted all along, but that’s the first time I’ve actually said it out loud.”

Anders: “The healing continues as the black bags are emptied. Just let it out and let it go. Here, I always keep a clean hankie nearby. I make people cry on purpose. Please, keep it. Your daughter won’t admit it, but she wants a hug from you.”

Chris: “You threw a lot of stuff at me all at once. I don’t want you to go over the whole thing again, but let me see if I have this right.

“God doesn’t punish us for our sins. We are in harmonious Heaven when we hit the mark or ignorant Hell when we miss. You don’t have to die to go to Heaven. It says it all in the Bible. Did I leave anything out?”

Anders: “That’s pretty good. You learn fast.”

Chris: “I am a genius.”

Anders: “You definitely are. Have you ever seen the green flash?”

Chris: “Is that some new superhero?”

Anders: “No. It’s what happens at sunset in the tropics. At the moment the sun sets, a green light flashes along the horizon. It is amazing.

“Let’s go back inside for a while. We can do a little more work, and then we’ll come back out here for the sunset. How does that sound?”

Chris: “Sunset sounds marvelous.”

Garden of Earthly Delights

XLI

Elias: "The garden is through this gate. Just so you know, the fence is to keep critters out, not to keep the vegetables in."

Mrs. K: "Do they ever try to run away?"

Elias: "No, auntie, they like it here."

Mrs. B: "This is an impressive garden. Is that area for a future crop after you get the weeds out?"

Elias: "That is the crop, auntie. What looks like weeds to you, we call volunteers. The land provides us with plenty."

Mrs. B:"Do you eat those weeds?"

Elias: "Those are edible plants, auntie. Some of them are herbs. Change the way you look at something, and it changes."

Mrs. B: "They still look like weeds to me."

Elias: "Have you ever read *As a Man Thinketh*, by James Allen?"

Mrs. B: "No, I don't believe I have."

Elias: "He said the human mind is like a garden. It can be wisely cultivated or allowed to run wild. Whether tended or neglected, it must bring forth. The soil will grow whatever we plant.

"It will grow food, medicine, or poison. They look the same to the untrained eye. It's good to know the difference. Some are good. Some are bad. We can keep our crops of good substance, or we can allow the wild plants to take over.

"The same with our minds. We must plant pure thoughts and pull out impure thoughts continually. Become a master gardener."

Mrs. B: "I've heard you reap what you sow."

Elias: "Yes. What do you want? Sow the seeds of what you want, and your garden will be full of earthly delights."

Anger Management

XLII

Anders: "It is beautiful out here. While you're feeling all floaty, let's go back inside to your power zone, where we can dig up some more secrets."

Chris: "You want to know all my secrets?"

Anders: "No, I want *you* to know your secrets."

Chris: "I already know my secrets. Why do we need to go there?"

Anders: "I'm talking about the secrets you hide from yourself."

Chris: "How can you hide secrets from yourself?"

Anders: "Your subconscious keeps many secrets below your conscious level of awareness. When we were in your power zone earlier, you uncovered a gem."

Chris: "Poor Lenny. Weird, how that affected me. All right, let's go exhume the bodies."

Anders: "You'll be happy you did."

They go back inside.

Chris: "Is this what you're calling my power zone?"

Anders: "Yes. This is the place where you have all the power of the universe at your fingertips or, more precisely, on the tip of your tongue."

Chris: "This is my God spot?"

Anders: "You have already energized this spot with manamana."

Chris: "I know what mana is. That girl at the ice stand told me it's energy, but why did you say it like that, manamana?"

Anders: "It's a higher frequency of energy. This area is blessed by the work you did here earlier. To make energy and add it to anything is called ho'o manamana.

"Because you've already done that kind of work here, you are in harmony with this spot. Each time you work through something else, you add more connections, making this a place of power for you."

Chris: "Can I take it with me when I leave?"

Anders: "You can't take my study with you, but I can show you how to gather that power into yourself so you can take it with you wherever you go. At some point, you may find yourself aware of how powerful you are. Then you won't be concerned about packing around balls of energy."

Chris: "Let's see … I was right … here in this chair."

Anders: "Your subconscious knows. You can probably feel the harmony when everything is just right."

Chris: "This feels pretty good, right here." She shifted the chair slightly while wiggling into her seat.

Anders: "Perfect. Take a nice deep breath, and as you let it out, allow yourself to go back into a very relaxed state of mind. That's right. As you continue to relax, I want you to remember the direction of your past. Just get an impression of the path leading back in time from where you are right *now*.

"Earlier, we went back along that path to find the seed of sadness, remember?" Christine nodded. "We reevaluated how you relate to that emotion in a perfectly safe way.

"Now, I would like to talk to you about a different emotion, and that is anger. If we run the anger program too often, or at too high a level, the toxins build up faster than our bodies can get rid of them.

"When you think about it, what kinds of things get you angry?"

Chris: "I get *really* mad when I think about that jackass I was married to for 30 years. Part of me feels guilty, like if I wasn't the way I am, he would have been better to me."

Anders: "Did he tell you that?"

Chris: "No. He never came out and said it that way. He would always remind me of how much he has done for me, and I never appreciate what he does."

Anders: "Do you think you appreciated the things he did?"

Chris: "Well, some of it. But most of the time, he would tell me he was doing something for me, or for my own good, but it was really for *him*. It was always something he wanted or, sometimes, it was something he thought made him look generous. He always made a big deal about it.

"To himself, he was as generous as St. Nick. Most of the time, he would give me something I didn't even want. And I'm supposed to be grateful for that? He can get stuffed."

Anders: "Would you like to get rid of underlying guilt, right now?"

Chris: "How can you get rid of guilt? Isn't it just a natural emotion?"

Anders: "It is natural. All our emotions have a positive intention. They are vibrational sensors reporting their findings in those frequencies in which they operate.

"Just like we did with sadness, we can go back to your first unresolved experience of that emotion, with the wisdom you have now, and reevaluate your feelings of guilt. We are not really getting rid of it, just shifting how you experience it."

Chris: "I was floating earlier."

Anders: "It is nice, isn't it? Remember how that felt and, while you're floating, see if you can call up the feeling of guilt. You can do that easily by remembering a time when you felt guilty for something you did or did not do. Get in touch with your feelings of guilt, right now. That's right."

Chris: "This isn't very comfortable. I don't like this feeling."

Anders: "I know, but you are doing great. Your body is vibrating on a guilt frequency, but you can float up out of your body, where you will not feel the vibration."

Chris: "That's better."

Anders: "As you float there, above your body, just remember; remember your first experience of guilt. Was it before, during, or after your birth?"

Chris: "After."

Anders: "What age were you?"

Chris: "I think I was about five or six."

Anders: "Which is it?"

Chris: "I was five … and a half."

Anders: "That half is very important when you're young. At our age, we round down. Are you back there now?"

Chris: "Yep. Just floating up here."

Anders: "Allow yourself to drift down into your body as you were then, now. See what you were seeing. Hear what you were hearing. Feel what you were feeling."

Chris: "I'm in the kitchen. Mommy, Daddy, and Tommy are out in the living room. I lit the gas burner on the stove. It's so cool. I just turn the knob, and the blue flames dance. They're so beautiful. I don't remember why, but I picked a paper napkin up from the counter and started to push the corner toward the flame, to see how close I could get it."

Anders: "Like any good scientist."

Chris: "It's too close—and catches on fire. What do I do? It's starting to burn my fingers. I have to get rid of it. I throw it into the trash can, turn off the burner, and run out to the living room.

"Pretty soon, Daddy yells, 'FIRE!' By now, yellow and orange flames are climbing out of the trash can. He fills a glass milk bottle with water at the sink and dumps it on the fire. The fire goes down and he runs outside with the smoking can.

"When he comes back in, he starts yelling at me. I already feel bad about it. He doesn't have to call me stupid. I'm not stupid."

Anders: "No, you're not. And you have wisdom now that you did not have back then. What lesson did you need to learn that you can help the younger you understand?"

Chris: "Don't stick paper in fire unless you want more fire."

Anders: "That is a valuable lesson, but what did you need to learn about guilt?"

Chris: "When you do something bad, you feel bad. … Daddy was scared. I think I feel more guilty about scaring him than I do about the fire."

Anders: "Whatever resources you have now, you can now have then, to help you have a better understanding of that feeling.

"Once you have that understanding, you can bring that understanding through any subsequent events, along your life's path. Allowing you to reevaluate that experience with a wisdom that allows you to learn what you needed to learn from that event. While releasing the guilt, clearing the energy blocks at each of those events, all the way back to now."

Chris: "My whole body is tingling."

Anders: "Just sit there and enjoy it for a while. Continue taking deep breaths, as deep as you can."

She adjusted her position in the chair. Sitting a little straighter, a little more upright, she began to take noticeably deeper breaths.

Anders: "We sat down here with the intention of clearing the emotion of anger. Let's do that now."

Chris: "I don't want to leave here. Where I am right now is perfect."

Anders: "You can come right back to here. In fact, we aren't really going to leave. We are going to stay right here in this state while you move around within it. After you process the root cause of anger, we can go back out onto the lanai. Okay?"

Chris: "Okay. Let's do it."

Anders: "Can you get in touch with your anger right now?"

Chris: "That's easy. I just have to think about Marcas. That does it every time."

Anders: "Remember a recent event that made you really mad? What are the qualities? Notice how that feels, and where you feel that in your body. Let's put Marcas in isolation for now. Make him smaller and further away.

"Right now, I would like you to float up out of your body. Just float right up, and see yourself, sitting in your power spot, down here in this chair. While you are floating up there, I wonder if you can remember the first time you felt anger. Was it before, during, or after your birth?"

Chris: "After."

Anders: "OK. After. How old were you?"

Chris: "I was just a baby, maybe like six months."

Anders: "Go ahead and let yourself travel back to that time. And when you get there, float down into your body then. Is anyone there with you?"

Chris: "I'm in my room, in my crib. It's cold. I'm crying. Tommy is in here. He took my blankie. It's not his anymore. He can't do that. Why is he being mean to me?"

Anders: "And that makes you angry?"

Chris: "I'm just a baby, and he is being unfair to me."

Anders: "You were a baby then. As an adult who has had children and grandchildren of her own, you have wisdom and understanding you did not have then. What are you aware of now, you were not aware of then, that would help that younger you with this situation?"

Chris: "Even though Tommy was older than me, he was a sweet little boy. He sure is clinging onto that blanket.

"Oh, Tommy! He wasn't being mean to me. He just missed his blankie. My big baby brother."

Anders: "Does that help you remember the event differently?"

Chris: "Yeah! That shines a whole new light on things. All these years … I'm sorry, Tommy. Please forgive me."

Anders: "Excellent. Now that you have that understanding, you can bring that understanding back through all the subsequent similar events, learning what you needed to learn, releasing the anger, removing the blocks to the Flow, all the way back to now.

"When you are back to now, you can stay in a state of deep relaxation while you energize your body enough to walk out to the lanai. When you're ready, let's go see if the whales are playing."

Outside, on the lanai.

Chris: "You know, I feel really good right now, and I don't want to jinx anything, but that Marcas still pisses me off. Can I say that?"

Anders: "Of course you can. You were married to the man for 30 years. There are vast, intricate webs of connections between the two of you. We just snipped a few cords. Each mental, physical, or emotional interaction between the two of you connects another thread. You could cut them too."

Chris: "Threads of *what*?"

Anders: "Aka. It's an invisible substance that's in and around everything. The more interactions you have with a person or a subject, the more connections you have. Threads with similar frequencies weave together, making strong cords."

Chris: "Oh, we had lots of interactions. He harped on me about everything. He just wouldn't let some things go. Those are probably some thick cords. Is there any way I can just, you know, cut them all at the same time? Get rid of him once and for all?"

Anders: "Sure, you can cut any aka cords you want. I must say, though, cutting the cords only cuts the current conduit between the two of you. Your subconscious will send out new threads until you fully forgive him. You still want to look at what is inside you that attracted him into your life in the first place."

Chris: "I can deal with me. I can't deal with him anymore."

Anders: "Stand up. I want you to get the full experience of this."

Chris: "For my own good, eh?"

Anders: "Yes. The more you get into the spirit of it, the more effective it will be. Bend your knees a little, like you are leaning against a barstool, almost sitting on it."

Chris: "Now I'm a barfly?"

Anders: "Focus. Just bend your knees a little bit and put your hands out in front of you, like you are holding a basketball in your hands. Now, bring your hands toward each other and begin to rotate them upward, as you lift the air in front of you straight up and out.

"There is energy in the air. Move it in your mind's eye as you move your hands through the air in bigger and bigger circles, reaching out, scooping up more energy and then bringing it to your center, and pushing it up, out the top of your head, like a fountain.

"You can bring that flow of energy into your body by shifting the focus of your mind. Feel that energy flowing inward and upward through your body, through your core, out the top of your head. Your hands continue to gather energy and direct its flow in ever increasing circles.

"Continue breathing deeply as the fountain flows through you and the rain of blessings come down around you. At this level of mind, you can see all the connections you have to everyone and everything glowing in the ether.

"Identify the cords you want to cut. Make them glow brighter or a different color. Separate them from the ones you want to keep. Everything is flexible in this state. You can separate them with your mind.

"Make those connections clearer and brighter. We want this to be *spectacular*. We want there to be no question of intention or doubt of outcome.

"You probably didn't notice the lightsaber by your side until now, did you? Take out your lightsaber and power it up. Wave it around a little. Careful that you don't accidentally cut cords you want to keep.

"Buwezzch. Buwezzch. With one fell swoop, you are going to cut the Marcas cords. Cut them off close to your body. Get ready. Here it comes. Raise your sword. *Swoosh*!

"Feel the power of cutting the ties that bind. Watch as the tangled web begins to drift off into space, getting smaller and smaller as it goes, drifting farther and farther away, until it is too small to see. Then, *poof*, it is gone completely."

Chris: "*That* was amazing. I feel like the clouds have opened up and the sun is shining."

Anders: "That really is the sun."

Chris: "It feels wonderful."

Everything Is Energy

XLIII

Mr. H: "Elias, you said everything is energy. How can this rock be energy? It doesn't move on its own."

Elias: "Maybe it does. It vibrates faster than we can see. Maybe it moves slower than we can see.

"Einstein said, 'Everything is energy and that's all there is to it.' All matter is made up of atoms. Every atom is made of protons, neutrons, and electrons. Energy."

Mr. H: "But why does it feel solid? How can I stand on top of energy without falling through?"

Elias: "Because what we think of as solid matter is fields of energy vibrating at specific frequencies in specific patterns. Magnetic repulsion prevents the fields from crossing into each other."

Mr. H: "So, when I clap my hands together, they won't just pass through themselves?"

Elias: "Yep. I'm still trying to figure out how to arrange the hydrogen atoms in my feet to repulse the hydrogen in the bay. I think that might be how you walk on water. That's my theory anyway."

Mr. H: "There must be other physical laws in play too."

Elias: "We see ourselves as physical structures, but we are energy vortices. My mind is the transmitter. My body is the receiver. I am a transceiver. My mind also translates the energy pattern into a form I can grasp.

"When this body dies, the transmitter is still transmitting. I can create a new man in my likeness and image. Everything begins with a thought vibration."

Mr. H: "How can you create a new man?"

Elias: "In the beginning was the Word. Each word has a specific pattern and frequency. Thought vibration sends out a specific wave pattern. Vibration produces energy. The pattern and frequency determine the form.

"I think therefore I am. My mind sends a thought pattern at a specific frequency to manifest the form you see now."

Not With That Attitude

XLIV

Anders: "Whether a result of evolution or by divine design, your body is capable of healing itself. We don't understand how a cut finger repairs itself. Yet it does.

"Your subconscious rebuilds your body, using a dynamic blueprint of your perfect self. As another healing protocol, I want to talk to you about fasting."

Chris: "Fasting? Isn't that the same as not eating?"

Anders: "Yes. Americans, generally speaking, eat too much food too often. Our bodies are capable of complex chemical reactions that we're not consciously aware of.

"Throughout history, fasting has been a remarkably effective medical protocol."

Chris: "You mean like the old saying 'starve a cold; feed a fever'?"

Anders: "Yes, exactly. When you have a cold, the degree of severity depends on a couple of things. Some viruses are more aggressive than others to begin with.

"The nature of the virus is one factor and the condition of your mind and body is another. You probably have about 20 pounds of undigested food in your guts right now."

Chris: "Twenty pounds? The drain's on the bottom, why doesn't it just keep going?"

Anders: "It's usually because the plumbing is clogged with sludge. Also, it takes about six to eight hours to digest a meal. And even if we don't snack, we eat about every four or five hours. But we gotta have our snacks, don't we?"

Chris: "I know I have to have my afternoon treat. I deserve it."

Anders: "It isn't a question of whether you deserve it. You definitely do. The question is, can your body burn the coal as fast as you are shoveling it in?"

Chris: "I don't eat with a shovel."

Anders: "No, but we eat too often. We eat too much and too much of the wrong things."

Chris: "Then why did God make chocolate, if we're not supposed to eat it?"

Anders: "Cacao is a superfood, but God didn't put sugar into it. Is it the cacao, or the sugar that you crave?"

Chris: "If I'm being honest, I tried unsweetened chocolate, you know, the kind for baking. No, thank you. That stuff is nasty."

Anders: "Were programmed and conditioned to consume sugar. We get a constant stream of messages telling us how happy we'll be if we eat or drink whatever they're selling. And most of what they're selling has added sugar. We've become addicted to sugar."

Chris: "Is that so terrible? It makes me feel good. I thought that was part of your whole philosophy. You said feeling good makes you feel better."

Anders: "Cancer feeds on sugar. A sugar rush is just like the rush of any other drug. It's a temporary artificial manipulation of the energies in your body.

"Human beings have discovered millions of things they can ingest, absorb, or insert that will change their state of mind. They want to change the vibration they feel in their bodies. Sugar does that quickly."

Chris: "That always worked for my kids. If they were grumpy about something, I just gave them a cookie, and they were happy. For a while anyway. Then they'd find something else to cry about later. But you can't just keep giving them cookies all day."

Anders: "When we have an oversupply of sugar, we can get an overgrowth of candida in our body. It's not really your body that's craving sugar, it's the bacteria that feeds on sugar calling for more."

Chris: "How do I get them to shut up?"

Anders: "Starve them out. Kill them off by cutting their food supply. A great way to begin fasting is to start eliminating excess sugar. Make conscious decisions about your consumptions."

Chris: "They put that stuff in everything, though."

Anders: "The more levels of processing these so-called food products go through, the worse the results are for your body. Candy bars don't grow on trees."

Chris: "If they did, I'd have myself an orchard."

Anders: "I'm just saying that our bodies are designed to process flora, fauna, and fungus. They tolerate the man-made chemical compositions called food products, but those are not food."

Chris: "The big producers have to process our food, or it will go bad. Tomatoes have to be canned at their peak or they won't last at all. I saw that on a documentary about our food supply."

Anders: "Some processing and additives are necessary to keep the food supply healthy. The further food gets from its natural state, the harder it is for our bodies to use it. And the more of *that* stuff we consume, the more toxins we accumulate in our bodies."

Chris: "Everybody talks about detoxifying these days. It's all the rage. Is that why you fast, or do you do it for religious reasons?"

Anders: "I fast mainly for health reasons, but the mind and body work together, so there are spiritual benefits as well. Every change of seasons, I fast for three days."

Chris: "Oh, I could never do that."

Anders: "Not with that attitude."

Chris: "Three days?! Nothing to eat or drink? How do you keep from falling over?"

Anders: "Your body adapts to the new habit. I drink water, black coffee, and green tea. Those who observe Ramadan fast for thirty days."

Chris: "But my friend, Sari … When do they do that?"

Anders: "It's usually right after Easter."

Chris: "I've known her for a few years. She never said a word."

Anders: "Fasting is highly personal. Part of the process is not talking about it."

Chris: "That's the first rule of fast club. Three days doesn't seem very long compared to thirty. So, you don't eat anything at all, for three days. Is there something magical about three days?"

Anders: "It's a running theme that keeps popping up. Your body goes through stages. After the first eighteen to 20 hours, your body goes into autophagy, which means it starts to eat itself."

Chris: "Aack! That sounds like starvation mode. Nothing about starvation sounds good to me."

Anders: "It is starvation mode. We have negative associations with starvation, and for good reason. But long before you die of starvation, your body will eat anything within it that is not the healthy you.

"Your organs, systems, and all cells work together to feed on parasites, bacteria, molds, and any other foreign organisms living in your body. The healthy cells consume unhealthy cells. It's like a self-cleaning function of the body."

Chris: "That all happens in the first day? Why don't you just do that?"

Anders: "I do, and I have friends who do. After dinner on Saturday night, they skip dessert and fast until Sunday dinner."

Chris: "If I don't get to eat for the next 24 hours, I want to have that last dessert."

Anders: "If your target is to starve parasites, it's a miss to feed them before the battle."

Chris: "Sin. The sound of an arrow whizzing past its mark."

Anders: "A 24-hour fast, once a week, is an amazing practice. It helps your body keep up with your overeating."

Chris: "Hey!"

Anders: Daddy"Don't take it personally. I meant it generally. What are we told about breakfast?"

Chris: "It's the most important meal of the day!"

Anders: "That's the mantra. Ask anybody. They'll tell you the same. We have had that message continuously tapped into our minds for over a hundred years.

"That myth didn't come out of medical research. It started as a propaganda campaign by a cereal company. And as with all propaganda, other people started seeing how they could also profit from the message, and it grew.

"Clever and enchanting new slogans were put in front of people. Catchy jingles were created, and people would sing them for no reason."

Chris: "Sometimes those earworms get in deep."

Anders: "The subconscious loves jingles because they're fun. It doesn't question whether they are true. It just keeps replaying them. When you examine them, many commonly held beliefs are simply myths. So many great lies."

Chris: "It seems like there is a lot of that going on with you. Religion, physicians and politicians, TV, they're all pushing lies. Do you believe anything?"

Anders: "'All the world believes a lie.' I have many beliefs. I think there are a lot of false doctrines that are accepted by the masses that are anything but for the public good.

"When the breakfast campaign began, nobody had a clue the impact it would have on society as a whole. They were happy they had a marketing campaign that caught fire. Other producers hitched a ride and were also successful.

"Bright and shiny new minds came in with brighter and shinier new ways to get the message out. Here we are, over a century later, and *everybody knows* breakfast is the most important meal of the day."

Chris: "And you're saying it's not?"

Anders: "Breakfast is the most important meal of the day because you're breaking your fast, and it is important what food choices you make. I prefer to break my fast around 2 PM."

Chris: "That's not breakfast. That's afternoon snack time."

Anders: "That's part of the socially programmed myth. Breakfast doesn't have to be eaten in the morning. If you wait a few hours to refuel, demand keeps up with supply."

Chris: "If you don't eat breakfast at breakfast time, it's not breakfast. Although I'm not opposed to having breakfast for dinner. I can have bacon, eggs, and pancakes anytime."

Anders: "You can break your fast at any hour. You want to be choosy when selecting the food you put in. Traditional breakfast foods aren't as good for your system as the ads would have you believe.

"Different combinations of foods create different chemical reactions in your body. You want to ease your digestive system back to work. To break an extended fast, I start with a little bone broth and add a pinch of black pepper.

"The collagen activates the enzymes, coats the stomach, and lubricates the plumbing. Black pepper stimulates saliva which gets the rest of the system working."

Chris: "After no food for a whole day, I think I could eat an extra-large meat-lovers pizza."

Anders: "Your stomach will start shrinking back to normal size, so you won't be able to eat as much as you used to."

Chris: "Thank God for that."

Anders: "That's just one of many benefits of fasting."

Chris: "There are many benefits to eating too. I could go on and on about that, but what else does fasting do?"

Anders: "Once your body gets caught up on processing your last eight meals, it burns up the stored glycogen in your muscles and then your liver. At that point, your body converts to operating on ketones and using stored fat for fuel."

Chris: "I've been hording it. I've got plenty of that. When does the fat start burning?"

Anders: "That kicks in about the same time as autophagy. Depending on the amount of sugar in your system, your body goes into a state of ketosis in the 20–24-hour range. Actually, I've found that if I eat keto for two days before fasting, it makes the fast much easier."

Chris: "It facilitates the fast?"

Anders: "Yeah, because you've already burned through the glycogen and your body is operating on ketones; it doesn't miss the meals as much. It will definitely remind you of the habit of the meals. Your subconscious may act like you are starving, but it knows better."

Chris: "When I get hungry, my subconscious is an award-winning prima donna. It gets overly dramatic and self-centered. And neither one of us cares who knows it."

Anders: "That's one of the psychological benefits of fasting. You learn to discipline the urges that used to control your life. You learn to break the associations that trigger responses. Each time, it's a new lesson in self-mastery.

"For a three-day fast, the first weekend of each season, I begin strict keto on Tuesday, with lots of fresh greens. Around one o'clock, on Thursday, I'll have a couple of eggs with some breakfast meat and cheese.

"At 2 PM, I have a citrus and fiber drink as a sweeper to brush out any lazy food particles. I put lemon, orange, and grapefruit juice, a half teaspoon of apple cider vinegar, and two tablespoons of psyllium fiber in a glass with water."

Chris: "What's that, that psyllium fiber?"

Anders: "The acids dissolve leftover food, and the fiber grabs hold to pull it out. Cleans you out like a bottlebrush. Any store that carries food supplements should have it. I like the orange-flavored one with the real sugar. It tastes great with the citrus."

Chris: "But you said sugar is bad. Doesn't that take you out of ketosis?"

Anders: "We all make our choices. I love the taste of it. That little bit of sugar temporarily flips me back to burning carbs, but I usually go right back into ketosis. If that's a concern for you, you can get unsweetened fiber sitting on the same shelf. The fast begins as soon as I stop eating.

"I continue ordinary activities. In the evening, I set goals for the next three months. On these three nights, as I fall asleep, I assume the qualities of having accomplished those goals.

"On the first morning when I wake up, it's been about seventeen hours since I've eaten anything. I have a glass of water, and two cups of black coffee. I normally have bullet-proof coffee, but the butter and oil have calories, so they're off-limits during a fast.

"The acid-wash and bottlebrush beverage from yesterday afternoon is ready to be flushed out of my lower intestines, taking with it the dead cells and undigested food that had been hanging around in there for a while.

"With some light exercise and normal activities, my body has shifted into ketosis and autophagy. Increased BDNF starts building new brain cells. By the time I finish my workout, it's increasing production of HGH, or human growth hormone."

Chris: "My friend, Amy, got an HGH treatment. She said it made her feel a lot younger, but I think it cost her around $5,000. So, now you're at 24 hours with no food. You must be pretty hungry."

Anders: "I have already conditioned my mind and body to having 2 PM as my normal breakfast time. The alarm for that habit is going off, but I haven't felt any hunger."

Chris: "What do you do if you do get those demon hunger pangs?"

Anders: "I have a cup of green tea. I sprinkle in ginger, salt, and crème of tartar, for the electrolytes."

Chris: "Like we had earlier? That was delicious! Then, the hunger goes away?"

Anders: "It really does. I also don't turn on the TV because they are continuously running commercials for food products and restaurants. I started to notice even the shows themselves were promoting eating. There are multiple, powerful suggestions to eat during every hour of TV programming."

Chris: "Those burgers look so much better on TV than they do when you actually get one."

Anders: "You wouldn't want to eat one of those picture-perfect burgers. They put cardboard between each layer to fluff it up."

Chris: "I know a Red Delicious tastes better than a Rome Beauty. Flavor over appearance. So, you're starving, and your body eats itself, right?"

Anders: "Your body knows the difference between a healthy cell and a foreign body. It knows the difference between good and bad bacteria. It eats parasites, molds, bacteria, viruses, cancer cells, malformed cells, and anything else that is not part of a healthy you."

Chris: "Hold on. Did you just say my body will eat viruses and cancer cells from itself?"

Anders: "Yep. The healthy cells that once had an overflowing food supply from consumption now start eating anything that is not a healthy cell. That includes microbes and cells your own mind created when it started sending corrupted signals to your system."

Chris: "How does it know the difference?"

Anders: "Remember, your subconscious mind has a blueprint for your body in a perfect state. Every 11 months, your body is completely renewed on an atomic level. None of the atoms in your body right now were part of you a year ago."

Chris: "If my body is completely new every year, why does it feel like it keeps getting older and older?"

Anders: "Aside from having the blueprint of your perfect body, it also has beliefs about the change orders it has received.

"We each have a health paradigm, which includes our beliefs about aging and longevity, recovery from injury, and the cause of disease. You may not like the current state of your body, but you created it through your beliefs."

Chris: "Can I uncreate it? How do I get my subconscious mind to use that perfect me blueprint?"

Anders: "Visualization. When was the last time you saw yourself as a healthy 22-year-old?"

Chris: "About 30 years ago when I *was* 22."

Anders: "Exactly. You have been rebuilding your body according to your beliefs. Once you can accept that your health is determined by your beliefs about health, you can start reevaluating those beliefs.

"You can form new, empowering beliefs. You can master your own health."

Chris: "I'm hearing that a year from now, I can be 53 or 22. I'm in. Where do I sign up for 22?"

Anders: "You can dramatically slow down the aging process. I am not aware of anyone who has reversed it. You may be the first, if you can believe it. Can you get from here to there in one year? It took thirty years to get from there to here.

"Can you believe you are 22? 'As a man thinketh in his heart, so is he.' The heart, in the Bible, means the subconscious mind.

"Your beliefs, your paradigms, are what you think in your heart. What you believe in your heart is who you are."

Chris: "How do you change your beliefs?"

Anders: "That is the big question, isn't it? The old beliefs you used to have, which no longer serve you, belong to the old you.

"You can start by believing that you can change your beliefs. For you to accept new beliefs, you must cross off the old you. You must crucify the old you for the new you to be born again."

Chris: "Like a born-again Christian? I don't want to be one of them boring goody-goodies."

Anders: "So, that's where she gets it. The other day, I was wondering how a person can call themselves a Christian unless they awaken to the Christ within and are born again. It is the foundation of his teachings.

"'Boring goody-goodies' might be one of the beliefs you want to reevaluate. Each person is an individual with individual beliefs. When you slap a group label on a person, you close *your* mind to their individuality."

Chris: "It makes it easier to keep people sorted if I keep them in groups."

Anders: "Just because a person is in a particular group, doesn't mean they think the same way as the rest of the group. They may agree on many concepts but disagree on others."

Chris: "Some groups seem like they are all a bunch of mindless zombies chanting the same stupid thing.

"I play Bingo on Tuesday nights because I like to play. It's fun, and sometimes I win. But oh Lord, all those people talk about is getting old and all their aches and pains. I get so sick of it."

Anders: "We were having an interesting conversation about fasting, when we got off on this fascinating discussion about beliefs.

"Since you want to change your beliefs about fasting, I will tell you that the only way you will ever change your beliefs is to reevaluate them. Ask yourself, 'Does this belief serve me?'

"When you examine your beliefs, you find some cannot stand the light of reason."

Chris: "I'm not clear on exactly how you do that."

Anders: "Do you remember when we were talking about how a sin is simply missing the target?"

Chris: "How could I forget that?"

Anders: "Define your target by knowing precisely what you want. That is your Heaven on Earth. Order is Heaven's first Law. Organize your mind toward that destination.

"Your limiting beliefs will be the first to pop up into your awareness. Those are the beliefs that tell you that you can't do something. Limiting beliefs define our bubbles and give us a sense of safety and stability.

"This is when you decide. Gut check time. Is this belief in harmony with my target?

"When you make decisions, you cut off what doesn't work."

Chris: "It sounds easy when you say it like that."

Anders: "It is simple, but it isn't easy if you don't know you can. 'You can't escape from a prison if you don't know you are in one.'

"Even some people who know they can escape, are more afraid of the unknown than they are of familiar ideas. Their awareness of their possibilities hasn't caught up with their capabilities."

Chris: "Well, I don't want to be jumping out of the frying pan into no damned fire."

Anders: "Nobody does. In the simplest terms, as basically as I can, I'll spell it out.

"*Decide* what you want. *Become* that person. *Feel* it in your heart. Take *action* in that direction.

"Actions that are on target move you closer to heaven. Actions that move you in another direction are a sin to that destination."

Chris: "And sin is punishable."

Anders: "The only punishment is that you don't get what you wanted."

Chris: "There you go again. You're messing with my beliefs."

Anders: "I'm just having you pull them out so you can decide for yourself if they serve your purpose."

Chris: "Maybe we should come back to this later. You were telling me what happens when you starve yourself on purpose. Your body eats cancer, viruses, and is a miracle cure for all that ails you."

Anders: "Skin tags, moles, warts, tumors, and anything else that is growing where it shouldn't be gets eaten. Fasting also reduces inflammation, breaks down insulin resistance, and builds new brain cells.

"Unhealthy foreign organisms get consumed while the good organisms flourish. All these benefits of autophagy begin after about 20 hours."

Chris: "Then you turn off your TV so you won't be tempted by commercials. What do you do then, go to bed early?"

Anders: "I use the time to define my goals. It's the beginning of a new season and a perfect opportunity for me to assess my accomplishments and set new targets for the quarter. I sit down with a pen and a pad of paper to flesh out my goals and cast a new spell."

Chris: "Oh, now you're a witch too? As I recall, the Bible doesn't look too kindly on witchcraft."

Anders: "Definitions and interpretations. When you spell out what you want, you are casting a spell. You see, writing causes thinking. You are arranging and organizing your mind to clarify your desires.

"Organizing your ideas helps solidify your ideal. A clearly defined idea will take form in the material world. False beliefs fall away. Thoughts become things."

Chris: "Have you ever done a vision board?"

Anders: "Absolutely. I love vision boards. Your subconscious mind thinks in images. It understands words as symbols. It communicates with pictures."

Chris: "What about when I talk to myself? I hear words and sentences. Where are those voices coming from?"

Anders: "Those are usually sound bites; phrases, and things we have heard ourselves or others say. I carry on conversations in my head all the time.

"I usually go to bed early because my body rebuilds, and my mind renews during sleep. I am giving my subconscious direction, and I want to give it the opportunity to fulfill my command."

Chris: "What about the next day? What happens next? You must be ready for some breakfast by then."

Anders: "When I wake up on the second morning, I've now been fasting for over 40 hours, and autophagy, ketosis, and HGH production are operating at high levels."

Chris: "How do you feel?"

Anders: "The second day is usually the easiest. I get up and go through my habitual morning routine, including a workout."

Chris: "Two days without eating, and you work out? Don't you get weak?"

Anders: "At that point, my body is operating extremely efficiently, and I'm full of energy. I have played golf, arguably better, in the middle of a three-day fast.

"Exercising stimulates circulation of the lymph, which is the garbage collection operation of the body. The blood has a pump to move it around, but the lymph relies on the movement of muscles to squish it around. It flows through the body, picking up dead cells and other waste products."

Chris: "Bring out ch'r dead! Bring out ch'r dead! Where does it dump the bodies then?"

Anders: "The lymph carries all that garbage away. Some of it goes out through the skin, some goes out in the toilet, a lot of it goes out through the lungs. We can really accelerate the elimination by breathing."

Chris: "I already do that. Bam! That was easy."

Anders: "You could learn to breathe better. Most of the time, our breathing is too shallow. You are usually only exchanging about the top third of the air in your lungs. That means more than half the air in your lungs is stagnant and toxic.

"If you want to be healthy, you have to breathe deeply. I like to do Chi Gung exercises to circulate energy, blood, and lymph, and the deep breathing helps purge my lungs."

Chris: "I like to dance. Does dancing do the same thing?"

Anders: "Yes. When you dance, you are pumping a whole bunch of other feel-good chemicals into your system because you are having a good time. Dancing is amazingly healthy and fun. People should dance more and breathe deeper. Really push out the stale air."

Chris: "What about belly dancing? That's fun. I took a class in that one time."

Anders: "Belly dancing and hula are fun and healthy. Dancers are also massaging and stimulating the organs in their bellies. Organs don't move around on their own."

Chris: "You don't want your organs moving around. They fit nicely where they are."

Anders: "They can be moved without being repositioned. I'm just talking about shaking them up with a little jiggle."

Chris: "Everybody likes a little jiggle, now and then."

Anders: "And it's healthy. After I get my circulation up, I meditate for a while."

Chris: "How long do you meditate?"

Anders: "It varies. I take this time to pray and meditate on my lists from the day before."

Chris: "Are you praying for God to give you the things on your list? 'I have been such a good boy Santa. Here is my list.'"

Anders: "Yes, and no. I am praying to the God-in-me for the things I want. My subconscious already knows I deserve what I ask for. I decided and spelled out what I wanted the day before. I use the list as a tool to think through and organize what I want.

"On this day, I perform a Prayer Action. I imagine myself *being* the person who has already accomplished those things. In my imagination, I see, hear, smell, taste, and touch the things that would be true now that this is already done.

"I flow mana into the image. I do the same as I fall asleep each night, in the assumption that I already have what I want.

"Most importantly, I vividly imagine the emotions I feel. This gets my mind and body tuned to the vibration of the frequency of that desired outcome.

"The more time I spend on that frequency, the more I resonate with the outcome I want, and the more we are magnetized to each other. That is an unstoppable force."

Chris: "Frequency? Like a radio frequency?"

Anders: "Radios, TVs, and cell phones all operate in different frequency ranges. Your life is a printout of your past beliefs that have set you vibrating at a certain frequency.

"The life you have now is on that frequency. The life you want is on another channel. Your physical brain is an electronic switching station. You use your mind to recalibrate your brain. Change the channel."

Chris: "Change your mind; change your life."

Anders: "As Neville Goddard says, *assume* the wish fulfilled. Assume the thing you want also wants you and is already done. Then let it go. Don't think of it in any other way than that it already exists. Just become *aware* of its presence. Give thanks that it is done."

Chris: "And that works for you? Do you always get what you want?"

Anders: "Every time. These laws are constants. The principles operate whether we are aware of them or not. Energy flows where attention goes.

"I energize the image with breathing techniques to charge it with mana. I convince myself that I want this outcome and make it a passion."

Chris: "Why don't you have a big ol' mansion with servants and fountains and birds flying all over the pavilion?"

Anders: "Is that what *you* want? I have what I want. Look around. I didn't have this two years ago. I can tell you it's a long way from the housing project in the north valley I lived in as a kid.

"They always give those hellholes such pretty names, with good intention to inspire heavenly ideals. The road to Hell is paved with good intentions. Astoria Gardens … makes it sound like Heaven's backyard.

"This is my Heaven right here. I see the new swimming pool forming right over there."

Chris: "It is heavenly here. Oka-ay. I see what you mean. Not everybody wants to live in a mansion. I guess I could be happy in a smaller house."

Anders: "I always end a prayer action with gratitude for all that I have and all that is on its way.

"The attitude of gratitude is a powerful amplifier. Then, I go do something in the garden or my workshop like any other Saturday afternoon. In the evening, I like to read."

Chris: "And you still aren't hungry? If I made it that far, 48 hours, I think I would start wondering how my shoes might taste with a little salsa."

Anders: "It takes persistence at first. It gets easier. After you've done it a couple of times, you learn to tell the difference between an impulse and actual hunger.

"I get a little hunger pang in my stomach every once in a while, but if I focus on something else, it goes away in a minute or so. A cup of green tea will do the job if it doesn't go away on its own.

"Sunday morning when I get up, it has been about 64 hours, and stem cell production is starting to ramp up. I have my water, coffee, exercise, and gratitude meditation.

"Then I'll pick one piece of literature and really study it for a couple of hours. It might be a chapter, a page, or even a paragraph from a book."

Chris: "A paragraph? I thought I was a slow reader. You know you read faster if you don't move your lips, don't you?"

Anders: "I read it over and over while I'm making notes. I may even write a page for my blog. My readers enjoy the breakdowns.

"Then, around 2 PM, I break my fast with a cup of bone broth. By the time we have Sunday dinner, my body is prepared to feast."

Chris: "Let the feast begin. That is really quite a weekend. Let's see, so your body eats all the bad stuff in it, including fat. You get HGH and stem cell treatments. Your brain rebuilds itself.

"It doesn't cost you anything to do it, and you save the money you would have spent on food. It's too bad you have to stop eating to do it. And you do that four times a year?"

Anders: "At the beginning of each new season, I cleanse my body and rearrange my mind."

Come Back Uncle

XLV

Mr. H: "Are you a Christian, Elias?"

Elias: "That question is more complicated than it sounds. I don't think you're supposed to ask me that. I may have said too much already."

Mr. H: "I'm not asking as a representative of the state. I'm just curious, that's all."

Elias: "During this visit, you are one and the same, uncle. Please come back later."

Mr. H: "I'm sorry. I didn't mean to offend you."

Elias: "No, uncle, you did not offend. You must end this visit as the State of Hawaii, change your clothes, and come back as you. Then, we talk good story uncle, in the state of ha wai 'i."

Mr. H: "That sounds nice."

Elias: "Come over on Sunday for the lu'au. One o'clock."

Mr. H: "Yes, I think I'd like that. If you're sure there's enough."

Elias: "We always have plenty."

Mr. H: "Mahalo."

Elias: "You are welcome to come earlier. Service begins at ten."

Mr. H: "I'm not sure if I can make it that early. I'm staying here, on big island, with my cousin this weekend."

Elias: "We stream it, so you can watch online. But you come back here, yeah?"

Mr. H: "I'll be here. Mahalo."

Elias: "Bring your cousin too."

Mr. H: "I'll ask him. Aloha, Elias."

Elias: "Aloha, uncle."

Manawa

XLVI

Truly: "Good morning, merry Christmas, and happy birthday."

Anders: "Birthday? You mean it's time? I thought he wasn't due for a couple more days. You're ready?"

Truly: "I don't know if I'm ready, but I'm fairly certain he is. I got up a couple of hours ago when my water broke. I've been feeling some tightening, too."

Anders: "A couple of hours? Why didn't you wake me up?"

Truly: "On this part of my journey, I walk alone. I've been meditating. Everything is fine. Last night, I felt some tightening, but there was no rhythm to it.

"I lay down on the bed and started doing my breathing. I got so relaxed, I fell asleep. Until he popped the hatch. Here, I made you some coffee."

Anders: "Thank you. I'll call Grace."

Truly: "She's on her way. I told her to hurry. I get the feeling he can't wait to come out."

Anders: "How are you feeling? Where is your mindset?"

Truly: "It's a perfect day. I'm excited and looking forward to this. If I'm being honest, I still feel a little bit nervous, but overall, I feel good."

Anders: "I know you feel good *and* empowered. You've retrained your mind and body. You're ready for the most natural childbirth you could imagine. A little bit of nervousness is okay. It lets you know that something is about to happen."

Truly: "Something is definitely about to happen. Bring Grace down when she gets here. I'm going to put on my music, start breathing, and head down to the water. I might even swim a little."

Anders: "Do you need anything else?"

Truly: "I'll call you if I need anything. I have my bag."

Anders: "We'll be down in a couple of minutes. This is going to be beautiful. Don't start without me."

Truly: "It has already begun."

Anders: "How many centimeters?"

Truly: "I didn't measure, but I'd say I'm definitely opening up. Contractions are coming a little harder and closer together."

Anders: "You look fabulous. You are literally glowing."

Truly: "Thank you. I'll see you in a few."

Anders: "Set your intention for this segment."

Truly: "I already have." Her voice trailed off as she walked out the door.

Down at the water, thankfully a short walk, an oversized flotation chair and a few air mattresses sat strapped to the dock.

Anders and his friend had designed and built a special dock configuration on top of a pu'u. One side of the dock was like any other dock, in that it was straight to allow boats to move along its length. On the southern side, a combination of lava rock and kava wood formed what looked like half of a party-sized hot tub, with deck, seats, and swimmers' step forming a C shape.

This pu'u, or little mound, formed by a bubble in molten lava, had popped, leaving a rim, usually just inches above the surface of the water, and formed the perfect foundation for the deck. The seaward side had collapsed, forming a natural doorway to the sea. It was a good place to gear up for snorkeling or to have a baby.

She walked out onto the deck; the sunshine graciously warmed her usual spot. As she managed to lower herself onto the bench with an assist from the handrail, she said out loud, "Elias, we aren't going to hurt each other, are we, baby? I'm going to stay calm, and you're going to stay calm, and you're going to come into this world peacefully. I'm just going to relax my body so you can slip out like a little fish. How does that sound to you?

"Wait until you see this place. It is amazing. I don't think you could have picked a better place on this planet. I'm just going put my feet in the water to see how it feels. I don't know if I'll ever get used to the water being warmer than the air, but that's what it's like here in the mornings. It's so nice. I think you're going to like it here, Elias.

"Mommy has to go away for a while. Remember, no matter how many miles separate us, we are always connected. Andy has plans for you. I don't know. He said you may have been the one who planned all this. You know, I already had plans of my own. The two of you will just have to carry out your plans by yourselves for a while."

Chris: "I hope I'm not too late."

Truly: "Oh, I forgot. Gramma Chrissy hasn't decided yet, but she'll probably be here too.

"Of course not, Mom. You know it takes longer than that."

Chris: "Well, you guys said it would go a lot quicker, so I didn't know what to expect. I came straight down here. How are you feeling, sweetie?"

Truly: "Exquisite."

Chris: "Can I get you anything? Would you like some …? Oh, here comes Andy and Gracie! Good morning! We're over here."

Anders: "Thanks Chris. Good morning to you."

Chris: "Who is this little angel?"

Grace: "This is my daughter, Naya."

Chris: "It's wonderful to meet you, Naya."

Naya: "I'm five. There's no school because it's Christmas."

Chris: "Well, we're happy you are here. I'd like to hold someone's hand for this. Can I hold yours?"

Naya: "Sure."

Chris: "Okay. Let's go sit down over here, out of the way, and put our feet in the water."

Anders: "How are you doing over there? Everything going according to plan?"

Truly: "It sure seems like it. I don't know if it's even possible to be more perfect than this. The sun is shining, the water is warm, Elias is ready … and so am I."

Grace: "Slow down a sec. Let's take a look at you first, sister. I want to see how you're doing. Can you get your leg up here on the bench?"

Anders: "Hang on. I'll put up the shade. The neighbors don't have to see everything."

Grace: "I want to check your temperature first anyway."

Truly: "It might read a little high. I've been sitting here in the sun."

Grace: "That's all right, I just want to make sure we're in the right ballpark."

Truly: "Hang on." *Ahhh. wheeeew. Ahhh wheeeew.* "Contraction." *Ahhh. wheeeew. Ahhh wheeeew.* "This is a strong one." *Ahhh. wheeeew. Ahhh wheeeew.* "Okay, I think that's it."

Grace: "All the signs say you're getting closer."

Truly: "Yeah. You better get your booties on."

Anders: "I can sense how relaxed you are, right now. Continue taking deeper breaths and allowing your body to do what it was naturally designed to do. You are looking forward to meeting your son in the outside world. His transition is also transformative for you."

Grace: "Now that we have some privacy, let's see how you're doing down there. You look pretty ripe, like you aren't wasting any time."

Truly: "No, I'm ready."

Grace: "I'd say you're about 10 cm already. Are you ready to get into the water yet?"

Truly: "Maybe after this contrac ... " *hmmmm. Hoooh, ahhh. wheeeew. Ahhh wheeeew.*

Anders: "Deeper breaths. Slow it down. You're doing an amazing job. Stay focused on how you want to be. Relax your muscles. Allow the tightening to run its course. It has a purpose. It's part of the process. Good."

Grace: "They're getting closer together now. He'll probably be here before breakfast."

Truly: "I hope so. We don't eat breakfast until after noon."

Grace: "Yeah. I meant before normal people's breakfast time. You two are ready right now."

Truly: "Yes we are."

Grace: "Let's do this."

Truly: "I'm already doing this. Too late to turn back now. He is coming. There's only one way to go from here."

Grace: "Andy, I still don't understand the hypno-stuff. Are you going to start hypnotizing her soon?"

Anders: "She has already been hypnotizing herself. All hypnosis is self-hypnosis. You'll just have to keep him from swimming away. I'll help her go deeper as we get closer."

Grace: "We can't get much closer without actually being there."

Anders: "All the things are ready. Truly, are you ready to get in?"

Truly: "He's ready to come out, so yeah, I'm ready to get in."

Anders: "That's the spirit. I'm ready. Take my hand. Now is the moment of power for his transition and your transformation."

Truly: "Do you have to be so dramatic?"

Anders: "Just keeping a positive mindset and using positive words. Come on in. The water's fine."

Truly: "Here comes another one." She does her breathing technique. "I feel like I want to push."

Grace: "Hold that thought. And that feeling. Breathe up."

Anders: "Let's get you situated here."

She eased herself into the water. She sat on the step between Anders' legs, and he placed his hands on each side of her belly.

Truly: "It's so warm in here."

Anders: "The black lava absorbs the sun. Close your eyes for a second. I'll add mana with a little reiki. Take a deep, deep breath … and as you let it out … feel your mind and body relax … even deeper.

"Remember your breathing techniques. In your mind's eye, direct the flow of energy through your body. That's right. Relax, and focus on this one thing.

"All of your energies flowing in harmony. You already know how beautiful this is. You have seen it. Remember?

"You can allow the muscles of your torso to lengthen and align as they also pull and separate and open the passage while at the same time, the pelvic muscles relax and become more elastic. Lifting … and opening. Breathing up.

"Your body is built for this. Your body is ready. You are in control. Just allow the birth to unfold naturally. Breathe. In through the nose … and out through the mouth."

Grace: "Okay. How are you feeling?"

Truly: "Like I want to push him out. I really feel like pushing."

Grace: "We want to time it with a surge. Wait for it."

Truly: "Don't have to wait. Here we go." *Hmmmm.*

Anders: "Breathe into it. Feel him moving with each breath as you continue to relax."

Grace: "I see his crown. He's on his way. I don't want you to push. I want you to work with the surge. Start at the top and allow the muscles to work like they know how. Breathe down into the flow."

Anders: "Can you see Elias in your mind's eye, moving into position? Can you feel your energy, his energy, and my energy in harmony, aligning and lighting his path? Relax and breathe down."

Grace: "Okay. Wait for the next surge. Deep breaths."

Truly: "Here we go."

Anders: "Each breath flows in, and as you exhale … imagine your breath also flows down through your body, surrounding your baby, opening and flowing out your pelvic floor."

Grace: "Here he comes."

Anders: "You don't have to force him out. Allow your muscles to work independently, elongating and contracting in perfect sequence. Let the flow of energy guide him. He knows the way."

Truly: "Your time is now, Elias. Little bullethead first. Slip and slide time. Keep your hands down, baby. Trust Gracie. She's got you." *Aaaaaagh*!

Grace: "Welcome to Earth, Elias. Aloha nui loa, keiki. This is your mama. I think you know each other already."

Truly: "I've been holding him in my belly all this time. I finally get to hold him in my arms. He is the most beautiful thing I have ever seen in my entire life."

Chris: "Me too, I feel like I was just born myself."

Anders: "Harmonious."

Tatsu Academy

XLVII

Mr. H: "Well, your facility seems more than suitable, and Elias is certainly remarkable, Dr. Starkstrom. We will report our findings to the committee. I am sure you will get approval for your school."

Mrs. K: "It's a wonderful thing you are doing here."

Anders: "These children are the future. I know that may sound like a cliché, but it is the literal truth. Someday our children will take the helm. It's up to us to provide clean fuel and accurate charts."

Mrs. B: "What did you say the name is?"

Anders: "Tatsu Academy."

Frankly, My Dear

XLVIII

Anders: "Is there a way for you to stay here with us for three months?"

Truly: "Three *more* months? I've already been here a month."

Anders: "I know, but I mean, can you continue your training remotely?"

Truly: "I took vacation time to come here a month early, and now I have six weeks of convalescent leave. Two and a half months is a lot of time to be out of the mix. I have a lot of catching up to do. Everybody in my class is working their butts off, *together*, while I'm here slacking in Hawaii."

Anders: "That may be their perception, but you have not been, nor will you be slacking."

Truly: "Some of those people are going to be fellow crewmembers, and all of us will be in the same fleet. It's important to struggle together during initial training. You can't replace that kind of bond."

Anders: "I'm asking you to stay here to lay the foundation for an irreplaceable bond between you and Elias. There will be new classes of cadets coming through."

Truly: "There will only be one *first* class of cadets coming through this program. And I'm in it."

Anders: "That is an important distinction. Let's define what we want and make a plan. If you return in six weeks, everything is fine with the Space Force, yeah?"

Truly: "That *is* the plan. Good talk, thanks."

Anders: "That is the current plan. I want to explore modifying it a little. I feel it's especially important for mom and baby to bond for the first three months."

Truly: "Where did you come up with that number? What is so magical about three months?"

Anders: "Intuition. I asked myself, and that was the number that came up."

Truly: "So, it's arbitrary. What does your intuition have to say about the bonding Elias and I have been doing for the past nine months?"

Anders: "That nine months, plus three months, equals twelve months. All three are multiples of three and form a magical arrangement."

Truly: "Well, six is also a multiple of three. The magical arrangement is for me to head back in six weeks. You don't even have any evidence that six additional weeks makes a difference."

Anders: "Honestly, I don't know if it makes any difference. Just so you know, you're mixing variables and ending up with a false product. Six weeks equals one-and-a-half months."

Truly: "So what? You said you were going to take care of him. Now you're nibbling. It's six more weeks this time. What about next time? I played that game enough with Marcas. I'm not going to allow it in my life anymore. You taught me that."

Anders: "I love it when you're decisive."

Truly: "Anyway, I was starting to get the impression that you didn't want me around anymore. Now you want me to change my plans and stay. You have already changed my life completely from what it was to who knows what."

Anders: "I didn't mean to leave that impression. Of course, I want you around. You and I were on the same divine frequency when we met. Things in resonance are magnetically attracted to each other.

"Whether you share my belief or not, I believe there were forces at work that brought us together. It's even possible that we made an agreement before we were born into this world to have these experiences, and *that* little one presided over the meeting. His plan."

Truly: "Mysterious ways. Then, why have you been so cold this morning?"

Anders: "I guess I have been cold compared to previous months. When I said I love you, I meant it unconditionally. The feeling of love is its own reward. I didn't mean to spook you. You're not obliged to love me back."

Truly: "I do love you, but you also know I had an entirely different plan for my life. Now, I have a son and an undefined relationship with you. It made me uncomfortable. That's why I acted that way."

Anders: "The way I saw it, if you meant the things you said, then I must be delusional, and I should just leave you alone. If you didn't mean the things you said, that's nonsense. I don't need any more nonsense in my life, so I should just leave you alone.

"Different equations, same product. The answer to both is that I should just leave you alone. I took my foot off the gas pedal and put it on the soft pedal."

Truly: "I didn't mean it the way you heard it. Why do you want me to give up more of my plans when you're not clear on yours?"

Anders: "I know what I want. I haven't changed my desired outcomes. New ideas reveal themselves to me as I go. I don't know if the question has ever been properly answered as to the ideal minimum time for a mother and child to bond."

Truly: "A lifetime."

Anders: "Right. We are always bonding with our mothers. The question came into my mind, I sent it upstairs, and the immediate response was three months. So, I put it to you."

Truly: "Maybe you could have started with that instead of coming after my agenda."

Anders: "Look at me. Always learning."

Truly: "You and Mom could bring Elias back to the mainland for those six weeks. That way, I can get back to my training and you can feel good about the two of us bonding for the full twelve months. How is that for a compromise?"

Anders: "Look at you. Problem solver."

Truly: "Mom needs to clean up some stuff anyway. She needs to settle up with Marcas and figure out what she wants to do with the house and everything. How are things going with her?"

Anders: "She still clings to some disempowering beliefs, but she's come a long way."

Truly: "Thank you for inviting her to stay."

Anders: "There's plenty of room. Who, but her, should live in the mother-in-law apartment?"

Truly: "I'm not sure how I feel about you calling her mother-in-law."

Anders: "I didn't. Just the apartment. I can tidy things up in my schedule to make that work. I usually spend my winters here."

Truly: "Six weeks here or there. I wonder why six weeks looks so much bigger to you when it affects your schedule. We are only talking about the second half of winter. You'll still be here for the first half."

Anders: "I'm a chameleon. I adapt quickly to achieve my desires. I'm good. In the meantime, I'm sure you have a plan to get back in shape. Good thing you didn't use pregnancy as an excuse to let yourself go. If you like, we can also do a script for your life."

Truly: "It's more interesting to live life *un*scripted."

Anders: "Unscripted is certainly more challenging. That's the way most people live, but you are not most people. You know you create your world by default or design."

Truly: "How long is that going to take? 'Cause right now, I just want to go down to the beach for a swim with the dolphins. Can we just chill for a little while?"

Anders: "It takes a lot less time than you might be hallucinating. But now is always a perfect time to chill. We can do it after you finish swimming. Let's head down to the dock. I've got Elias.

"Your subconscious knows what it wants. Writing it out brings agreement with your conscious mind. When the two of you agree, there are no limits to what you can do."

Truly: "That sounds familiar. Did you tell me that before?"

Anders: "Probably. It is one of the basic tenets of my beliefs.

"The conscious mind relates to the material world, while the subconscious mind is connected directly to spirit. The difference between what we know consciously, as the five senses perceive, and what spirit knows, creates conflict within. Agreement between conscious and subconscious is harmony.

"All this stuff is in the Old Testament and retold in a different way in the New Testament. People think the Bible is a history book, so some people reject it outright and some follow it literally, but most people just don't know what to think."

Truly: "So they don't think."

Anders: "Most people are conditioned to allow others to think for them. *That* is the systemic problem.

"When you understand the Bible is a book about you and your psychology, you will perceive the stories in a whole new way. The Bible is happening right now, in each of us. Every character represents a state of mind."

Truly: "Yeah. You said that before. How is the Bible about me? Which stories?"

Anders: "One of the most misunderstood stories is the tale of the crucifixion."

Truly: "That was brutal. I was always told to praise Jesus because he suffered to wash away all our sins."

Anders: "Jesus was a master of mind and body. He did not suffer physical pain."

Truly: "He died on the cross that we might live."

Anders: "Do you understand what that means?"

Truly: "They drilled it into us in Sunday school. I mean, it kinda makes sense. Since the fall of man, we are all sinners. So, God sent us Jesus to take the punishment for everyone. Then we start with a clean slate.

"Then, apparently, we just keep sinning until he comes back to do it again. Only this time, he won't be the one suffering."

Anders: "It does have a certain logic to it."

Truly: "I feel like there are a lot of holes in the story."

Anders: "That is because the story has been presented to us as a historical report. It is actually a metaphor for individual awakening.

"The second coming of Christ is when you accept who you are. It is the awareness that NOW is all there is. Past mistakes were learning experiences.

"Forgive and forget, then move forward. To release your old beliefs, you must take the action of killing off your old self, so the new self might live. Cross off the old man."

Truly: "I'm a woman."

Anders: "I hadn't noticed."

Truly: "Butthead. There is no doubt in my mind that this discussion is far from over. Having said that, I believe with all my heart that I am going for a swim. Don't let your son get too much sun."

Anders: "I'm putting up the shade. Have fun."

As Anders dipped Elias into the water, he could see the fins of dolphins swimming alongside Truly. "Elias, we have a lot of work to do, but it's going to be an amazing adventure.

"You sure do love the water, don't you? Mama looks like she's having fun out there."

Truly swam back to the dock. Flopping her flippers on the deck, she asked, "Does life get any better than this?"

Anders: "I keep working on it. Looked like there were a lot of them out there today."

Truly: "Yes! It was fabulous. Kayakers kept chasing after them, so they kept swimming away, but a few of them came back to swim with me. I could do that every day!"

Anders: "Yeah, that never gets old. I still remember my first time, about 20 years ago, right here in this bay. You *can* do that every day."

Truly: "I see why you moved here."

Anders: "Your presence is always welcome. Come here anytime and stay as long as you want."

Truly: "I will be here, for the next few weeks anyway. I don't want you to think I'm crazy, but I think the dolphins were talking to me."

Anders: "I don't think that's crazy at all. What did they say?"

Truly: "Well, they didn't actually speak with words, but I understood them. They wanted to know why Elias wasn't swimming with me."

Namaka

XLIX

As the kūpuna walked down the driveway toward their car, Elias said to his papa, "Uncle looks more like Namaka now. More green and blue. Does that mean he's happy?"

Anders: "I believe he is, Elias. He didn't know what to expect from you, kiddo. He still has a little bit of vog in his head, but his energies are more in harmony."

Elias: "Aunties look happier too."

Anders: "Elias, give praise to everyone you meet. Always leave them with the feeling that their lives are a little bit better for having met you and be thankful for whatever they have made you aware of."

Elias: "Harmonious."

We Now Return You to
Your Regularly Scheduled Programming.

Recommended Reading

As a man Thinketh: The Original 1902 Edition (The Wisdom Of James Allen)
James Allen

The Neville Collection: All 10 Books by a Modern Master
Neville Goddard

Rev. Ike's Secrets For Health, Joy and Prosperity, For YOU: A Science Of Living Study Guide
Rev. Ike

The Secret of the Ages: The Master Code to Abundance and Achievement
Robert Collier

The Robert Collier Letter Book: Fifth Edition
Robert Collier

Working With The Law
Raymond Holliwell

The Power Of Your Subconscious Mind
Dr. Joseph Murphy

The Fallacy of Old Age: Dr. Joseph Murphy LIVE! (audio)
Dr. Joseph Murphy

The Amazing Laws of Cosmic Mind Power [Revised/Expanded Edition]
Dr. Joseph Murphy

The Magic of Believing: The Classic Guide to Unlocking the Power of Your Mind
Claude Bristol

Thought Vibration: The Law Of Attraction In The Thought World
William Walker Atkinson

The Kybalion: The Definitive Edition
William Walker Atkinson

The Classic Ralph Waldo Trine Book Collection (Deluxe Edition) - In Tune With The Infinite;
What All the World's A-Seeking; This Mystical Life of Ours; The Greatest Thing Ever Known
Ralph Waldo Trine

The Silva Mind Control Method
Jose Silva

The Law of Psychic Phenomena: A Systematic Study of Hypnotism, Spiritism, Mental Therapeutics, Etc.
Thomson Jay Hudson

The Classic Thomas Troward Book Collection (Deluxe Edition)
The Hidden Power And Other Papers On Mental Science
Thomas Troward

Genevieve Behrend Collection: (3 Books): Your Invisible Power, How to Live Life and Love
it, Attaining Your Desires By Letting Your Subconscious Mind Work For You
Genevieve Behrend

The Complete Works of Florence Scovel Shinn: The Game of Life, Your Word is Your Wand, The Secret Door to Success ,The Power
of the Spoken Word
Florence Scovel Shinn

The Doors of Perception and Heaven and Hell
Aldous Huxley

The Finding of the Third Eye
Vera Stanley Alder

You Were Born Rich
Bob Proctor

Change Your Paradigm, Change Your Life
Bob Proctor

The Science of Getting Rich: Original Retro First Edition
Wallace D. Wattles

Think and Grow Rich: The Landmark Bestseller Now Revised and Updated for the 21st Century (Think and Grow Rich Series)
Napoleon Hill

NLP/Hypnosis:

Time Line Therapy And The Basis Of Personality (Pedagogy for a Changing World)
Tad James and Wyatt Woodsmall

NLP: The New Technology of Achievement
Steve Andreas

Heart of the Mind - Engaging Your Inner Power to Change with Neuro-Linguistic Programming
Connirae & Steve Andreas

Core Transformation: Reaching the Wellspring Within
Connirae and Tamara Andreas

Trance-Formations: Neuro-Linguistic Programming and the Structure of Hypnosis
Richard Bandler

Get the Life You Want: The Secrets to Quick and Lasting Life Change with Neuro-Linguistic Programming
Richard Bandler

Frogs into Princes: Neuro Linguistic Programming
Richard Bandler

Using Your Brain--For a Change: Neuro-Linguistic Programming
Richard Bandler

Reframing: Neuro-Linguistic Programming and the Transformation of Meaning
Richard Bandler

Teaching Excellence: The Definitive Guide to NLP for Teaching and Learning (NLP for Education)
Dr. Richard Bandler and Kate Benson

Persuasion Engineering
Richard Bandler and John LaValle

Patterns of the Hypnotic Techniques of Milton H. Erickson, M.D. Volume 1
John Grinder, Judith DeLozier, and Richard Bandler

Patterns of the Hypnotic Techniques of Milton H. Erickson, M.D., Vol. 2
John Grinder, Judith DeLozier, and Richard Bandler

The Structure of Magic, Vol. 1: A Book About Language and Therapy
Richard Bandler and John Grinder

The Structure of Magic II: A Book About Communication and Change
Richard Bandler and John Grinder

Hypnotherapy
Dave Elman

HypnoBirthing, Fourth Edition: The breakthrough natural approach to safer, easier, more comfortable birthing - The Mongan Method, 4th Edition
Marie F. Mongan

Quantum Healing (Revised and Updated): Exploring the Frontiers of Mind/Body Medicine
Deepak Chopra M.D.

Ageless Body, Timeless Mind: The Quantum Alternative to Growing Old
Deepak Chopra

Energy Medicine: Balancing Your Body's Energies for Optimal Health, Joy, and Vitality
Donna Eden and David Feinstein

Answer Cancer
Steve Parkhill

New Age Hypnosis
Bruce Goldberg

Secrets of Speed Seduction Mastery
Ross Jeffries

The Multi-Orgasmic Man: Sexual Secrets Every Man Should Know
Mantak Chia

Awaken Healing Energy Through The Tao: The Taoist Secret of Circulating Internal Power
Mantak Chia

Chi Gung: Chinese Healing, Energy and Natural Magick
L.V. Carnie

Opening the Energy Gates of Your Body: Chi Gung for Lifelong Health (Tao of Energy Enhancement Series)
Bruce Frantzis

Huna: The Ancient Religion of Positive Thinking
William R. Glover

Golf in the Kingdom
Michael Murphy

Huna Code in Religions
Max Freedom Long

What Jesus Taught in Secret
Max Freedom Long

Urban Shaman
Serge Kahili King

Huna: Ancient Hawaiian Secrets for Modern Living
Serge Kahili King

The Richest Man In Babylon - Original Edition
George S. Clason

Brave New World
Aldous Huxley

1984
George Orwell

Futility, Or The Wreck Of The Titan: By Morgan Robertson - Illustrated
Morgan Robertson

Of Mice and Men
John Steinbeck

The Complete Hitchhiker's Guide to the Galaxy Boxset: Guide to the Galaxy / The Restaurant at the End of the Universe / Life, the Universe and ... and Thanks for all the Fish /
Mostly Harmless
Douglas Adams

Los autoestopistas galácticos: Guía del autoestopista galáctico, El restaurante del fin del mundo, La vida, el universo y todo lo demás (Spanish Edition)
Douglas Adams

The Prince and the Pauper: Original Illustrations
Mark Twain

The Picture of Dorian Gray
Oscar Wilde